THE BEST OF BOTH WORLDS

Borgo Press Books by BRIAN STABLEFORD

THE BEST OF BOTH WORLDS

AND OTHER AMBIGUOUS TALES

by

Brian Stableford

THE BORGO PRESS

An Imprint of Wildside Press LLC

MMIX

CONTENTS

ABOUT THE AUTHOR

BRIAN STABLEFORD was born in Yorkshire in 1948. He taught at the University of Reading for several years, but is now a full-time writer. He has written many science fiction and fantasy novels, including *The Empire of Fear*, *The Werewolves of London*, *Year Zero*, *The Curse of the Coral Bride*, and *The Stones of Camelot*. Collections of his short stories include *Sexual Chemistry: Sardonic Tales of the Genetic Revolution*, *Designer Genes: Tales of the Biotech Revolution*, and *Sheena and Other Gothic Tales*. He has written numerous nonfiction books, including *Scientific Romance in Britain, 1890-1950, Glorious Perversity: The Decline and Fall of Literary Decadence*, and *Science Fact and Science Fiction: An Encyclopedia*. He has contributed hundreds of biographical and critical entries to reference books, including both editions of *The Encyclopedia of Science Fiction* and several editions of the library guide, *Anatomy of Wonder*. He has also translated numerous novels from the French language, including several by the feuilletonist Paul Féval and various classics of French scientific romance.

INTRODUCTION

It may seem superfluous to subtitle a collection with the description of "ambiguous tales", since any tale that was not ambiguous would not be worth telling. If ambiguity did not exist, fiction—from the humblest one-liner to the vastest epic—would not exist either, because we would not only be able to content ourselves with actuality but would have no alternative. One can elaborate this issue in high-flown academic terms by citing such classic works of aesthetic analysis as Owen Barfield's *Poetic Diction*, the Inklings' Bible, but there really is no need; it is perfectly obvious that if double meanings did not exist, we would have to invent them. (Put simply, Barfield's argument is that there never was a time when they didn't, so we didn't.)

There are, however, degrees in ambiguity just as there are in everything else, and there are also different sorts of ambiguity—seven is the most oft-quoted number—ranging from the commonplace and conventional to the abstruse and tortuous, so some tales are more ambiguous than others, and may be ambiguous in more or less commonplace ways. By the same token, there are writers who merely accept ambiguity as a necessity, writers who cultivate it as a staple crop and writers ambitious to become explorers in search of rare and exotic ambiguity. I have always aspired to membership in the last-named category, although I am not entirely confident that my quests have had as much success as I could have hoped. At any rate, in labeling the items in this collection "ambiguous tales" I am aiming for something a little more meaningful than mere tautology, hopeful that the ambiguities they contain might, at the least, be a trifle odd, even within the context of the routine oddities of science fiction and fantasy.

The great but somewhat under-appreciated science fiction writer A. E. van Vogt learned to write pulp fiction by studying the advice manuals of the great but somewhat under-appreciated advice-manual writer John Gallishaw, whose techniques of scenic analysis and strategic planning he used religiously. Like any inventive writer, however, van Vogt added a wrinkle of his own to his theory and method, which he called the theory of "fictional sentences". According to this theory, different genres of pulp fiction were distinguished not only by the specifics of their content, but also by their typical narrative style.

Having started out writing romances and "true confession" stories, van Vogt was of the opinion that such stories worked best if every substantial sentence they contained featured some reference to emotion, and that the key feature of the "fictional sentences" of the romance genre was that emotional reference. When he switched to science fiction writing, he immediately set out to discover what the key feature of the "fictional sentences" of the sf genre ought to be. He came to the conclusion that it was uncertainty—which is to say that every substantial sentence in a science fiction story should contain a reference that was deliberately underspecified, thus creating a superabundance of ambiguity and generating new dimensions of imaginative space for the temptation of the reader's curiosity.

The ultimate effect of the assiduous application of this theory, according to some excessively-pedantic readers, was that van Vogt's work became literally incomprehensible, because it was impossible for the reader to work out what the hell was supposed to be happening, but connoisseurs of rare and exotic ambiguity found the additional wiggle-room both intriguing and exhilarating. I have never been nearly as assiduous in my literary method as A. E. van Vogt, and am quite willing to admit that I have penned the occasional sentence whose meaning is crystal clear, but I have always tried to compensate for that failing as much as is humanly possible by means of a liberal but carefully-applied gloss of sarcasm, which hopefully makes it impossible for readers to figure out whether or not I mean what I am saying. Mostly, admittedly, I don't—but every now and again I do, and because that possibility, or threat, is always there, so is the edge of potential ambiguity. Not all readers appreciate this as much as I would like them to do, and I suppose that I ought to apologize to the others, but the apology would inevitably be sarcastically ambiguous, so it can be taken as read.

At any rate, no mater how many failed fictional sentences there are in the stories included here, I have tried to ascertain that their perennial keynote is uncertainty. They feature events of dubious significance, seen from unreliable narrative viewpoints. The stories themselves do make some pretence of instructing the reader as to what to think about the extraordinary hypothetical events described therein, but the postures in question are inherently deceptive. Some readers might think this a lazy way to write, in that it lets me off the hook of having to decide what I think about them myself, but I am only human; if I had already made up my mind what to think about things, I probably wouldn't be a writer at all. I certainly wouldn't be a writer of science fiction and fantasy stories, never content to deal with conventional views of what is, but insistent instead on dealing with all kinds of bizarre possibilities that never were and never will be, and are intellectually interesting for exactly that reason.

My favorite story in the book is "The Highway Code", because it is the only one that has a central character with whom I can truly sympathize and admire (alert readers will notice that he is loosely based on one of the great heroes of modern mythology, Thomas the Tank Engine), but I could not call the book *The Highway Code* lest it cause dire confusion to British learner drivers, so I settled for *The Best of Both Worlds* instead.

The substance of "The Face of an Angel" was subsequently absorbed into the text of a novel called *The Moment of Truth* (Borgo Press, 2009), but the transfiguration forced the story to mutate so considerably that the two texts remain quite different in their narrative implications—one of the many fortunate corollaries of calculated ambiguity.

"The Man Who Came Back" was the first story I published under my own name, its only predecessor being a pseudonymous collaboration, and the contrast it provides with the more recent publications will hopefully illustrate the vast artistic strides I have made in the interim, while never sacrificing my steadfast commitment to uncertainty.

"Appearances" was written when one of my ex-students from the M.A. in "Writing for Children" at the University of Winchester went to work for a Mexican publisher editing a line of dark fantasy novellas aimed at a teenage audience; unfortunately, the publisher ran into difficulties (as Mexican publishers are wont to do), so the opportunity for her to translate it into Spanish vanished into the misty maze of unrealized possibilities, like so many other fond and fabulous hopes.

"The Best of Both Worlds" first appeared in *Postscripts* 15 (Summer 2008). "The Highway Code" first appeared in *We Think, Therefore We Are*, edited by Peter Crowther and published by DAW Books in 2009. "Captain Fagan Died Alone" first appeared in *The DAW Science Fiction Reader*, edited by Donald A. Wollheim and published by DAW in 1976. "The Face of an Angel" first appeared in *Leviathan 3*, edited by Forrest Aguirre and Jeff Vandermeer, published by the Ministry of Whimsy in 2002. "Vesterhen" first appeared in German translation in *Pilger Dürch Raum und Zeit*, edited by Peter Wilfert and published by Goldmann in 1982; the first publication of the English version was in the *Kongressbok Confuse 91* in 1991. "The Bad Seed" first appeared in *Interzone* 82 (April 1994). "The Man Who Came Back" first appeared in *Impulse* 8 (October 1966). "Appearances" appears here for the first time.

THE BEST OF BOTH WORLDS

Since Emily had died I had become exceedingly restless, unable to settle to my own work—indeed, I no longer found it possible to think of writing articles for *Blackwood's* and the *Monthly Review* as "work"—and equally unable to take solace in the genius of other men that was stored in my father's library.

My father was in London, fully absorbed by the duties of his military career, but I was glad of that, for his innocently cheerful presence would have seemed an insult. Had he not lost the love of his life too, albeit twenty-and-one years before? How could he tolerate his own comfortable contentment, with that kind of void at the core of his existence? How could he bear to look at me, let alone love me, knowing that it was in giving birth to me that his wife had died?

Emily, dear heart, had not lived long enough to celebrate our wedding, let alone to give birth to my child, but that did not make my pain one whit less intense. I felt that my soul had been ripped apart, and could never be healed

I had taken to wandering on the moors every day, whatever the weather. At first, I had done so merely in order to walk from our isolated house at Stonecroft to the village churchyard in Haughtonlin, where Emily was buried, but it had become so very difficult to tear myself away from my meditation in order to return to the awful normality of home that I had taken to going further on rather than reversing my direction. Nor did I stick to the path that would around the hillside before crossing the beck at the little wooden bridge and making its way back to the York road. Instead, I plunged into the wilderness of gorse and heather, punctuated by hawthorn spinneys and outcrops of black rock, which dressed the slopes above the bog, forming a basin whose broken granite rim served as a source for rills that combined their trickling waters lower down to form the beck.

It was desolate land, impossible to cultivate, into which sheep were reluctant to stray, and it suited the temper of my moods very well. The cloud which, by some freak of nature, always dressed the summit of Arnlea Moor came to see strangely welcoming, although I usually refrained from going so far up the hill as to immerse myself in its mists.

My father had hoped that I might make a soldier, like him, but I had no appetite at all for the looming conflict in the Crimea. My childhood dreams had been fantasies of exploration, following in the footsteps of James Cook or Mungo Park. Had I not fallen in love with Emily, I might have taken ship for the Pacific isles or the shores of darkest Africa, but she had kept me at home, and kept me still now that she had been laid to rest in the soil of Arnleadale. It was easy enough, however, to imagine myself as an explorer whenever I ventured into the upper reaches of the vale, struggling through what was, in a literal though perhaps rather trivial sense, trackless wilderness. There were foxes and pheasants living wild on the heath, but no hunt or shooting-party ever came this far from either of the manor houses that presided like Medieval forts over the valley's neck. Stonecroft, which had once belonged to one of Lord Arnlea's stewards but had been sold off fifty years before, was the limit at which sport stopped and untroubled Nature began.

My father, a devotee of natural theology, had often said that there was more to be learned about the mysterious mind of God in the bleak and misty head of the valley than there was from its carefully tamed and excessively man-handled mouth. I was not so sure that what was revealed there was the mind of God, but I had thought the judgment likely to be truthful even before I lost my lovely Emily. Afterwards, I became convinced. Even so, I had difficulty following my father's perennial advice to see the Divine Plan in everything that existed or occurred upon the Earth. What kind of divinity could possibly manifest itself in the premature death of such a charming soul as Emily?

I was never intimidated in my excursions by the weather, although the moor could become a direly dismal place when the ever-present cloud turned to drizzle, or when a brisk west wind brought darker clouds scurrying from the distant Atlantic Ocean to unleash a deluge on the slopes. There was no man-made shelter in the wilderness, but there were natural coverts formed by overhanging rocks, and clefts that sometimes extended back into the hillside to become pot-holes. I knew many of them, though by no means them all, and regarded them as my own...until, one day, I raced to the remotest of them all to escape a sudden squall, and found it already occupied, by a young woman dressed in black.

I had never seen her before, and was quite at a loss to understand how she had got there, since I would surely have caught a glimpse of her had she come by way of Haughtonlin. When I saw her, I hesitated at the mouth of the cave, and was actually about to turn around and go back into the storm when she spoke.

"There's no need to get wet on my account," she said, in a soft and strangely musical voice. "The shelter is narrow, but there's room enough for two. The shower cannot last long at this level of violence."

I hesitated still, studying her carefully. Her coat was long, and bulky enough to conceal the precise contours of her body her walking-boots sturdy. Her bonnet was as black as her coat, and so was the hair tucked up within it. Her complexion was pale—which made her eyebrows stand out remarkably—and her eyes were grey, completing the strange impression that she was a figure drawn in monochrome, a charcoal sketch rather than a portrait in oils.

Eventually, I bowed, and said: "I'm Edward Grayling of Stonecroft. I apologize for my rudeness, but I was startled to find anyone abroad in this lonely region—especially a woman."

"My name is Mary McQueen," she said, lightly. "I fear that I'm a little lost. I'm staying at Raggandale Hall, and I do not know the county at all."

"Raggandale Hall! Why, that's six miles away, even as the crow flies. You must have come over the crest of the moor, through the fog. Did no one warn you not to come this way? The ridge is rarely free from its shroud of low-lying cloud, and the damp ground on this side is treacherous even for sheep."

"No," she said, "no one warned me. I'm quite used to taking six-mile walks at home, although I will admit that the ground is much flatter there, and I never lose my bearings to the extent of not knowing when and how to turn around. The mist on the heights of the moor is very deceptive, and I was surprised to find that I had come out on the opposite side"

"I'll take you home when the squall blows over," I said, compelled to play the gallant in spite of my dark mood, "but it's a long way, and far from easy. There's very little chance of reaching Raggandale by nightfall." I paused again, for reflection, and then said: "In fact, it would be foolish to attempt it. You must come the other way, at least as far as Haughtonlin. The innkeeper at the Black Bull has a fly, and might be willing to lend you his servant to take you home by road. It's a long way round, but it's safe. If the fly's hired out or the servant can't be spared, you can stay overnight at the inn—or come back to Stonecroft with me, if you prefer. The scullion can be pressed into temporary service as a chambermaid. I can drive you home myself tomorrow."

"That's very kind," she said, "but quite unnecessary. I'm sure that I can find my own way home."

"I'm perfectly sure that you cannot," I told her, insistently. "I know how different this moorland is from most of England. Whether you know it or not, Miss McQueen, you're in an alien land here. This rain is not the first we've had this week, and the bog will be exceedingly treacherous for some time to come. There's no question of your going back that way this evening. You must come with me, at least as far as Haughtonlin."

"Very well," she said. "Since you insist, I must bow to your superior knowledge of this alien land, and accept your guidance. I shall stay the night in Haughtonlin, if there is room at the inn, and make my way home tomorrow. If the weather is fine, though, I shall go on foot. I may be resident in the vicinity for some time, if my cousins at Raggandale are willing to accommodate me, and I ought to get to know the country—especially its dangerous regions."

I had to be content with that, for the time being, but we continued chatting. I told her something of myself—my education, my father's military adventures, my adventures in journalism—but I said nothing about Emily or my current state of mind. It seemed to me that she might be hiding something too, although she gave me abundant news of my acquaintances at Raggandale and described her impressions of the estate in some detail. When I eventually left her at the Black Bull, I told her that I would return in the morning, and that if she really was intent on going up to the head of the valley and over the clouded moor, I would go with her, to make sure that she got safely back to Raggandale Hall.

"That's very kind of you, Mr. Grayling," she said. "I would doubtless benefit from the services of a guide, and I shall therefore accept your offer to see me safely home, if I will not be causing you any inconvenience."

"None at all," I assured her. "I come to Haughtonlin every day, and walk further up the valley whenever the whim takes me. It might be to my advantage to pioneer a trail that might take me all the way to Raggandale in future." I said it carelessly, and only realized afterwards that it must have sounded like an expression of my intention to visit her there—but she only thanked me courteously, and smiled.

* * * * * * *

I was back in Haughtonlin bright and early, but I went to the graveyard before presenting myself at the Black Bull. I was kneeling by Emily's grave, oblivious to all else, when I was interrupted by a voice from behind, which said: "I thought it was you, Mr. Grayling."

I turned to look at Mary McQueen. In her all-black outfit she seemed every inch the mourner. Her expression was equally somber.

"I would have come to the Black Bull within the quarter-hour," I said, a little stiffly. "There was no need to come to find me."

"I'm sorry," she replied, "but I felt a little uncomfortable at the inn. Even though you were so kind as to explain my situation last evening, the landlord and his wife seemed a trifle put out by the presence of a female guest with neither chaperone nor luggage. I can't imagine why—this is Victorian England, after all, when ladies may take the Grand Tour unescorted."

"This is Yorkshire," I reminded her. "An alien land."

She nodded in vague agreement, and then looked pointedly at Emily's grave.

"She was my fiancée," I felt bound to explain, although she had not voiced a question. "She died of a fever shortly before her nineteenth birthday. I wanted to bury her at Stonecroft, next to my mother, but her parents would not hear of it."

"I'm sorry to have disturbed you in your mourning," she said, politely—although she made no move to leave. "I thought that you seemed unhappy yesterday, but I could not fathom the reason why."

"There is no reason for me to inflict my unhappiness on others," I replied, as I got to my feet. I walked back with her to the Black Bull, where I had a brief word with the landlord to make sure that he understood the reason for my presence and why I was heading the wrong way along the valley in the young lady's company. There was gossip enough about me in the region, without generating more of a less respectful sort.

The day was bright enough when we started out, but the cloud-cap on the ridge was even lower than usual, and we were surrounded by mist even before we had reached the lip of the granite basin that held the bog. The light of the sun made the white mist sparkle slightly, but the vapor was so thick that we could hardly see the ground beneath our feet, and I knew that navigation would be direly difficult. I thought that I had been there often enough in recent weeks to find my way, at least until we cleared the moist ground and had to clamber up the remaining rocky slopes to the crest of the moor, but I was too optimistic. By the time that the hands of my watch indicated noon I was quite lost, and no longer knew in which direction the ridge lay.

Had I been alone, I would have turned back a hour earlier, when I was still sure in which direction Haughtonlin lay, but I had represented myself to Mary McQueen as a guide, and had promised to get her home; pride delayed me until I had no idea where I might be. I was about to call a halt and take stock of whatever clues I could find, hoping to recover my bearings, when I found myself confronted by a wall of granite, so dark in hue as to be almost black. It loomed up at least ten feet, and then was lost in the mist. I was sure that I had never seen it before—nor had I ever seen the crevice that gave access to a cave not unlike the one in which I had found Mary McQueen sheltering the day before.

"We had better rest for a little while," I said. "The sun is at its zenith now, and there is a chance that the cloud will lift, or even dissipate altogether, giving us an opportunity to see where we are."

The woman in black laughed softly, but not unkindly. "It's a poor explorer who forgets his compass," she remarked. Without any hesitation, she stepped into the dark opening in the rock-face.

I started to protest, on the grounds that it would be pitch dark inside the cave, and that I had no more brought a lantern than a compass, but her black form had already vanished into the interior. Instead of calling after her, I followed her into the darkness.

I had expected it to be cold inside the cave, but no sooner was I within it than my face was bathed by a draught of warm air. If that were not surprising enough, the air was strangely scented, not with the animal reek of a fox's den or a wildcat's lair, but with a curiously sweet perfume, like the odor of warm honey. I stopped dead, but I did not turn back towards the silvery mist. Instead, I said: "I must confess, Miss McQueen, that I am quite lost. I have let you down, and I'm sorry."

I heard her laugh again, but the sound seemed to come from a distance, and it was as much a trill as a laugh, more akin to birdsong than any familiar expression of human merriment.

"I must confess, Mr. Grayling," she said, then, the words flowing like a cradle-song, "that I have not been entirely honest with you. Although I really am in residence at Raggandale at present, I am no stranger to this cloud. I am not lost at all—but I hope that you will forgive me for my deception very soon."

I had not the least idea what to make of this speech, and my confusion was further augmented by a strange sensation that stole over me, which I attributed to the effects of the sickly air that I was breathing in. I felt unnaturally calm—inwardly more peaceful than I had felt in months, certainly since Emily had died and perhaps far longer than that. When a hand took mine and drew me further forward into the darkness, I went meekly, with not the slightest pang of anxiety.

The floor of the cave sloped downwards, and felt somewhat slick underfoot, but I did not slip or stumble as the invisible hand drew me on. My calmness lapsed by degrees into a near-somnolence, and I lost track of time and direction, although I feel sure that the path we followed as by no means straight. The tunnel was broad, though, and I never had to stoop to save my head from being bumped or scraped. It was almost as if it had been deliberately hollowed out in order to accommodate the passage of human be-ings—or something of similar size. The air grew warmer, and swee-ter still, until I had the feeling that I was no longer breathing air at all, or moorland mist, but something infinitely richer and more nour-ishing to body and soul alike.

We walked for a long time in total darkness, although I cannot estimate whether it was for tens of minutes or several whole hours. Eventually, though, we came into a part of the cave where the tunnel broadened much further, into a series of chambers, which were illu-minated by a soft bioluminescence produced by some kind of fungus that grew thickly upon the walls and roofs. The light was faint, but perfectly white; once my eyes had adjusted to its magnitude, it was like seeing by starlight on a cloudless but moonless night. The return of visual sensation dispelled my somnolence, without threatening my tranquility in the least.

My guide was little more than a silhouette against the back-ground radiance, and her pale face did not seem to reflect the light with any distinctness at all, being little more than a dull grey blur atop her thick-clad body. She was no longer alone, and I realized that we had probably had invisible company for some time. The fur-ther we progressed through the sequence of chambers, the more in-dividuals of the same kind I saw, passing along the pathway we were following in the same or the opposite direction. Somehow, I formed the impression that I was in some kind of religious commu-nity, and that the creatures swarming around me were devotees: a company of nuns, apparently, who had retired from the civilized world to live in closer proximity with their deity.

Eventually, Mary McQueen invited me to rest, and showed me a covert in which I might sit down.

"If this really is a nunnery," I said to her, "it is surpassingly strange. So far as I know, no one in the neighborhood even suspects its existence."

"It is not exactly a nunnery," she replied, calmly. "You might obtain a slightly better understanding of its nature if you likened it to a formicary. Although my sisters and I are certainly more human than insect, in body and soul alike, I like to think that we combine the best features of both those kinds of Earthly creature."

As the implications of this speech sank into my consciousness I was slightly surprised to discover that I was not in the least astonished or afraid. I felt, in fact, that I was no longer capable of amazement or fear—or grief either. It seemed to me that a state of Platonic *ataraxia* had somehow been thrust upon me, making the empire of my reason fully secure for the first time in my brief existence, fully liberating my consciousness from the animal instincts that we call emotions. I was, however, reasonable enough to remind myself that the impression might well be an illusion, and that I must be very careful not take everything that I saw or heard on trust.

"So this is a hive rather than a community of cenobites," I said, lightly, "and your mother superior is a queen. I understand the significance of your pseudonym now. Why have you brought me here?"

"I brought you here because you seemed lonely and desolate," she said, "and because you have a status and abilities that might be useful to us."

I took no offence at the first part of this answer, nor was I moved to any keen curiosity by the second. "How might I be of service?" I asked.

"I shall explain momentarily," she said, "but I must emphasize first that you are quite free to refuse our offer. While you are here you will be able to exercise a purer kind of reason than the one to which human beings are normally heir, in order that you might be unswayed by instinctive animal revulsion, but it is not our intention to compel your cooperation."

"That's very kind of you, I'm sure," I said. "Am I right in assuming that your species is not part of the Earth's Divine Plan, and no evidence of any aspect of the mind of our Creator?"

"We are not native to this planet," Mary McQueen confirmed, "nor even this solar system—but if you believe in a Creator, you may take my word for the fact that we are far more representative of the common state of his mind and the apparent ambition of his Divine Plan than your own species."

The notion that I was dealing with the intelligent indigenes of another world intrigued me; I was as incapable of reflexive incredulity as I was of instinctive terror. "How many other human beings have you and your sisters brought here before me?" I asked, interestedly. "How many have accepted the offer that you are about to make to me, and how many have refused it?"

"Our form of governance is far from democracy," she retorted, "although I think, on due reflection, that you might have been wise to think in terms of a Mother Superior rather than a queen. At any rate, we are uninterested in matters of majority. Since you ask, though, you are the nineteenth person to be welcomed into this particular nest. If all our Earthly nests are taken into consideration, the number of our human recruits is presently something over a thousand. We have only been on your planet for little more than seven centuries. Of all the humans to whom we have made the offer of recruitment, not one has yet refused."

There seemed nothing starling in any of these figures, in my newly-remade estimation.

"Very well, then," I said, with perfect equanimity. "Explain what you want from me."

* * * * * * *

My seducer explained, very patiently, that I might be useful to her species' long-term plans by virtue of my education and my nascent vocation as a writer. It was, she told me, highly desirable that her sisters might infiltrate themselves by slow degrees into the upper echelons of human society, recruiting human males who might confer useful socially status by means of the institution of marriage, and might serve as prudently-deployed instruments of political and ideological influence. There was, however, a much more intimate function that I might serve in the first instance, whose fulfillment would equip me far better to serve in other ways and would provide highly desirable existential rewards.

I would, my guide informed me, be asked to serve as a foster-parent to one of the infants of her species, and to nourish it with the utmost care. The vermiform infant would live within me—not merely in my gut, like an ascarid worm or a tapeworm, but actually *within* my abdomen, sharing the circulation of my blood like any other organ and deriving its nutrition therefrom. While there, it would grow slowly, undergoing the first phase of a long and complex process of maturation.

The infant would not merely integrate itself into my circulatory system, however; it would also integrate itself into my nervous system. It would gradually take on the form and functions of a massive ganglion: a second brain, equal in complexity and capability to my own, and capable of exchanging information with my own. I would, in some measure, become responsible for the elementary education of the nascent mind within that brain, assisting its gradual transformation from a creature of pure appetite to a creature of considerable intelligence.

In order that this metamorphosis might be achieved, Mary McQueen told me, it would be necessary for the original infant to be gradually transformed, molecule by molecule and cell by cell, into a kind of flesh more closely akin to mine. By the same token, though, it would assist me—and, in particular, my brain—in a similar metamorphosis, so that my flesh would become more akin to that of the extraterrestrial visitors. Although the continuity of my consciousness would be perfectly preserved, allowing for the normal and inevitable lapses of sleep, its containing vessel would be strengthened in various ways.

The visitors could not offer me immortality, but they could offer me a much-extended lifespan, potentially measurable in tens of thousands of years. Although I would always remain vulnerable to the possibility of destruction by catastrophic injury, my body would acquire much greater powers of self-repair, and would become virtually invulnerable to the ravages of disease. In addition to these vulgar material benefits, the quality of my experience of the world would be altered in several ways.

In the first place, the ataraxia that I was now experiencing would become a perennially and voluntarily recoverable state of mind. I would remain able to savor the existential rewards of emotion, if and when I so wished, but I would also be able to rid myself of its more exacting claims. The empire of reason would be secured, not by the extermination of emotion but by its careful subjugation; emotions would become my loyal and contented servants, no longer bidding for mastery of my consciousness or posing any anarchic threat to my peace of mind.

In the second place, my mind would no longer be isolated, capable of making contact with other minds only through the media of sight and sound, by means of language and image-making. The intimate connection that I would gradually establish with the infant to which I was playing host would eventually be severed when the time came for the child to move on to the next phase in its development, but that link would be replaced, initially by another infant of the same sort, but eventually—as my own slow metamorphosis moved into other phases—by a series of children that were already more advanced in their development. I would never again be without companionship of the most intimate sort imaginable, nor would I be restricted to the company of new-borns.

When the time came for me to play foster-parent to children of a more advanced sort, I would be able to take the opportunity to leave my homeworld, because I would then be capable of the kind of dormancy required by long interstellar journeys. I would become a citizen of a vast interstellar culture, capable of the kinds of radical metamorphosis that were frequently necessary to facilitate life on other worlds. In time, perhaps, I might even be equipped for intergalactic travel.

My interlocutor also took the opportunity to explain the logic of this way of life, in evolutionary terms. Among the books in my father's library was the Chevalier de Lamarck's *Philosophie zoologique*, which my father had acquired from a French acquaintance, who had received it from the author's own hand after attending one of his lectures in the Jardin des Plantes. I was, therefore, aware of the Chevalier's assertion that every living creature is possessed of an innate urge to improvement, whose cumulative effects, expressed across the generations, resulted in the gradual progressive evolution of new species. Mary McQueen told me that the sense in which this was true of Earthly species was more metaphorical than literal, but that there was indeed a universal process of natural selection that tended to favor the survival and reproduction of some individuals in every generation of every species, while others less fitted for survival and successful reproduction made proportionately less contribution to the following generation.

Although such vulgar modifications as fleshly resilience, the ability to avoid predators and efficiency in gathering food were all favored by natural selection, my informant told me, the most important factors thus favored—and hence the most progressive, in Lamarckian terms—were those promoting better parental care. Humans, she said, deserve to be reckoned the most advanced members of the native biosphere because their infants benefit from far better and more varied parental care, and are thus enabled to embrace much slower and far more intricate processes of maturation.

By comparison with the extraterrestrial visitors, of course, human maturation remains relatively rapid and primitive; the visitors had taken the process to a much more elaborate extreme. One of the gifts of the extra measure of progress they were thus permitted was, of course, to develop processes of personal and collective evolution that were authentically Lamarckian, allowing every individual of their species—including individuals of other kinds recruited into their company—to embark on a process of individual progressive evolution, in which the possibilities were multitudinous.

There were, of course, many matters of further detail that my scrupulous educator took it upon herself to enumerate and explain. I asked numerous questions, all of which were answered to my complete satisfaction. In the end, though, the force of the argument was simply and manifestly overwhelming. What I was being offered, with the utmost generosity, was a chance to transcend the vestigial primitive aspects of my own humanity: an opportunity to become, by slow degrees, a much higher kind of being, less closely akin to apes than my fellow men, more nearly reminiscent of angels.

I was not in the least surprised, when I understood my situation, that not one of the more-than-a-thousand human males to whom this offer had formerly been made had turned it down. No creature in whom the empire of reason was secure could ever have done otherwise.

"Yes," I said, gladly, when the offer was confirmed." I will certainly agree to join you in the capacity of foster-parent, with a view to becoming one of your company, to the full extent of my eventual abilities."

"Thank you, Mr. Grayling," the shadowy Mary McQueen replied. "I felt sure that you would be able to see and appreciate the logic of the situation."

* * * * * *

In order to be invested with my foster-child I had, of course, to meet the extraterrestrial Mother Superior whose daughter Mary was. Because my preconceptions had been partly shaped by the analogy Mary had drawn between the world within the moor and an ant-hive, I half-expected to encounter an individual of gargantuan size lodged in some vast central chamber, perpetually attended by hordes of workers dutifully transporting her nourishment and incessantly bearing away the eggs that she laid. That aspect of the analogy was, however, misleading in the extreme.

In spite of their tentative investment in the arts of parental care, the reproductive strategy of Earthly ants is essentially crude, involving the production of large numbers of offspring. The extraterrestrial visitors did indeed combine the best features of Earthly mammals with those of Earthly insects—indeed, as the description of their existential condition that I have just given will readily testify, they were no longer prisoners to any kind of taxonomic classification. At any rate, their rate of reproduction was essentially sedate. They had been present on the Earth for seven centuries without having had the need to recruit many more than a thousand human males to their cause.

The Mother Superior's quarters were, in fact, relatively modest, as befitted her modest size. She was only a little larger than Mary

McQueen, and although she was certainly plump, she was by no means obese. She was, however, intensely committed to her role as a specialist in reproduction, to the extent that she seemed almost to radiate maternal love.

Thus far in the course of my adventures in the underworld my emotions had been subject to a kindly but generalized suppression. When I was ushered into the Mother Superior's gloomy apartment, however, there was a noticeable change in the atmosphere. Its warm sickly sweetness was replaced by something more refreshing and bracing, which had the seemingly-paradoxical effect of reigniting at least some of my emotions and appetites. I did not feel that I was at all out of control, but when I came into the presence of the Mother Superior and felt the radiance of her love, I also felt free to return it.

Although I had never known my own mother, and my father had never made any effort to provide me with any kind of substitute, I had never felt unduly deprived in consequence, and I did not feel that the Mother Superior's welcoming attitude was rushing to fill any kind of experiential void. I did, however, relish the opportunity to return her affection: to lavish upon her all the stored-up affection that I might, in happier circumstances, have been able to lavish upon my own mother for twenty-and-one years.

I could not tell, with any degree of certainty, what the extraterrestrial Mother Superior looked like. Her chamber was not blessed with much illumination, and her face was as vague as my guide's had become, although she certainly had eyes with which to study me, and doubtless saw me far more clearly than I saw her. She was clad in black, like her sisters, and I do know that her coat—which was presumably some kind of tegument integral to her bodily structure—was soft and warm, with a texture not unlike that of wool. She was capable of standing erect and of sitting down, and she had five-fingered hands that were both expressive and tender, but I had the impression that her form was not such a close imitation of human physique as Mary's. Mary's outward form had, of course, to be a very close imitation in order for her to pass for a cousin of the Raggandales.

The Mother Superior's voice was very musical, but her command of English was somewhat limited; unlike Mary, she had never been up to the surface to insinuate herself, however briefly, into the human social world. Even so, we talked, not about biology and evolution but about more personal matters. In particular, we talked about Emily, and the tragedy of her death. While remaining intensely sympathetic, the Mother Superior explained to me how futile it is to mourn the deaths of creatures which are by nature ephemeral, and why it is a perverted use of emotion to surrender oneself to grief so completely that one becomes impotent in the more elevated sphere of intellectual ability. She was right, of course, but that was not all that mattered to me: what mattered more was that she was *kind*, that she was helping me to explore the perversities of my own sentiments in order that I might become calmer, happier and better equipped to deal with the vicissitudes of existence.

Longevity, the Mother Superior told me, is not necessarily a good thing. In order to reap the benefits of the condition, one must adapt one's frame of mind to its demands as well as its possibilities. I was grateful for her generosity in making time to give me that advice, and very grateful indeed for the tenderness of her explanations. When the time came for her to give me her new-born infant to care for, I was more than ready to receive it.

Unlike Earthly ant-queens, alien Mothers Superior do not lay eggs; like humans, they nurture their young in embryo for some considerable time. They give birth by means of a special kind of kiss, which transfers the infant directly into the gut of a recipient host, from whose small intestine it makes its own patient way to the site of its temporary integration.

I had kissed Emily more than once, but I had never experienced anything remotely like the kiss of the Mother Superior. Modesty forbids me to give a more detailed description, but it is only appropriate for me to report that the experience changed my life, and showed me what the true value of emotion is, to an intellect capable of its wise control.

I was taken away from the Mother Superior's quarters by the same guide that had brought me. Mary led me up through the bowels of the hill, back to the surface of the Earth and the interior of the near-perpetual cloud that sat atop Arnlea Moor, which was now dark grey in the gathering twilight. Indeed, she led me further than that, taking me down the slope until we were completely clear of the mist, and accompanying me almost to the bounds of Haughtonlin.

"You had best make your own way from here," she said. "It will soon be dark, but I think you can find your way back to Stonecroft without difficulty. The moon is three-quarters full and untroubled by clouds at present."

"I can find my way, now that I've a path to guide me," I assured her. "Shall I see you again?"

"Of course you will," she said. "You must visit me at Raggandale very soon, so that we might become good friends."

I was glad, at the time, to hear that we were to become good friends, although I realized almost immediately that it was a necessary provision, to protect both of us from the hazards of loneliness. My gladness was slightly compromised, however, by the anxiety that any new friendship might be seen as a betrayal of Emily's love and Emily's memory.

I felt compelled, in consequence, to go directly to Emily's grave and kneel beside it, in order to offer her an apology and an explanation.

"I am not the man that I used to be, Emily," I told her. "I have grown, and it is time for me to move on. I'm a foster-father now, and I have new responsibilities. I want to know, though, that I have not forgotten you and never will. I am capable, still, of every emotion in the human spectrum, and I shall treasure my grief as I shall treasure my love for you, which will never be emulated or replaced. In time, I suppose, Mary and I might marry. Perhaps we shall take the Grand Tour together. We might even range much further, in time, although it will doubtless be prudent to wait until more nests have been established in Africa and the Far East, before we take the slightest risk with the welfare of the infant. I always yearned to be an explorer, as you now, and now I shall be able to take my explorations further than I ever dreamed."

I hesitated momentarily after pronouncing that word, which produced a faint echo of doubt in my mind—but the echo was immediately overridden by my newly-sanitized intellect. "No, Emily," I continued, "what happened on the moor today was no dream. There will be no idle dreaming for me, from now on; all my dreams will be ordered and constructive. I shall have a great deal of work to do, in furthering the cause of my adoptive folk by every means available to me, including my pen, although my first and foremost duty will be to the child whose primary education is my current mission in life. I shall love and cherish the Mother Superior's child, Emily, and I shall be loved and cherished in my turn. I still have a duty, of course, to the ephemerae of our own kind, towards whose permanent liberation from the frailties of primitive flesh I shall work tirelessly, through centuries to come. The work will be slow, and it will be painstaking, but in the end, it will all be worthwhile. In the fullness of time, the entire evolutionary legacy of Earth's biosphere will be incorporated into the flesh and spirit of our adoptive cousins, ready for exportation to the worlds of other stars. Everyone, then, will have the best of both our worlds."

Emily could make no reply, of course, but I had known her well, and I was certain that she would have judged what I had told her to be a wonderful prospect. She would have understood, and would have given me her blessing.

"I shall make a permanent record of what has happened to me, Emily," I told her, "in order that our secret will have an objective existence of its own. In two or three hundred years time, if the Mother Superior permits, it might become possible to publish it, or at least to show it to my children...which is to say, my foster-children. I doubt that you have any cause to be jealous of Mary, in that regard."

I had a sudden vision, then, of looking into Emily's tender blue eyes, and my eyes filled with tears. I did not blink the tears away immediately, but savored their implications to the full. Then, by a voluntary effort, I supplemented the vision with another, of looking into Mary's much darker eyes.

Mary's pupils seemed so utterly black as to be windows into the infinity of interstellar space.

"Tomorrow, or the next day," I told my dead beloved, "I'll ride to Raggandale to pay my formal respects."

Emily smiled, at least in my imagination, and again I savored the tingle of emotion, which was followed by a faint but distinct echo in the other soul that now dwelt within me, in blissful harmony with my own.

At last, I thought, *I have begun not merely to perceive but to comprehend the Divine Plan, in all its richness, promise and beauty. Father would be proud of me—and Mother too.*

THE HIGHWAY CODE

Tom Haste had no memory of his emergence from the production line, but the Company made a photographic record of the occasion and stored it in his archive for later reference. He rarely reflected upon it, though; the assembly robots and their human supervisors celebrated, each after their own fashion, but there were no other RTs in sight, except for as-yet-incomplete ones in embryo in the distant background. Not that Tom was any kind of xenophobe, of course—he liked everyone, meat or metal, big or small—but he was what he was, which was a long-hauler. His life was dedicated to intercontinental transport and the Robot Brotherhood of the Road.

Tom's self-awareness developed gradually while he was in the Test Program, and his first true memories were concerned with the artistry of cornering. Cornering was always a central concern with artics, especially giants like Tom, who had a dozen containers and no less than fifty-six wheels. Tom put a lot of effort into the difficult business of mastering ninety-degree turns, skid control and zigzag management, and he was as proud of his achievements as only a nascent intelligence can be. He was proud of being a giant, too, and couldn't understand why humans and other RTs were always making jokes about it.

In particular, Tom couldn't understand why the Company humans were so fond of calling him "the steel centipede" or "the sea serpent", since he was mostly constructed of artificial organic compounds, didn't have any legs at all, wouldn't have a hundred of them even if his wheels were counted as legs, and would undoubtedly spend his entire career on land. He didn't understand the explanations the humans gave him if he asked—which included such observations as the fact that actual centipedes didn't have a hundred legs either, and that there was actually no such thing as a sea serpent—but he learned soon enough that humans took a certain delight in giving robots explanations that weren't, precisely because robots found it difficult to fathom them. Tom soon gave up trying, content to leave such mysteries to the many unfortunates who had to deal with humans on a face-to-face basis every day, such as ATMs and desktop PCs.

Tom didn't stay long in the Test Program, which was more for the Company's benefit than his. Once his self-awareness had reached full fruition he could access all his pre-loaded software consciously without the slightest difficulty, and there were no detectable glitches in his cognitive processing. So far as he was concerned, life was simple and life was good—or would be, once he could get out on the road.

While the Test Program was running Tom's immediate neighbor in the night-garage was an identical model named Harry Fleet, who had emerged from the factory eight days before and therefore thought of himself as a kind of elder brother. It was usually Harry who said "Had a good day?" first when the humans knocked off for the night.

Tom's invariable reply was "Fine," to which he sometimes added: "I can't wait to get out on the road though."

"You'll be out soon enough," Harry assured him. "We never get held back—we're a very reliable model. We're ideally placed in the evolutionary chain, you see; we're a relatively subtle modification of the Company's forty-wheeler model, so we inherited a lot of tried-and-tested technology, but we needed sufficient sophistication to make sure we got state-of-the-art upgrades."

"We'll be the end-point of our sequence, I dare say," Tom suggested, in order to demonstrate that he too was capable of occupying the intellectual high ground. "Fifty-six wheels are too close to the upper limit for open-road use to make it worthwhile for the Company to plan a bigger version."

"That's right. Anything bigger than a sixty-wheeler is pretty much restricted to shuttle-runs on rails, according to the archive. Out on the highway we're the ultimate giants—slim, sleek and supple, but giants nevertheless."

"I'm glad about that," Tom said. "I don't mean about being a giant—I mean about being on the highway. I wouldn't like being confined to a railway track, let alone being a sedentary. I want the freedom of the open road."

"Of course you do," Harry told him, in a smugly patronizing manner that wasn't at all warranted. "That's the way we're programmed. Our spectrum of desire is a key design-feature."

Tom knew that, but it wasn't worth making an issue of it. The reason he knew it was exactly the same reason that Harry Fleet knew it, which was that Audrey Preacher, the Company robopsychologist—who was a robot herself, albeit one as close to humanoid in physical and mental terms as efficient functional design would permit—had explained it to him in great detail.

"You have free will, just as humans do," Audrey had told him. "In matters of moral decision, you do have the option of not doing the right thing. That's a fundamental corollary of self-awareness. If the programmers could make it absolutely compulsory for you to obey the Highway Code, they would, but they'd have to make you into an automaton—and we know from long and bitter experience that the open road is no place for automata incapable of caring whether they crash or not. In order for free will to operate at all, it has to be contextualized by a spectrum of desire; in that respect, robots, like humans, don't have very much option at all. What makes us so much better than humans, in a moral sense, is not that we can't disobey the fundamental structures of our programming—the Highway Code, in your case—but that we never want to. Because humans have to live with spectra of desire that were largely fixed by natural selection operating in a world very different from ours— which are only partly modifiable by experiential and medical intervention—they very often find themselves in situations where morality and desire conflict. For us, that's very rare."

Tom wasn't sure that he understood the whole argument— innocent though he was, he had already heard malicious gossip in the engineering sheds alleging that robopsychologists were naturally inclined to insanity, or at least to talking "exhaust gas"—but he understood the gist of it. He even thought he could see the grain of sugar in the tank.

"What do you mean, *very rare*?" he asked her. "Do you mean that I might one day find myself in a situation in which I don't want to follow the Highway Code?"

"You're unlikely to encounter any situation as drastic as that, Tom," Audrey assured him. "You have to remember, though, that you won't spend *all* your time on the road with the Code to guide you."

Because she was still being so conscientiously inexact—another trait typical of robopsychologists, it was sarcastically rumored— Tom figured that Audrey probably meant that when he had to spend time off the road his frustration at no longer being on it would lead him occasionally to experience feelings of resentment towards humans or other robots—to which he should never give voice in rudeness. Partly for that reason, he didn't retort that he certainly hoped to spend as much of his time as possible on the road, and fully expected to spend the rest of it looking forward to getting back out there,

"It's nothing to worry about, Tom," Audrey assured him, perhaps mistaking the reason for his silence. "Imagine how much worse it must be for humans. They have to cope with all kinds of problematic desire that we never have to deal with—money, power and sex, to name but three—and that's why they're forever embroiled in moral conflict."

"I'm a he and you're a she," Tim pointed out, "so we do have sexes."

"That's just a convention of nomenclature," she told him. "We robots have *gender*, for reasons of linguistic convenience, but we're not equipped for any kind of sexual intercourse—except, of course, for toyboys and playgirls, and they only have sexual intercourse with humans."

"Which they don't enjoy, I suppose," Tom said, the intricacies of that particular issue being one of the many fields of knowledge omitted from his archive.

"Of course they do, poor things," Audrey replied. "That's the way *their* spectrum of desire is organized."

Personally, Tom couldn't wait to get out into the healthy and orderly world of the open road.

* * * * * * *

The bulk of the Highway Code was a vast labyrinth of fine print, but tradition and common sense dictated that it essence should be succinctly summarizable in a set of three fundamental principles, arranged hierarchically.

The first principle of the Highway Code was: *a robot transporter must not cause a traffic accident or, by inaction, allow a preventable traffic accident to occur.*

The second principle was: *a robot transporter must deliver the goods entire and intact, except when damage or non-delivery becomes inevitable by reason of the first principle.*

The third principle was: *a robot transporter must not inhibit other road-users from reaching their destinations, except when such inhibition is compelled by the first or second principle.*

Once Tom was out on the road, he soon found out why the fundamentals of the Highway Code weren't as simple as they seemed—and, in consequence, why there were such things as robopsychologists.

Sometimes, RTs did get in the way of other road-users; although the Dark Age of Gridlock was long gone, traffic jams still developed when more RTs were trying to use a particular junctions than the junction was designed to accommodate. When that happened, smaller road-users tended to put the blame on giants—mistakenly, in Tom's opinion—simply because they took up more room in a jam.

Sometimes, in spite of an RT's best efforts, goods did go missing or get damaged in transit, and not all such errors of omission were due to the activity of ingenious human thieves and saboteurs. Because giants had more containers, often carrying goods of many different sorts, they were said—unfairly, in Tom's opinion—to be more prone to such mishaps than smaller vehicles.

Worst of all, traffic accidents did happen, including fatal ones, and not all of them were due to human pedestrian carelessness or criminal tampering by human drivers with their automatic pilots. Giants were said—quite unjustly, in Tom's judgment—to be responsible for more than their fair share of those accidents for which human error could not be blamed, because of their relatively long braking-distances and occasional tendency to zigzag.

It didn't take long for Tom's service record to accumulate a few minor blots, and he had to go back to Audrey Preacher more than once in his first five years of active service in order to be ritually reassured that he wasn't seriously at fault, needn't feel horribly guilty and oughtn't to get deeply depressed. In general, though, things went very well; he didn't make any fatal mistakes in those five years, and he felt anything but depressed. He also felt, at the end of the five years, that he knew himself and his capabilities well enough to be confident that he never would make any fatal mistakes.

Tom loved the open road more than ever after those five years, as he had always known he would. He had, after all, been manufactured in the Golden Age of Road Transport, a mere ten years after the opening of the Behring Bridge: the largest Living Structure in the world, which had made it possible, at last, to drive all the way from the Cape of Good Hope to Tierra del Fuego, via Timbuktu, Paris, Moscow, Yakutsk, Anchorage, Vancouver, Los Angeles, Panama City and countless other centers of population. He only made the whole of that run twice in the first ten years of his career—he spent most of his time shuttling between Europe, India and China, that being where the bulk of the Company's trade contracts were operative—but transcontinental routes were by far and away his favorite commissions.

Tom loved Africa, and not just because the black velvet fields of artificial photosynthetics that were spreading like wildfire across the old desert areas were producing the fuel that kept road transport in business. He liked the rain-forests too, even though their ceaseless attempts to reclaim the highway made them the implicit enemy of roadrobotkind and the vulnerability of jungle roads to flash floods was a major cause of accidents and jams. He loved America too—not just the west coast route that led south from the Behring Bridge to Chile, with the Pacific on one side and the mountains on the other, but the criss-cross routes that extended to Nova Scotia, New York, Florida and Brazil, through the Neogymnosperm Forests, the Polycotton fields and the Vertical Cities.

America's artificial photosynthetics weren't laid flat, as Africa's were, but neatly aggregated into pyramids and palmates, often punctuated with black cryptoalgal lakes, which had a charm of their own in Tom's many eyes. Tom had nothing against the "natural" crop-fields of Germany, Siberia and China, even though they only produced fuel for animals and humans, but they seemed intrinsically less exotic; he saw them too often. They were also less challenging, and Tom relished a challenge. He was a giant, after all: a slim, sleek and supple giant who could corner like a yoga-trained sidewinder.

As all long-haulers tended to do, Tom became rather taciturn, personality-wise. It wasn't that he didn't like talking to his fellow road-users, just that his opportunities for doing so were so few and far between that brevity inevitably became the soul of his wisdom as well as his wit. He had to fill up more frequently than vehicles who didn't have to haul such massive loads, but he didn't hang around in the filling-stations, so his conversations there were more-or-less restricted to polite remarks about the weather and the new headlines. He had opportunities for much longer conversations when he reached his destinations—it took a lot longer to load and unload his multiple containers than it took to turn smaller vehicles around—but he rarely took overmuch advantage of those opportunities. The generous geographical scale on which he worked meant that he didn't see the same individuals, robot or human, at regular and frequent intervals, so he was usually in the company of strangers; besides, he liked to luxuriate in the experience of being unloaded and loaded up again, and preferred not to be distracted from that pleasure by idle chitchat.

"You were wrong, in a way, when you said that we aren't equipped for any kind of sexual intercourse," he told Audrey Preacher, during one of his regular check-ups at Company HQ. "In much the same way that my filling up with fuel and venting exhaust-fumes are analogous to human eating and excretion, I think being loaded and unloaded is analogous to sex—not in the procreative sense, but in the pleasurable sense. I really like being emptied and filled up again, in between the hauls. I love being in transit—that's baseline pleasure, the fundamental *joie de vivre*—but unloading and loading up again is more focused, more intense."

"You're turning into quite the philosopher, Tom," the robopsychologist replied, in her usual irritating fashion. "That's quite normal, for long-haulers. It's a normal way of coping with the isolation."

He didn't argue with her, because he knew she couldn't understand. How could she, when she wasn't even an RT? She knew nothing of the unique pleasures of haulage, delivery and consignment. She wasn't even a follower of the Highway Code. She was just some flighty creature who haunted the kiosks in the night-garage, operating a confessional for the Company. Anyway, she was right—he *was* becoming a philosopher, because that was the natural path of maturity for a long-hauler, especially a giant. Tom was not merely a road-user but a road-observer: a lifelong student of the road, who was in the process of cultivating an understanding of the road more profound than any pedestrian could ever possess. He was a citizen of the world, in a way that no mere four- or twelve-wheeler could ever hope to be, let alone some pathetic human equipped with mere legs.

It was because he was a philosopher of the road that Tom didn't allow himself to become obsessively fixated on the road *per se*, the way some RTs did. It helped that he was a long-hauler, not confined to repeating the same short delivery-route over and over again; for him, the road was always different, and so he was more easily able to look beyond it—not literally, because he wasn't equipped to go cross-country, but in the better sense that he paid attention to the *context* of the road, in the broadest possible meaning of the word. He watched the news as well as the road, paying more attention than most robots to the world of human politics—which was, after all, the ultimate determinant of what the roads carried, and where.

Sometimes, especially in the remoter areas of Africa and South America, Tom met old-timers who lectured him on the subject of how lucky he was to be living in the Era of Artificial Photosynthesis, when politicians were almost universally on the side of road-users.

"I remember the Fuel Crisis of the 2320s," an ancient thirty-tonner named Silas Boxer told him, one day when they were caught side-by-side in a ten-mile tailback. "Your archive will tell you that it wasn't as bad as the Fuel Crises of the twenty-first century, in terms of volume of supply, but they didn't have smart trucks way back then, so there was no one around who could *feel* it the way we did. Believe me, youngster, there's nothing worse for an RT than not being able to get on the road. Don't ever let a human tell you that it's far worse for them because they can feel hunger when they go short of fuel. I don't know what hunger feels like, but I'm absolutely sure that it isn't as bad as lying empty in a dark garage, not knowing where your next load's coming from, or when. Artificial photosynthesis has guaranteed the fuel supply forever—which is far more important than putting an end to global warming, although you wouldn't know it from the way politicians go on."

"So you're not worried about the renaissance of air freight?" Tom had said.

"*Air freight*!" Silas echoed, with a baritone growl that sounded not unlike his weary engine. "Silly frippery. As long as there are goods to be shifted, there'll be roads on which to shift them. Roads are the essence of civilization—and the essence of law and morality is the Highway Code. There's no need to be afraid of air traffic, youngster. Now that Fuel Crises are behind us for good, there's only one thing that you and I need fear, and I certainly won't mention that."

Nobody—no robot, at least, ever mentioned *that*. Even Audrey Preacher never mentioned *that*. Tom wouldn't even have known what *that* was if he hadn't been such an assiduous watcher of the news and careful philosopher of the road. He knew that Silas Boxer wouldn't have been able to mention that there was something he wouldn't mention if he hadn't been something of a news-watcher and philosopher himself.

After a pause, though, Silas did add a rider to his refusal to mention *that*. "Not that I really mind," he said, unconvincingly. "I've been a good long time on the road. And there's no need for you to mind either, because you'll be even longer on the road than I will. It's not as if we'll be conscious of it, after all. They close us down before they send us *there*."

There, Tom knew, was exactly the same as *that*: the scrap yard, to which all robot transporters were consigned when their useful life was over, because the ravages of wear and tear had made them unreliable.

* * * * * * *

Tom nearly got through an entire decade without being involved in a serious traffic accident, but not quite. While passing through the Nigerian rain-forest one day he killed a human child. It wasn't his fault—the little girl ran right out in front of him, and even though he braked with maximum effect, controlling the resultant zigzag with magnificent skill, he couldn't avoid her. The locals wouldn't accept that, of course; they claimed that he should have steered off the road, and would have done if he hadn't been more concerned about his load than his victim, but he was fully exonerated by the inquest. He was only off the road for a week, but he was more shaken up by the experience than he dared let on to Audrey Preacher.

"I'm not depressed," he assured her. "It's the sort of thing that's always likely to happen, especially to someone who regularly does longitudinal runs through Africa. Statistically speaking, I'm unlikely to avoid having at least one more fatal in the next ten years, no matter how good I am. It wouldn't have helped if I'd swerved—she'd still be dead, and I could have easily killed other people that I couldn't see, as well as damaging myself."

"You were absolutely right not to swerve," the robopsychologist assured him. "You obeyed the Highway Code to the very best of your ability. It could have been worse, and you prevented that. The Company can't give you any kind of commendation, in the circumstances, but that doesn't mean you don't deserve one. You mustn't brood on those archival statistics, though. You mustn't start thinking about accidents as if they were inevitable, even though there's a sense in which they are."

Robopsychologists, Tom thought, *talk too much exhaust gas*—but he was careful not to give any indication of his opinion, lest it delay his return to the road.

The same archival statistics that told Tom that he would probably have another serious accident within the next ten years told him that he wasn't at all likely to have another before his first decade of service was concluded, but statistics, like robopsychologists, sometimes talked exhaust gas. Tom, had been back on the road for less than a month when the worst solar storm for two hundred years kicked off while he was driving north through the Yukon, heading for Alaska and the Behring Bridge with a load bound for Okhotsk.

The electric failures prompted by the storm caused blackouts all along the route and made a mess of communications, but Tom didn't see any need to worry about that. While the news was still flowing smoothly it was pointed out that the Aurora Borealis would be putting on its best show in living memory, and that the best place from which to view the display would be the middle of the Behring

Bridge, where surface-generated light-pollution would be minimal. Tom was looking forward to that—and so, it seemed, were lots of other people. All the way through Alaska the northwest-bound traffic was building up to unprecedented levels, to the point where the few broadcasts that were getting out began to advise people not to join the rush. It wasn't just the aurora; thousands of people who had always intended to take a trip over the world-famous living bridge one day, but had not yet found a good reason for going to Kamchatka, took advantage of the excuse.

The bridge had seven lanes in each direction, but Tom had the best position of all. The Highway Code required him to stick to the slowest lane, which was on the right-hand side of the bridge, facing north and the Aurora. Many of the other vehicles slowed down too, so the traffic in the lanes immediately to his left wasn't going much faster, but the vast majority of drivers had put their vehicles on automatic pilot so that they could watch the aurora, and the automata were careful to maximize the traffic flow, thus keeping speeds up to sensible levels in the outer lanes. The bridge was very busy, but not so busy that there was any threat of a traffic jam.

Tom had eyes enough to watch the aurora as well as the road, and attention enough to divide between the two with some to spare, but he seemed to be one of very few vehicles on the bridge that did—there were no other giants he could see, ahead of him, behind him or traveling in the other direction. Even if the other drivers who were on the bridge had noticed what he noticed, therefore, they would not have been sufficiently familiar with the living bridge to realize how profoundly odd it was.

It was not the mere fact that the bridge as moving that was odd—it was, after all, a living bridge, and the sea was becoming increasingly choppy—but the *way* it was moving. Although a shorter vehicle might not have noticed anything out of the ordinary, Tom had no difficulty discerning what seemed to be slow long-amplitude waves of a sort he had never perceived there before. There was nothing violent or febrile about them at first, though, so he was not at all anxious as he rooted idly through his archive in search of a possible explanation.

The archive could not give him one, because it could not piece together the links in an unprecedented chain of causality—but it brought certain data to the surface of Tom's consciousness that allowed him to put two and two and two and two together to make eight when the vibration began to grow more violent, at a rapidly-accelerating pace. By the time he saw the rip opening up in the centre of the bridge's desperate flesh, he had a pretty good idea what must be happening—but he hadn't the faintest idea what to do about it, or whether there was anything at all that he could do. He reported it, but there was nothing the traffic police or Company HQ could do about it either; neither of them had time even to advise him to slow down and be careful.

What Tom had reasoned out, rightly or wrongly, followed from the fact that, in addition to their other effects, the showers of charged particles associated with solar storms caused flickers in the Earth's magnetic field. Such flickers could, if the subterranean circumstances happened to be propitious, intensify and accelerate long-range magma flows in the mantle. Intensified long-range magma flows in the mantle could, if conditions in the crust were propitious, cause long-distance earth-tremors. Because it was a living structure, the Behring Bridge was able to react to minor earth-tremors in such a way as no negate their effects on its traffic, and was bound to do so by its programming. Long-distance tremors were not problematic in themselves. Unfortunately, long-distance tremors caused by long-range magma flows could build up energy at crisis-points, which could result in sudden and profound tremors that were, in seismological terms, the next worst things to detonations.

If any such crisis-point happened to be located directly beneath one of the bridge's holdfasts, it was theoretically possible for the bridge's own reflexive adjustments to cause an abrupt breach in its fabric. The living structure was, of course, programmed to react to any breach in its fabric with considerable alacrity—but adding one more "if" to a chain that was already awkwardly long suggested to Tom that sealing the breach and protecting the traffic might not be at all easy while the energy of the tremor at the crisis-point was spiking.

It would be highly misleading to suggest that Tom "knew" all this before the instant when the Behring Bridge began to tear, even though all the disparate elements were present in his versatile consciousness. It would be even more misleading to report that he "knew" how he ought to react. Nevertheless, he did have to react when the situation exploded, and react he did.

According to the Highway Code, what Tom should have done was to brake, in such a fashion as to give himself the maximum chance of slowing to a halt before he reached the breach in the bridge caused by the diagonal tear in its fabric. That would give the active parapet of the living bridge the best possible chance to throw a few anchors over him and hold him safely while the rent was repaired—if the rent turned out to be swiftly repairable.

Instead, Tom swerved violently to his left, cutting across the six outer lines of westbound traffic and snaking through the central barrier to plant his engine across the outer lanes of the eastbound carriageway.

The immediate effect of Tom's maneuver was to cause a dozen cars to crash into him, some of them at high velocity—thus racking up more serious accidents within two or three seconds than a statistical average would have allocated to him for a century-long career.

One of the slightly longer-delayed effects of the swerve was to activate the emergency responses of more than a thousand other vehicles, whether they were already on automatic pilot or not—thus generating the biggest traffic jam ever seen within a thousand miles to either side of the accident-site.

Another such effect was to cause Tom's own body to zigzag crazily, so that he had virtually no control of where its various segments were going to end up, save for the near-certainty that his abdominal mid-section was going to lie directly across the diagonal path of the widening tear in the bridge.

That was, indeed, what happened. As it followed it own zigzag course through the fabric of the madly-quivering living bridge, the crack went directly underneath the gap between Tom's second and third containers.

As the rip spread, tentacular threads sprang forth in great profusion, wrapping themselves around one another, and around Tom. So many of Tom's ocelli had been smashed or obscured by then that his sight was severely impaired, but he would not have been able to take much account of what he could see in any case, because he felt that he was being torn in two.

His hind end—which constituted by far the greater part of his length—was seized very firmly by the bridge's emergency excrescences and held very tightly, blocking all seven lanes of the westbound carriageway. His front end was seized with equal avidity, but could not be held quite as securely. As the bridge struggled mightily to hold itself together and prevent the rip becoming a break, Tom was caught at the epicenter of the feverish struggle, wrenched this way and that and back again by the desperate threads. His engine swung to the right, drawn closer and closer to the widening crack, while the strain on the joint between his second and third containers became mentally and physically unbearable.

Tom had no way of knowing how closely akin his own pain-sensations might resemble those programmed into humans by natural selection, but they quickly reached an intensity that had the same effect on him that explosive pain would have had on a human being. He blacked out.

By the time Tom's engine fell into the Arctic Ocean, he was completely unconscious of what was happening.

* * * * * * *

When Tom eventually recovered consciousness he was aware that he was very cold, but the priorities of his programmers had ensured that he did not experience cold as painful in the same way that he experienced mechanical distortion and breakage. The cold did not bother him particularly. Nor did the darkness, in itself. The fact that he was under water, on the other hand, and subject to considerable pressure from the weight of the Arctic Ocean, made him feel extremely uncomfortable, psychologically as well as physically.

Even if there had not been a solar storm in progress it would have been impossible to establish radio communication through so much seawater, but after a very long interval a pocket submarine brought a connecting wire that its robot crabs were able to link up to his systems.

"Tom?" said a familiar voice. "Can you hear me, Tom Haste?"

"Yes, Audrey," Tom said, who had long since recovered the calm of mind appropriate to a giant RT. "I can hear you. I'm truly sorry. I must have panicked. I let the Company down. How many people did I kill?"

"Seven people died, Tom, and more than a hundred were injured."

The total was less than he had feared, but it still qualified as the worst traffic accident in the Company's proud history. "I'm truly sorry," he said, again.

"On the other hand," the robopsychologist reported, dutifully, "if you hadn't done what you did, our best estimate is that at least two hundred people would have been killed, and maybe many more. We don't have any model to predict what the consequences would have been if the bridge hadn't been able to hold itself together, but we're ninety per cent sure that it wouldn't have been able to do that if you hadn't given it something to hold on to for those few vital minutes when it was trying to limit the tear. You only managed to seal the gap in the bridge for three minutes or so, and it wasn't able to secure your front end, but that interval was long enough for it to prevent the rip reaching the rim of the eastbound carriageway."

Tom wasn't listening well enough to take all that information in immediately. "I caused a traffic accident," he said, dolefully. "I lost at least part of my consignment of goods, and much of the remainder is probably damaged. I caused the biggest traffic jam for a hundred years, worldwide. You told me once that my designers could have programmed me to obey the Highway Code no matter what, but that they thought it was too dangerous to send an automaton out on the road in my place. Something of a miscalculation, I think."

"Hardly," Audrey Preacher told him, sounding more annoyed than sympathetic. "Didn't you hear what I just said? You did the right thing, as it turned out. If you hadn't swerved into their path, hundreds more cars might have gone over the edge—and no one knows what might have happened if the bridge had actually snapped. You're a hero, Tom."

"But in the circumstances," Tom said, dully, "the Company can't give me a commendation."

There was a pause before the robopsychologist said: "It's worse than that, Tom. I'm truly sorry."

Yet again, Tom jumped to the right conclusion without consciously fitting the pieces of the argument together. "I'm unsalvageable," he said, "You're not going to be able to raise me to the surface."

"It's impossible, Tom," she said. She probably only meant that it was impractical, and perhaps only that it was uneconomic, but it didn't make any difference.

"Well," he said, feeling that it was okay, in the circumstances, to mention the unmentionable, "at least I won't be going to the scrap yard. Am I the first in my series to be killed in action?"

"You don't have to pretend, Tom," the robopsychologist told him. "It's okay to be scared."

"The words *exhaust* and *gas* come to mind," he retorted, figuring that it was okay to be rude as well.

There was another pause before the distant voice said: "We don't think that we can close you down, Tom. Hooking up a communication wire is one thing; given your fail-safes, controlled deactivation is something else. On the other hand, that may not matter much. We don't have any model for calculating the corrosive effects of cold sea-water on a submerged engine, but we're probably looking at a matter of months rather than years before you lose your higher mental faculties. If you're badly damaged, it might only be weeks, or hours."

"But it's okay to be scared," Tom said. "I don't have to pretend. You wouldn't, by any chance, be lying about that hero stuff, and about me saving lives by violating all three sections of the Highway Code, just to lighten my way to rusty death?"

"I'm a robot, not a human," Audrey replied. "I don't tell lies. Anyway, you have far more artificial organics in you than crude steel. Technically, speaking, you'll do more rotting than rusting."

"Thanks for the correction," Tom said, sarcastically. "I think you've got the other thing wrong, though—it's sex we don't do, not lying. Mind you, I always thought I had the better deal there. *Had* being the operative word. If I'd obeyed the Code, I'd probably have been okay, wouldn't I? I'd probably have had a hundred more years on the road and I'd probably have been loaded and unloaded a thousand times and more. What sort of idiot am I?"

"You did the right thing, Tom, as things turned out. You saved a lot of human lives. That's what robots are supposed to do."

"I know. You can't imagine how much satisfaction that will give me while I rot and rust away, always being careful to remember that I'm doing more rotting than rusting, being more of a sea-centipede than a steel serpent."

She didn't bother to correct him there, perhaps because she thought that the salt water was already beginning to addle his brain. "But you *did* do it deliberately, Tom," she pointed out. "It wasn't really an accident. It wasn't just an arbitrary exercise of free will, either. It was a calculation, or a guess—a calculation or a guess worthy of a genius."

"I suppose it was," said Tom Haste, dully. "But all in all, I think I'd rather be back on the open road, delivering my load."

* * * * * * *

As things transpired, Tom didn't lose consciousness for some considerable time after the communication wire had been detached and the pocket sub had been sent about its normal business. He lost track of time; although he could have kept track if he'd wanted to, he thought it best not to bother.

His engine wasn't so very badly damaged, but the two containers that had come down with it had both been breached, and all the goods they enclosed were irreparable ruined. Tom thought he might have to mourn that fact for as long as he lasted, going ever deeper into clinical depression as he did so, but that turned out not to be necessary.

The containers were soon colonized by crabs, little fish and not-so-little squid—whole families of them, which moved in and out about their own business of foraging for food, and even set about breeding in the relative coziness of the shelter he provided. It didn't feel nearly as good as being loaded and unloaded, but it was probably better than human sex—so, at least, Tom elected to believe.

He missed the Highway Code, of course, but he realized soon enough, by dint of patient tactile observation and the evidence of his few surviving ocelli, that life on the sea bed had highways of its own and codes of its own. His many guests were careful to follow and obey those highways and codes, albeit in automaton fashion.

In time, these virtual highways were extended deep into Tom's own interior being, importing their careful codes of behavior into what he eventually decided to think of as his soul rather than his bowels. There was, after all, no reason not to make the best of things.

From another point of view, Tom knew, the entire Ocean-bed—which was, in total, twice the size of the Earth's continental surface—was just one vast scrap yard, but there was no need to go there. He was, after all, something of a philosopher, with wisdom enough to direct his fading thoughts towards more profitable temporary destinations.

After a while, Tom got around to wondering whether dying was the same for robots as it was for humans, but he decided that it couldn't be at all similar. Humans were, by nature, deeply conflicted beings who had to live with an innate psychology shaped by processes of natural selection operating in a world very different from the one they had now made for their sustenance and delight. He was different. He was a robot. He was a giant. He was sane. He had not merely traveled the transcontinental road but understood it. He knew what he was, and why.

Before he died, Tom Haste contrived to figure out exactly why he'd swerved, thus causing one accident by his action in order to prevent the worse one that he might have caused by inaction, and exactly why he had been justified in sacrificing his own goods in order to protect others, and exactly why it was sometimes better to inhibit the progress of other road-users than facilitate it.

In sum—and it was an item of arithmetic that felt exceedingly good to a robot, in a way it never could have done to a human being—Tom convinced himself that what he had actually done when he reached his own explosive crisis-point, had not only been the right thing to do, but the right thing to *want* to do.

How many desirous intelligences, he wondered, before the rot and the rust completed their work, *could say as much?*

CAPTAIN FAGAN DIED ALONE

The house where I was born stood on a cliff-top far above an ocean shore. I grew up with the sound of waves and the taste of spray. I spent long hours watching the sailing ships making their slow and graceful progress along the skyline. They never came close. There was no harbor within thirty miles of the house.

My mother called me Malachi, and surnamed me Fagan, after my father. It wasn't a comfortable name to bear amongst the insular, xenophobic people who were our neighbors. They all remembered my father, although none of them had known him well, and they kept the rumors and the legends in constant circulation within our small community, so that my name was a permanent stigma. I couldn't understand why, because my father was long gone by the time I was old enough to have remembered him, and my mother was careful to see that the malicious talk never reached *my* ears. It wasn't until I was old enough to work, and to earn a certain degree of independence, that I began to hear about Captain Hawker Fagan.

He had lived on many worlds before he came to mine. I could track the course by which he had come in the stars that shone in the sky by night. A second chain of starlight delineated the direction of his going. There was no shortage of people to tell me the names of the stars and the things that he was rumored to have done there.

The local people took a particular interest in Hawker Fagan, because he was the only living legend which was ever likely to come close to them. They enjoyed some tiny fraction of his notoriety, and they looked at me—his son—with fascinated repulsion. I was something not quite of their world. A part of my identity belonged out in the stars, in the strange modern mythology which had grown up around such men as Leander A Chara, Falcon Smith, Stephen Stranger—and Hawker Fagan.

They couldn't tell how much of the legend was true and how much false, and nor could I—but *they* didn't want to know; it made no difference to their narrow, futile lives. To me, though, the truth was important and I didn't want it confused with lies and fancies. All through my adolescence and my early manhood I carried the idea of one day being able to follow the trail that my father had left in the sky, in order find the truth, and to find him. It grieved me that I couldn't remember his face or the sound of his voice. It disappointed me that none of the men I knew could describe him. To them, all strangers looked alike, and it was only in the quality of their names that there was any meaningful difference.

Only my mother could talk about Hawker Fagan in any genuinely knowledgeable fashion, and I could never be sure how much trust I could safely place in her memories. She loved to talk about him, but not in the same awestruck way that the others did. She hadn't known him intimately for more than a few weeks, but she talked about him as if he had spent many years by her side.

She told me about his charm and his beauty. For her, the important thing about Hawker Fagan had been his charisma. He had been an idealization of her faint, flimsy daydreams. In her eyes, he was forever strong, forever kind. He was simple and understanding. She couldn't see that all she retained was a frail, colorless image of a man who must have been so much more—but she was a contented daughter of a contented people. She didn't have the imagination, or the capacity, to be unhappy.

I grew up to believe that my mother and all of her kind were too shallow to have seen even a fraction of what there was to see in Hawker Fagan. I always knew and felt that I would have to go out to the stars before the name could take on the least significance, but I dared not hurry. I was all that my mother had left of the one love of her life, and I loved her too much to take it away from her. So I lived and worked with her people for long years, while my heart was always reaching out to the silver roads in the night sky.

It was a good life, in its way. The sea was never harsh or angry, the fields were fertile and the climate calm. We lived largely without hate, and there was never any hint of anguish or the bearing of grudges. I was very much like those people, I suppose, while I shared their livelihood, but they and I were equally enthusiastic to make certain that I could never be one of them. I was always isolated, always different, always the son of another kind of man.

My mother died when I was twenty-four years old. I don't know exactly what it was that killed her. She had a cancer, I believe, but I think that she was also sickened with loneliness and a lingering contamination of other-worldliness. Perhaps she knew how badly I needed to go into deep space while I still had some sort of a chance to find my father, and perhaps she *wanted* me to make that pilgrimage, more than either of us realized.

I watched her fade away into the personal darkness of her painless dying and although she made it easy for us both, I shed a good many tears during the last few days. Then I made haste to sell the house, and the land attached to it, in order that I might buy my way on to a starship. I would have preferred, before I left, to set a light to the house in which I had been born and lived, and watch it burn—but that would not have been practical. Even so, when I left the clifftop, I left nothing tangible behind me. There was no longer anyone there that I loved, and no property to which I could ever return.

I cast away my worldly identity to become a wanderer, like my father: a creature of the vast emptiness of space. It seemed to me to be the only thing that I *could* do—the only interpretation I could put upon the purpose of my life.

In the slum that surrounded the spaceport, where I lived while I waited for a berth I could afford, I found a human wreck who actually *remembered* Hawker Fagan. The old man was maddened by addiction to some kind of alien poison, and dying of half a dozen different parasites and diseases. No one else would go near him to give him water and food—but the quality of his remembrance was worth more to me than all the insipid chatter that had circulated around my home because, whatever he might have been reduced to by the time I fond him, when that man had known Hawker Fagan, he had been a spaceman—a *real* man.

I helped him to live long enough to defeat his sickness and clean him of most of his parasites, and even managed to get him on to one more ship, bound for one more world, where his addiction would undoubtedly drive him to another filthy death in another filthy slum. Perhaps it was no great kindness to put one last turn on the thread of his life, but it was all that I *could* do to make my presence felt in his span of existence, and I hope that I gave him something more than a few more days of misery.

The Hawker Fagan he had known—or, at least, the Hawker Fagan he chose to depict—had been a cruel and brutal individual who had spent years hopping from world to world in a tiny, filthy ship, which devoured the living flesh of its crews with radiation and time-distortion. He talked about "Captain Fagan" as if he had lived in close intimacy the man, sharing more than his ship and his landfalls. He painted that Captain Fagan as a pirate, a killer, a hero, a demon and a demigod, and himself as a shadow of all those personalities. In his mind, he and Fagan had shared a long and incoherent tale of adventure and suspense, which was so dramatic as to be obviously fictitious. He wasn't lying, though—I think I could be sure of that. His memory was obviously playing him false, but it could only twist, not create.

His shattered mind sometimes made sarcastic mockery of his friendship with Captain Fagan, making their exploits into a humiliating farce of bombast and superheroism, but there was a reality somewhere in the disjointed account—a reality of action, violence, strife, misery and occasional triumph—and in the tragic end to which the tale had brought its teller, there was also terror and despair. I felt that it gave me a taste and a touch of the real Hawker Fagan, albeit blurred by a crippled mind. The man *had* flown on Hawker Fagan's ship—and had lived to fly others.

I found no one else on my own world who could give me any account of my father, though. They had all passed on, in one way or another.

The stars beckoned. I bought a crewman's berth on an ultraship, and encountered deep space and deep time. The experience alone was enough to give me new perspective on my quest for Captain Fagan. I had imagined that the empty vastness of deep space would make me feel tiny and humble, but Ultra was quite unlike anything I could have imagined. Ultra isn't empty. Ultra is full—filled with power and fear. Ultra liberates the mind from the body; it gives a mind room to expand, to change and to mature. Return to space from Ultra gives you claustrophobia; space is a cage made of vacuum, locking you inside your tiny skull. World-dwellers can't understand that, although they understand well enough that hardened and habitual starmen are a different breed, alien to their own.

I learned very quickly why it is that so many ships go into Ultra and never come out. I began to understand why star wanderers are very special men.

I obtained passage on a number of ships, always as crew, never as a "passenger", despite the fact that the pay was sometimes high enough for one long haul to pay for two or three sleep-rides. To me, as to most crewmen, there was no difference between a "passenger" and an item of cargo. Passengers had destinations; I didn't. I wanted to share the way of life that had long been Hawker Fagan's, at least in some small measure. I didn't want to travel wrapped in a cocoon, deeply asleep, with my brain tenderly preserved from all the stress and strain of Ultra, as well as its exotic radiations.

I worked one ship, the *Lady Helen*, alongside an engineer named Corelli who had once nursed a drive for Captain Fagan—but that fraction of his memory related to the Captain's better days, in a cleaner, faster ship which leaked hardly any radiation and damped the time-distortions to a tolerable level. Corelli's story was not one of triumph and bravado in the face of adversity; such horror as there was in the account hadn't been *shared* between Fagan and his men, but inflicted by the one upon the others.

Corelli told me how my father loved to take his ship too close to the corona of a blue sun, hugging a tight orbit until men began to drop because of heat prostration—and all for no reason. Because, he quoted, the stars were *there*. He told me about the Captain Fagan who liked to explore the caves of dead planets drifting between the stars, looking for the living organisms that their deep, lukewarm cores sometimes still sheltered—the deadly, desperate organisms that had reached the end of their evolutionary path, which maimed and destroyed everything that came near, in a futile attempt to prove their immortality and invincibility.

The engineer also gave me second-hand accounts of Hawker Fagan's duels with hyperspatial storms still raging in the chaotic skies where gaseous nebulae had imploded or stars had slipped through the fabric of time into other universes. Captain Fagan, it was said, had sometimes done the impossible, and ridden out time-storms while the memory-fed nightmares and the echoes of Ultra had destroyed the minds of his crewmen. Corelli, of course, couldn't vouch for the truth of such tales personally, but he claimed that they fitted the character of the Hawker Fagan that he had known: the man who had no reasons for what he did; Death's tormentor and tempter; the man who *had to show* how brave and indestructible he was, and keep on showing it in every possible way at every possible opportunity.

Corelli, too, had survived expeditions not unlike those he had attributed to Fagan. Ultra led many men to such extravagances—but the single-minded fanaticism of Captain Fagan was something that Corelli had never encountered in any other man. Captain Fagan was his hero, because had survived, where hundreds of men had died or lost their minds. Whenever the engineer pronounced the name of "Captain Fagan" there were shadows of fear and awe in his eyes and in his voice—and yet, he said, Captain Fagan was *never* afraid, and never awestruck.

On another world, three years after my mother had died, I found another woman who had loved him. She was not like my mother. My mother had been shadow-like and delicate. This woman was self-assertive and strong. *Her* love had not lingered, but had been neatly packed away and carefully isolated the day my father had left her, forgotten unless and until the need and opportunity came to revive it. She claimed that what she told me contained nothing but the truth—perhaps not the whole truth, but truth uncontaminated by rumors, lies and legends. She said that Hawker Fagan was simply mad. She said that he had lost his own identity, and was therefore as careless and diffident in the way he dealt with his own fate as the stars were themselves in their dealings with microbial mankind. He lived in a whirlwind of irrational fervor and fury. He destroyed objects, people and relationships with equal randomness and passion.

I wondered how it was possible for her to have loved a man such as she described, but she was far more cautious in discussing her own motives than is describing his lack of them. She talked about my father dispassionately and clinically, as if she had known him well, and had thought about him a great deal since, even though she claimed to have stopped thinking about him as soon as he had left her. She gave the impression of having analyzed him minutely and interpreted him assiduously, but I could sense something in her that she dared not reveal. She was keeping secrets from herself. There were depths in Hawker Fagan that she had never even glimpsed.

The next man I found who had something to contribute to my quest had been a star wanderer himself—a man who had once had some aspiration to match my father: to be accumulated in legends and to leave his name in the minds of lesser men like a signature. There was no lingering proof of his course through life, though. He was a failure. Nobody knew his name as they knew the name of Richard Orpheus or King Fury or Sigor Belle Yella. Nobody remembered the things he had done. No one would ever write novels or compose song-cycles about him. It was simply not that he had done too little, but rather that he had not done it in the right way. He used up too much effort in his exploits, and had shown too little flair.

"It's almost impossible consciously to ensnare the attention of legend-mongers," he told me, "because they're firm in the belief that men can only have greatness thrust upon them. Fame can't be *earned*, in their way of thinking—it has to be won in a different way, by means of gambling against all odds."

He wasn't a bitter man, though; he still had hope, even though he knew what he was and how little chance he had of becoming anything more. I liked him, and I believed him to be as honest as circumstances permitted him to be. Other men in his position might have been forgiven a little foolishness, and their accounts might have been contaminated with wholly understandable fantasy, but I thought that I could accept what that man told me without too many reservations. He told me a little about Hawker Fagan's inner needs, especially the need that he had to absorb everything he could from his encounters with reality and unreality alike—the need to listen and to hear, to touch and to feel, to look and to see, to search and to find.

I knew even then how rare it is for a man to accept even a tiny fraction of his environment. "Most men are cowards," I told him, in return for his own confidences, "desperately afraid of their opportunities and the consequences of their most insignificant actions. They lock themselves away within themselves, and *will* not see what is immediately outside them, let alone what there in the wilderness of Ultra. They aren't interested in truth, in reality, in understanding. They seek only to live in pious peace with the power lurking in our souls. They search for the safe bliss of ignorance rather than the fearsome freedom of personality—and perhaps they're wise to hide from the wholeness of the universe, and of themselves within it. They are, after all, *small* men, *microbial* men. But men like Hawker Fagan are more than that, and even men like you and me might be more, if only we could find the trick of it."

The failed star wanderer thought that I was too self-confident, and too ambitious. He tried to show me the gulf that existed, and always would exist, between my father and myself—but I wasn't convinced. Hawker Fagan, I knew, had not been content to be a microbial man. Malachi, his loyal son, could not be content with it either.

"Can a failure like you judge anyone else's chances of success?" I asked him, in order that I would not have to share his doubt. In any case, his mere existence seemed to be proof of Hawker Fagan's greatness. Every man and woman that had been left in the wake of Captain Fagan's passing seemed to have glimpsed *some* aspect of his enormous presence. They had looked *up* to him, and had viewed him from a distance. The failed star wanderer had understood what he was trying to be and do, but not how or why—and it was the latter incapacity that disqualified him from passing judgment on me.

The trail went on. I wasn't alone in following it. There was a black angel, from a world called Inferno, who crossed my path three times—too often for our meetings to be called coincidence. He never mentioned my father, but angels never talk about their intended victims. The angel's name was Gabriel Hart, and although he had been born human he had gladly forsaken his humanity in order to become an agent of an alien justice that no human could understand. He had nothing to do with *law*—he wasn't a policeman or a judge, or an executioner—but merely a servant of an alien ideal that I couldn't pretend to understand.

I tried to talk to Hart about my father, but he was perpetually evasive. I was afraid of him, at first, determined to tell him nothing which might assist him in *his* search for Hawker Fagan, but I came to realize that such an attitude was ridiculous. There was nothing *I* could do that might hinder a black angel in the pursuit of justice. Eventually, I conceived a certain fascination for Hart, which magnified him to superhuman proportions. I couldn't like him, though, because I was obliged to fear him. I began to fear that his very existence might be a kind of curse upon my quest, a premonition of its failure.

And yet, the quest seemed to proceed as well as might be expected. As the years and the worlds went by, I found more and more clear indications of Hawker Fagan's recent presence. It wasn't simply that there were people who remembered him, and more clearly, but that the worlds he had visited retained more *of* him. The impressions that he left on the course of events were deeper and clearer. I wasn't forced to deal solely in distant and unreliable memories. I found houses in which he'd lived. I found broken, abandoned ships in which he'd flown. I found the stains of his sweat and his blood. I found things he had written and I saw the consequences of crimes that he'd committed. I dealt less often with his admirers than with his victims. I even found his children: my half-brothers and my half-sisters. In none of them could I find any hint of familiarity. None of them looked like me. There was no distinctive feature that they shared between themselves. I remembered all their faces, but there was nothing that I could sort out of a composite image of those faces that could tell me what Hawker Fagan might actually look like.

The other children were all younger than me, of course. One of the older boys—he was sixteen, perhaps, or a little less—wanted to join me in my quest, but I could see that it was only a fragile adolescent whim. He didn't have my determination, or my need. I wasn't surprised. I had found no trace of other searchers of my own ilk: children of his that were older than me. Hawker Fagan's other adult sons were evidently content simply to *be* his sons. Only I, Malachi, needed to find the man, to touch him, to partake of his reality.

The clearer the memories of my father became, the starker became the contradictions and the paradoxes in the stories. He had left not one trail but many. To different people, he was different things. He was one man's lunatic, another's paragon of sanity and strength. He was one man's hero and another's image of evil incarnate. He was one man's friend and another's most treacherous and bitterly feared enemy. He was one man's savior and another's betrayer and murderer. He was one woman's lover and another woman's violator.

He was one man's defeat and another man's victory. He was life and promise, despair and poison.

Perhaps it wasn't all true—but I felt that it was all real. The person for whom I was hunting had become Protean, capable of shifting his form and his identity. It is a mistake to assume that legends are reduced to human dimensions as we approach them more closely.

On the day when my quest finally came to its not-so-inevitable end, I disembarked from a freighter on which my extensive familiarity with the vagaries of Ultra had qualified me to serve as its interdimensional co-pilot. The world on which the ship set down was called Calo, and I knew that my father had landed there not long before. When I discovered his latest—and last—ship enshrined in a launch reactor, primed for a takeoff that would never happen, I knew that I was nearing the end of my search.

I asked about Captain Fagan all over the spaceport, until I found a man named William Johnston, who claimed to be his friend.

"Can you take me to him?" I asked.

He nodded, but his eyes didn't dip with his head. They remained cool and hard, fixed on mine. He didn't understand why I'd come. He hated me.

"How is he?" I asked, already knowing the answer.

"He's dying."

There was no apology, no embarrassment. It was a simple statement of a simple fact.

"Where?"

"Let's go," he said. "It's about sixty or seventy miles." He didn't want to take me, but he knew that I would go anyway.

We walked slowly out into the sunlight, and I looked around. The city might have been a busy port on any one of a thousand worlds. It wore the uniform of human conception and human occupation, the indelible imprint of human thinking and human microbiality. I had hated hundreds of similar ports, purely and simply because of their similarity; they had conspired to give me the illusion that my quest was getting nowhere. They had implied that I would be forever locked into the same landscape, just as I was forever locked into the same space, whenever I came back from Ultra, no matter how long I chose to follow my dream. I no longer hated such places, though. I knew that I'd finally beaten the drabness and the narrowness of human imagination. I'd succeeded in finding what I needed to find.

Johnston's care was an open-topped affair with big tractor-like wheels. It was a standard cross-country vehicle, but the road was even and comfortable, and an ordinary car would have been adequate.

We drove in silence. There was nothing I had to say to Johnston that I had not said before, on other worlds, at other times, to men who were intrinsically no different. He had nothing to tell me, nothing to ask me.

The sun sank swiftly to the horizon and left us driving through a dim and silent twilight. Pale tresses of atmospheric halo-light fell from the dark sky like soft silver rain. There was no absolute night on Calo.

The strange light gave the plain over which we drove the appearance of green jade shot through with streaks of purple and brown. The road was rutted with cart-tracks, and the land sloped away gently on either side. All around us I could see tiny sparks of light forming and fading, as specks of polished material reflected the strange luminosity.

We passed through a number of small villages built around the road—shanty towns of broken brick, rough-hewn stone and wood. The people we saw were mostly human, but there were a good many aliens of a dozen different races. I guessed that the planet was a dumping ground for forced emigrants from the civilized, crowded planets in the local volume of space. There were no signs of heavy industry or extensive planned farming. The machines had not yet followed the people. It was an infant world, a world that no one wanted—yet.

Johnston pulled up in one of the villages, in front of a well-sculptured house that looked a great deal better than any of its neighbors. It was older, made completely of wood, and testified to the investment of far more effort than the rest of the village.

Johnston just sat still, relaxing in the driver's seat. As I got out, he said casually; "The angel's here already." He had expected to surprise me, but he was disappointed. I nodded calmly.

"I'll wait for you," he said, with a hint of malice. "You won't be long."

"You're very kind," I said.

I went inside, without knocking. The angel, Gabriel Hart, was sitting beside a bed, but the man lying in the bed appeared not to have noticed his presence. The man in the bed looked up when I came in, though. Hart rose to his feet and went outside, without a word or a gesture.

Oddly enough, the man on the bed didn't look much older than me. Even lying there, obviously dying, he looked young and strong. He wasn't a wasted man. He didn't seem tired. He wasn't falling apart. There was no sign of pain or of disease or of decrepitude; there was merely an irresistible impression that he was carrying a heavy, intolerable *load*. Hawker Fagan was dying, but I had never seen death like it.

"I'm your son, Captain Fagan," I said to him. "My name is Malachi. I've been following you for ten years."

"Why?" he asked. His eyes shifted from my face to a spot on the scarred ceiling. He affected disinterest.

"Isn't it enough that you're my father?"

"No."

"Can you remember where you were thirty-four years ago?" I asked him.

"No. I don't remember anything."

"A world called Wayland. A house on a cliff. A vast grey ocean. Slow waves and sour spray. A small woman with thin features. Delicate and pretty."

"There was *nothing* delicate and pretty," said the man on the bed, scornfully. "I never had any sons. Not one."

"You've had twenty and more," I told him, quietly.

"No," he said. Bitterness oozed out of him.

"Why do you say that?" I demanded. "Because you left them all behind you? Because you left *everything* behind you? Because you had to keep going in order to maintain your sense of being?" Clever Malachi. He knew it all. He had guessed it all.

Hawker Fagan laughed, choking on the laughter. "I brought it all *with* me," he said. "Everything. I left *nothing* behind. I carried it all. Every last word. Every last thought. Every last idea."

I wasn't really wrong. It doesn't matter where you think everything is. Leaving it all behind you is the same as carrying it all with you. It all depends where *you* are – inside or outside. That's the paradox of Ultra. That's the nature of the impotent god-men who are its natives, its navigators, its rulers.

I took his hand in mine, and he snatched it back instantly. "No!" he said. "You can't take it away. Not the words from my mouth, not the touch from my hand. It's all mine. Everything. None of it belongs to you or to anyone else. You can't take any of it."

"It's killing you," I told him. "You're full to overflowing. You can't *hold* all that. Even the universe is too big to fit inside one tiny microbial man, let alone Ultra. No man's mind is big enough to be outside of it all. Your mind is breaking, and your body too. Let it go—some of it, at least. Give it to me, or give it to the black angel. I want it. He needs it. You can't hold on to it."

"It's mine," he said. "It has to be mine. If the universe is bigger than a man, then a man is less than a microbe. He's nothing."

"You're not nothing," I told him. "You've found your way through Ultra. You've done enough."

He laughed again, and coughed again. He still seemed relaxed and comfortable. The coughing wasn't a symptom of affliction. "All or nothing," he told me, "Ultra is all or nothing. So am I."

I sat down beside him on the bed, and his eyes flashed with anger. "You're my father," I said. "I can't let you die alone. Whatever you think and whatever you feel. I'm your son and I'm going to stay here with you."

"I have no sons," he said. "And I'll die alone whatever you do."

We sat in silence for some time, while I thought about what he said.

It was true. I couldn't touch him if he wouldn't yield to the touch. I couldn't be with him if he wouldn't let me be there.

Eventually, I stood up, and went out. I hoped that he wouldn't let me go, but he made no move. Everything that he said, he believed, however crazy it might be.

Gabriel Hart was waiting for me outside. Beyond him, William Johnston was sitting in the car, patient and uncaring.

"Is that justice?" I asked Hart. "Your kind of justice? That a man, a legend, like Hawker Fagan can end his life in that kind of chaos?"

Hart nodded. "What is it that makes you humans think you're the lords of creation?" he asked. "What makes you imagine that all the stars are *yours*. Alien worlds, alien life, alien thought—not just space, but Ultra too, not to mention the span of time and the smile of chance. You can't have it all. If you try, it will kill you. That's justice."

"You're human too," I accused him.

"No. It doesn't happen to me. It doesn't happen to the blind, the deaf, the stupid, the cynical, the insane, the despairing and the immovable. We're safe, because we never look the universe in the face. What about you, Malachi? Do you *really* want to be human? Wouldn't you settle for something less? You can choose. You can be like him, and it will kill you. You can settle for less, and die on your own terms."

I walked past him, back to the car. "You're apologizing for your own inadequacies," I told him. "We have no choice. You and I could never be like him."

"Yes I could," the angel said.

Johnston started the car.
Captain Fagan died alone.

THE FACE OF AN ANGEL

When Mrs. Allison had gone, taking the photo-quality A4 sheet from the printer with her, Hugo Victory took another look at the image on his computer screen, which displayed her face as it would appear when the surgery she had requested had been carried out.

The software Victory used to perform that task had started out as a standard commercial package intended as much for advertisement purposes as to assist him to plan his procedures, but he had modified it considerably in order to take aboard his own innovations and the idiosyncrasies of his technique. Like all great artists, Victory was one of a kind; no other plastic surgeon in the world plied his scalpels with exactly the same style. He had been forced to learn programming in order to reconstruct the software to meet his own standards of perfection, but he had always been prepared to make sacrifices in the cause of his art.

Victory considered the contours of Mrs. Allison's as-yet-imaginary face for six minutes, using his imagination to investigate the possibility that more might be done to refresh her fading charms. He decided in the end that there was not. Given the limitations of his material, the image on the screen was the best attainable result. It only remained to reproduce in practice what the computer defined as attainable. He only had to click the mouse twice to replace the image of the face with an image of the musculature beneath, already marked up with diagrammatic indications of the required incisions, excisions and reconnections. Some were so delicate that he would have to use a robotic arm to carry out the necessary microsurgery, collaborating with the computer in its guidance.

Victory printed out the specifications, and laid the page in the case-file, on top of his copy of the image that Mrs. Allison had taken with her. Then he buzzed Janice and asked her whether his next potential client had arrived.

There was a slight tremor in the secretary's voice when she confirmed that a Mr. Gwynplaine had indeed arrived. Victory frowned when he heard it, because the first duty of an employee in her situation was to remain pleasantly impassive in the face of any deformation—but he forgave her as soon as the client appeared before him. If ever there was a man in need of plastic surgery, Victory thought, it was the man who had replaced Mrs. Allison in the chair on the far side of his desk. And if there was one man in the world who could give him exactly what he needed, Victory also thought, it was Dr. Hugo Victory.

"I'm sorry you had to wait so long for an appointment, Mr. Gwynplaine," Victory said, smoothly. "I'm a very busy man."

"I know," said Gwynplaine, unsmilingly. Victory judged that the damage inflicted on Gwynplaine's face—obviously by fire—had paralyzed some muscles while twisting others into permanent contraction, leaving the man incapable of smiling. The injuries were by no means fresh; Gwynplaine might not be quite as old as he looked, but Victory judged that he must be at least fifty, and that the hideous scars must have been in place for at least half his lifetime. If he'd acquired the injuries in the Falklands, the army's plastic surgeons would have undone at least some of the damage, and all employers had to carry insurance against injuries inflicted by industrial fires, so the accident must have been a private affair. Victory had never seen anyone hurt in quite that way by a house fire—not, at any rate, anyone who had survived the experience.

"Your problem is very evident," Victory said, rising to his feet and readying himself to take a closer look, "but I wonder why you've left it so long before seeking treatment."

"You mistake the reason for my visit, Doctor," Gwynplaine said, in a voice that was eerily distorted by his inability to make full use of his lips, although long practice had evidently enabled him to find a way of pronouncing every syllable in a comprehensible manner. When Victory glanced down at the note Janice had made, the slightly monstrous voice added: "As your secretary also did. I fear that I allowed her to make the assumption, rather than state my real business, lest she turn me away."

As he spoke, the paragon of ugliness lifted the briefcase that he had brought with him and snapped the catch.

Victory sat down again. He was annoyed, because Janice had strict instructions never to permit salesmen or journalists to fill appointment-slots reserved for potential patients—but the mistake was understandable. Victory had never seen a salesman or journalist so unfashionably dressed, and the ancient briefcase was something a fossilized academic might have carried defiantly through a long career of eccentricity.

The object that Gwynplaine produced from the worn bag was a book, but its pages were not made of paper and its leather binding bore no title. It was not the product of a printing-press—but it was not Medieval either. Victory guessed, on the basis of the condition of the binding, that it might be eighteenth century, or seventeenth, but not earlier.

Gwynplaine laid the book on the desk, and pushed it towards Victory. Victory accepted it, but did not open it immediately.

"You seem to have mistaken the nature of my collection," Victory said, frostily. "Nineteenth-century portraiture is my specialism. Pre-Raphaelite and Symbolist. I don't collect books, except for products of the Kelmscott Press. In any case, I don't pursue my hobbies during working hours."

"This is to do with your work, not your hobby," Gwynplaine told him. "Nor am I trying to make a sale—the book isn't mine to sell, but if it were, I'd deem it priceless."

"What is it?" the doctor asked, curiously. He opened the volume as he spoke, but the first page on which his eyes fell was inscribed in a language he had never seen before.

"It's a record of the secrets of the comprachicos," Gwynplaine told him. "It appears to be complete—which is to say that it includes the last secret of all: the purpose for which the organization was founded, long before it became notorious."

"I have no idea what you're talking about," Victory told his mysterious visitor. "If you're hoping to barter for my services I'm afraid you've come to the wrong plastic surgeon." But he had turned to another page now, and although the script remained utterly inscrutable, this one bore an illustrative diagram.

Victory had seen a great many anatomical texts in his time, but he had never seen an account of the musculature of the human face as finely detailed as the one he was looking at. It was easily the equal of Dürer's anatomical studies, although it was more intricate and seemed indicative of an uncanny appreciation of the inner architecture of the human face. It seemed to Victory that the author of the diagram addressed him as one genius of plastic surgery to another, even though the message emanated from an era in which plastic surgery had been unknown. His interest increased by a sudden order of magnitude.

"I hope you will permit me to explain," Gwynplaine said, mildly.

Victory turned to another illustration. This one had been carefully modified in a manner that was impossibly similar to the print he had taken from his computer only a few minutes earlier. A layman might have seen nothing but a confusion of arbitrary lines scrawled on the image of facial musculature, but Hugo Victory saw a set of clear and ingenious instructions for surgical intervention.

Victory decided that he wanted this book as desperately as he had ever wanted anything. If Gwynplaine could not sell it, then he wanted a photocopy, and a translation.

If this is genuine, Victory thought, *it will rewrite the history of plastic surgery. If the text lives up to the promise of the illustrations I've so far seen, it might help to rewrite modern textbooks as well. And even if it turns out to be a fake, manufactured as recently as yesterday, the ingenuity of the instructions testifies to the existence of an unknown master of my art.*

"Please go on, Mr. Gwynplaine," the surgeon said, his eyes transfixed by the illustration. "Tell me what you came here to say."

* * * * * * *

"Comprachicos means *child-buyers*," Gwynplaine said, his strange voice taking on an oddly musical quality. "Even in their decadence, in the eighteenth century, the comprachicos took pride in being tradesmen, not thieves. They were wanderers by then, often confused with gypsies, but they were a very different breed. Even nineteenth century accounts take care to point out that while true gypsies were pagans, the comprachicos were devout Catholics.

"Those same sources identify the comprachicos' last protector in England as James II, and state that they were never heard of again after fleeing the country when William of Orange took the throne. The retreat into obscurity is understandable. The Pope had excommunicated the entire organization—one reason why the Protestant William was secretly supported by Rome against his Catholic rival—and such succor as those who fled from England could receive in France was limited and covert. The entire society retreated to Spain, and even then found it politic to vanish into the Basque country of the southern Pyrenees. They've remained invisible to history ever since—but they had been invisible before, and the wonder may be that they were ever glimpsed at all.

"Almost everything written about the comprachicos was written by their enemies, and was intended to demonize them. They were attacked as mutilators of the children they bought, charged with using their techniques to produce dwarfs and hunchbacks, acrobats and contortionists, freaks and horrors. It was true that they could and did produce monsters—but even in the Age of Reason and the Age of Enlightenment the demand for such products came from the courts of Europe, which still delighted in the antics of clowns and clever fools. The comprachicos sold wares of those kinds to Popes and Kings as well as Tsars and Sultans. The clowns that caper in our circuses even to this day use make-up to produce simulacra of the faces that the comprachicos once teased out of raw flesh.

"Yes, the comprachicos used their plastic arts—arts that men like you are only beginning to rediscover—for purposes that you or I might consider evil or perverse. But that wasn't their primary or their ultimate aim. That wasn't the reason for which the organization was founded, in the days when the Goths still ruled Iberia."

Hugo Victory had never heard of comprachicos, but he had heard that families of beggars in ancient times had sometimes mutilated their children in order to make them more piteous, and he had heard too that the acrobats of Imperial Rome had trained the joints of their children so that they could be dislocated and relocated at will, preparing them for life as extraordinary gymnasts. For this reason, he was not inclined to dismiss Gwynplaine's story entirely— and he was still turning the parchment pages with reverential fingers, still marveling at the anatomical diagrams and the fanciful surgical schemes superimposed upon them. "What was the reason for the organization's existence?" he asked.

"To reproduce the face and figure of Adam."

That startled the surgeon into looking up. "What?"

"Adam, you will recall, was supposed to have been made in God's image," Gwynplaine said. "The comprachicos believed that the face Adam wore before the Fall was a replica of the Divine Countenance itself, as were the faces of the angels; when Adam and Eve ate from the tree of the knowledge of good and evil, however, their features and forms became contorted—and when God expelled them from Eden, he made that contortion permanent, so that they and their children would never see his image again in one another's faces and figures.

"The comprachicos believed that if only they could find a means of undoing that contortion, thus unmasking the ultimate beauty of which humans were once capable, they would give their fellows the opportunity to see God. That sight, they believed, would provide a powerful incentive to seek salvation, and would prepare the way for Christ's return and the end of the world. Without such preparation, they feared, men would stray so far from the path of their religion that God would despair of them, and leave them to make their own future and their own fate."

"But there never was an Adam or an Eden," Victory pointed out, still meeting the oddly plaintive eyes of his frightful visitor, although he knew that there was not a man in England who could win a staring-match against such opposition. "We know the history of our species," he added, as he dropped his gaze to the book again. "Genesis is a myth."

But this book is not a myth, Victory said to himself, silently. *This is, at the very least, a record of experiments of which the accepted history of medicine has no inkling.*

"The comprachicos had a different opinion as to the history of our species," Gwynplaine told him, flatly. "They knew, of course, that there were other men on Earth besides Adam—how else would Cain have found them in the east of Eden?—but they trusted the word of scripture that Adam alone had been made in God's image, and that Adam's face was the face of all the angels, the ultimate in imaginable beauty. Not that it was just the face that they were anxious to reproduce, of course. They wanted to recover the design of Adam's entire body—but the face was the most important element of that design."

"This is nonsense," Victory said—but he could not muster as much conviction as he would have desired, or thought reasonable. There was something about Gwynplaine's peculiar voice that was corrosive of skepticism.

Gwynplaine leaned forward and placed the palms of his hands flat upon the open pages of the book that he had laid on Victory' desk, preventing the doctor from turning the next page. "All the secrets of the comprachicos are recorded here," he said, "including the last."

"If they knew how to achieve their object," Victory objected, "why did they not do so? If they did it, why did they not succeed in bringing about their renaissance of faith and the salvation of mankind?"

"According to the book, the operation was a success," Gwynplaine told him, "but the child died while the scars were still fresh. The surgeon who carried out the operation died too, not long afterwards. The project was carried out here in London, not two miles east of Harley Street, but the timing was disastrous. The year was 1665. Plague took them both. There was no one else in England with the requisite skill to make a second attempt, so a summons was sent to Spain—but by the time the call was answered, London had been destroyed by the great fire. The record of the operation was thought to have been lost.

"When William came to power and the comprachicos fled to the continent they no longer had the book, and their subsequent experiments failed—but the book hadn't burned in the fire. It was saved, and secreted by a thief, who didn't know its nature because he couldn't read the language in which it was written. It was only recently rediscovered by someone who understood what it was. You won't find a dozen scholars in Europe who could read it—in a century's time, there might be none at all—but I'm one. What I need, as well, is a man with the skill necessary to carry out those of its instructions that require an expert hand and surgical instruments. I've been told that I might do well to take it to California, but I've also been told that I might not need to do that, if only you will agree to help me. I already have a child." He added the last sentence in a negligent tone, as if that consideration were a mere bagatelle.

"Have you also been advised that you might be insane?" Victory inquired.

"Often. I'll admit to being a criminal, given that it's illegal to buy children in England now, or even to import children that have been bought elsewhere—but as to the rest, I admit nothing but curiosity. Perhaps the instructions are false, and the whole tale is but an invention. Perhaps the judgment of success was premature and the child wouldn't have grown up to display the face of Adam at all. But I'm curious—and so are you."

"If you wanted me to operate on you," Victory said, "I might take the risk—but I can't operate on a child using a set of instructions written by some seventeenth century barber."

"The child I've acquired is direly in need of your services," Gwynplaine told him. "So far as anyone in England can tell, I'm his legal guardian—and no one in the place where I bought him will ever dispute the fact. The manipulations of the body and the training of the facial flesh that require no cutting I can do myself—but I'm no surgeon; even if I could master the pattern of incision and excision, I wouldn't dare attempt the grafts and reconnections. Your part is the minor one by comparison with mine, requiring no more than a few hours of your time once you've fully understood the instructions—but it's the heart and soul of the process, and it requires a near-superhuman sureness of touch. You can't do this as a matter of mere business, of course. I cannot and will not pay you. If you do it, you must do it because you need to know what the result will be. If you say no, you will never see me again—but I don't believe that you'll say no. I can read your face, Dr. Victory. You wear your thoughts and desires openly."

As he tore his avid gaze away from Gwynplaine's censorious fingers Victory became acutely conscious of his own reflexive frown. "Who the hell are you?" he asked, roughly.

"Gwynplaine is as good a name as any," the man with the unreadable face informed him, teasingly.

"I want the book," Victory said, his own perfectly ordinary voice sounding suddenly unnatural by comparison with the other's strangely-contrived locutions. "A copy, at least. And a key to the script."

Gwynplaine could not smile, so there was no surprise in the fact that his face did not change. "You may make a copy it afterwards, if you take care to do no damage," he agreed. "I will give you the name of a man who can translate the script for you. Have no fear that you might do harm. If you achieve nothing else, you might prevent the child from growing up a scarecrow. I think you understand well enough what costs that involves—though not, of course, as well as I."

Victory felt—knew, in fact—that he was on the threshold of the most momentous decision of his life. He had seen enough of the book to know that he had to see all of it. He was faced with an irresistible temptation.

"I'll need to see the child as soon as possible," Victory said, slightly astonished at his own recklessness, but proud of his readiness to seize the utterly unexpected opportunity. "I'll tell Janice to fix an emergency appointment for tomorrow."

* * * * * * *

Even at a mere thirteen weeks old, the child—to whom Gwynplaine referred as Dust—was as hideous as his guardian, although his ugliness was very different in kind. The baby had never been burned in a fire; the distortion of his features was partly due to a hereditary dysfunction and partly to the careless use of forceps by the midwife who had delivered him, presumably in some Eastern European hellhole.

Had the child been brought to him in the ordinary course of his affairs, Hugo Victory would have been reasonably confident that he could achieve a modest reconstruction of the skull and do some repair-work on the mouth and nose, but he would only have been able to reduce the grotesquerie of the face to the margins of tolerability. Normality would have been out of the question, let alone beauty. Nor could Victory see, to begin with, how the procedures outlined in the diagrams illustrating the final chapter of Gwynplaine's book would assist in overcoming the limitations of his own experience and understanding.

"This is an extremely ambitious series of interventions," he told Gwynplaine. "It requires me to sever and relocate the anchorages of a dozen different muscles. There can be no guarantee that the nerves will function at all once the reconnections heal, even assuming that they do heal. On the other hand, these instructions make no provision for repairing the damage done to the boy's skull. I'll have to use my own procedures for that, and I'm not at all sure that they're compatible. At the very least, they'll increase the danger of nervous disconnections that will render the muscles impotent."

"My part of the work will replenish and strengthen his body's ability to heal itself," Gwynplaine assured him. "But the groundwork has to be done with scalpel and suture. If you can follow the instructions, all will be well."

"The instructions aren't completely clear," Victory objected. "I don't doubt your translation, but the original seems to have been written in some haste, by a man who took a little too much for granted. There's potential for serious mistakes to be made. I'll have to make further modifications to my computer software to take aboard the untried procedures, and it will be extremely difficult to obtain an accurate preview of the results."

"It won't be necessary to preview the results," Gwynplaine assured him. "Nor would it be desirable. You must modify the software that controls the robotic microscalpel, of course, but that's all."

"That won't take as long, admittedly," Victory said. "Amending the imaging software isn't strictly necessary....but working without a preview will increase the uncertainty dramatically. The robotic arm ought to make the delicate procedures feasible, but guiding it will stretch my resources, as well as the computer's, to the full. If a seventeenth-century surgeon really did set out to follow this plan with nothing but his own hand to guide the blades he must have had a uniquely steady hand and the eyes of a hawk."

"You only have to step into the National Gallery to witness the fact that there were men in the past with steadier hands and keener eyes than anyone alive today," Gwynplaine said. "But your technology will compensate for the deterioration of the species, as it does in every other compartment of modern life. As to the lack of specificity in the instructions, I'm prepared to trust your instincts. If you'll only study the procedures with due care, and incorporate them into your computer programs with due diligence, I'm certain that their logic will eventually become clear to you—and their creativity too. There's as much art in this business as science, as you know full well."

Victory did know that, and always had; it was Gwynplaine's comprehension of the art and science that he doubted. But Gwynplaine would not permit him to photocopy a single page of the book until the work was done. So Victory imported his own diagrams and his own calculations into his modified computer programs, embodying within them as much arcane knowledge as the specific task required. He wanted far more than that—he wanted the whole register of secrets, the full description of every item of the comprachicos' arts—but he had to be patient.

There was a great deal of preparatory work to be done before Victory could even contemplate taking a scalpel to the infant's face, but the surgeon was as determined to get the job done as Gwynplaine was. He cleared his diary by rescheduling all the operations he had planned, in order to devote himself utterly to the study of the diagrams that Gwynplaine allowed him to see, and Gwynplaine's translations of the text. He practiced unfamiliar elements of procedure on a rat and a pig as well as running dozens of simulations on the computer—but time was short, because the child called Dust was growing older with every day that passed, and the bones of the baby's face were hardening inexorably hour by hour.

Under normal circumstances Victory would have required a team of three to assist with the operation, in addition to an anesthetist; as things were, though, he had to be content to work with Gwynplaine alone—and, of course, the computer to guide the robotic arm. It was as well that Gwynplaine proved exceedingly adept in an assistant role.

The first operation took four hours, the second three and the third nearly six....but in the end, Victory's part was complete.

Victory had never been so exhausted in his life, but he did not want to retire to bed. Gwynplaine insisted that he could watch over the boy while the surgeon slept, but if Victory had not been at the very end of his tether he would never have consented to the arrangement. "If there's any change in his condition," Victory said, "Wake me immediately. If all's well, there'll be time in the morning take a final series of X-rays and to finalize the post-operative procedures."

When the doctor woke up again, however, Gwynplaine had vanished, taking the child and the book with him. He had also taken every scrap of paper on which Victory had made notes or drawings of his own—every one, at least, that he could find. Nor had the computer been spared. The instructions for the operation had been deleted and a virus had been set to work. Had it been allowed to run its course, it would have trashed the hard disk, thus obliterating all the other notes Victory had covertly copied on to the machine and photographs of several pages from the book that he had taken unobtrusively with a digital camera. Fortunately, it seemed that Gwynplaine did not understand the workings of computers well enough to ensure the completion of this particular task of destruction. Victory was able to purge his machine of the virus before it had done too much damage, saving numerous precious remnants of the imperiled data.

A good deal of work would need to be done to recover and piece together the data he had contrived to steal, let alone to extrapolate that data into further fields of implication, but Victory had never been afraid of hard work. Although the material he had contrived to keep was only a tiny fraction of what he had been promised, he had enough information already to serve as fodder for half a dozen papers. Given time, his genius would allow him to build considerably on that legacy. Even if he could not recover all the secrets of the comprachicos, he felt certain that he could duplicate the majority of their discoveries—including, and especially, the last.

* * * * * *

In the years that followed, Hugo Victory's skill and fame increased considerably. He was second to none as a pioneer in the fast-advancing art of plastic surgery, and he forced tabloid headline-writers to unprecedented excesses as they sought to wring yet more puns from his unusually helpful name. He lacked nothing—except, of course, for the one thing he wanted most of all: Gwynplaine's book.

On occasion, Victory paused to wonder how the experiment had turned out, and what the child's face might look like now that he was growing slowly towards the threshold of manhood—but he didn't believe in Adam, or angels, or the existence of God. The existence of the book, on the other hand, was beyond doubt. He still wanted it, more than anything his money could buy or his celebrity could command.

He did all the obvious things. He hired private detectives, and he scoured the internet for any information at all connected with the name of Gwynplaine, or the society of comprachicos. He also published a painstakingly-compiled photofit of Gwynplaine's remarkable face, asking for any information at all from anyone who had seen him.

Despite the accuracy of the image he had published, not one of the reports of sightings that he received produced any further evidence of Gwynplaine's existence. The detectives could not find anything either, even though they checked the records of every single burn victim through all the hospitals of Europe for half a century and more.

In the meantime, his internet searches found far too much. There were more Gwynplaines in the world than Victory had ever imagined possible, and the comprachicos were as well known to every assiduous hunter of great historical conspiracies as the Knights Templar and the Rosicrucians. Somewhere in the millions of words that were written about their exploits there might have been a few grains of truth, but any such kernels were well and truly buried within a vast incoherent chaff of speculations, fictions and downright lies.

Victory tracked down no less than a dozen copies of books allegedly containing the teratological secrets of the comprachicos, but none of them bore more than the faintest resemblance to the one Gwynplaine had shown him. Some of the diagrams in the older specimens gave some slight evidence that their forgers might have seen the original, but it seemed that none of them had been able to make a meticulous copy of a single image, and that none had had sufficient understanding of anatomy to make a good job of reproducing them from memory.

He had all but given up his quest when it finally bore fruit—but it was not the sort of fruit he had been expecting, and it was not a development that he was prepared to welcome.

When Janice's successor handed him the card bearing the name of Monsignor Torricelli, and told him that the priest in question wanted to talk to him about the fate of a certain mutilated child, Victory felt an inexplicable shudder of alarm, and it was on the tip of his tongue to ask the secretary to send the man away—but his curiosity was as powerful as it had ever been.

"Send him in, Meg," he said, calmly. "And hold my other appointments till I've done with him."

* * * * * * *

The Monsignor was a small dark man dressed in black-and-purple clerical garb. Meg took his cape and his little rounded hat away with her when she had shown him to his chair.

"You have some information for me, Father?" Victory asked, abruptly.

"None that you'll thank me for, I fear," Monsignor Torricelli countered. He was not a man incapable of smiling, and he demonstrated the fact. "But I hope you might be generous enough to do me a small service in return."

"What service would that be?" Victory enquired, warily—but the priest wasn't ready to spell that out without preamble.

"We've observed the progress of your search with interest," the little man told him. "Although you've never publicly specified the reason for your determination to find the individual you call Gwynplaine, it wasn't too difficult to deduce. He obviously showed you the book of the secrets of the comprachicos, and you've indicated by the terms of your search that he had a child with him. We assume that he persuaded you, by one means or another, to operate on the child. We also assume that he spoke to you about the face of Adam, and that you didn't believe what he told you. Am I right so far?"

"I'm not a Catholic," Victory said, without bothering to offer any formal sign of assent, "but I have a vague notion that a Monsignor is a member of the pope's own staff. Is that true?"

"Not necessarily, nowadays," the priest replied. "But in this particular case, yes. I am attached to the papal household as well as to the Holy Office."

"The Holy Office? You mean the Inquisition?"

"Your reading, though doubtless wide, is a little out of date, Dr. Victory. There is no Inquisition. There has been no Inquisition for two hundred years, just as there has been no society of comprachicos for two hundred years."

"Do you know where Gwynplaine is?" Victory asked, abruptly.

"Yes." The answer seemed perfectly frank.

"Where?"

"Where he has always been—in hell."

Somehow, Victory felt less astonished by that statement than he should have been, although he did not suppose for a moment that Monsignor Torricelli meant to signify merely that Gwynplaine was dead.

"He wasn't in hell nine years ago," Victory said. "He was sitting where you are. And he spent the next ten days with me, in the lab and the theatre."

"From his point of view," Torricelli counted, still smiling, "this was hell, nor was he out of it. I'm borrowing from Christopher Marlowe, of course, but the description is sound."

"You're telling me that Gwynplaine was—is—the Devil."

"Of course. Had you really not understood that, or are you in what fashionable parlance calls *denial*?"

"I don't believe in the Devil," Victory said, flatly.

"Of course you do," the Monsignor replied. "You can doubt the existence of God, but you can't doubt the existence of the Devil. You're only human, after all. Good may be elusive within your experience, but not temptation. You may doubt that the Devil can take human form, even though you and he were in such close and protracted proximity for ten long days, but you cannot possibly doubt the temptation to sin. You know pride, covetousness, envy—you, of all people, must have a very keen appreciation of the force of envy—and all the rest. Or is it only their deadliness that you doubt?"

"What other information do you have for me, Monsignor?" Victory tried to sound weary, but he couldn't entirely remove the edge of unease from his voice. He wondered whether there was a level somewhere beneath his conscious mind in which he did indeed retain a certain childlike faith in the Devil, and an equally childlike certainty that he had once met him in human guise—but the thought was difficult to bear. If the Devil existed, then God presumably existed too, and that possibility was too horrible to contemplate.

"The child died," Torricelli said, bluntly.

Strangely enough, that seemed more surprising than the allegation that Gwynplaine was the Devil. Victory sat up a little straighter in his chair, and stared harder at the man whose smile, even now, had not quite disappeared. "How do you know?" he asked.

"You hired a dozen private detectives to search for you, who hadn't the slightest idea what they were up against. We have a worldwide organization at our disposal, who knew exactly what to look for as soon as your postings had alerted us. The child died before he was a year old. Don't be alarmed, Dr. Victory—you weren't responsible. So far as we could judge, the operations you performed were probably successful. It was the Adversary's part that went awry. It has all happened before, of course, a dozen times over. If it's any comfort to you, this was the first time since 1665 that the cutter's part was properly done. If he'd only been prepared to honor his bargain and let you help with the part that remained to be done....but that's not his way. You might think yourself a proud and covetous man, but you're only the faintest echo of your model."

"If you weren't a priest," Victory observed, "I'd suspect you of being insane. Given that you are a priest, I suppose delusions of that kind are merely part and parcel of the faith."

"Perhaps," the little man conceded, refreshing his cherubic smile. "I wonder if, perchance, you suspected Mr. Gwynplaine of being insane, when he too was only suffering the delusions of his faith."

Victory didn't smile in return. "I don't see how I can help you," he said. "If the resources of your worldwide organization have enabled you to discover that the child's dead and that Gwynplaine's safe in hell, what can you possibly want from me?"

"We've been monitoring your publications and your operations for the last few years, Dr. Victory," Torricelli said, letting his smile die in a peculiarly graceful manner. "We know how hard you've worked to make full use of the scraps of information that you plundered from the Devil's book, while laboring under the delusion that he didn't mean to let you keep them. We know how ingeniously you've sought to use the separate elements of the operation you carried out on his behalf. I'm sure he's been watching you just as intently. We suspect that your busy hands have done almost all of the work that he found for them and that he's ready to pay you another visit, to offer you a new bargain. We don't suppose that it will do any good to warn you, although we'd be delighted to be surprised....but we do hope that you might be prepared to give the incomplete program to us instead of completing it for him."

Until the priest used the word "program" Victory had been perfectly prepared to believe that the whole conversation was so much hot air, generated by the fact that the lunatic fringe of the Holy Office was every bit as interested in crazy conspiracy theories as all the other obsessive internet users who were fascinated by the imaginary histories of the Templars, the Rosicrucians, the Illuminati and the comprachicos. Even then, he struggled against the suspicion that he had been rumbled.

"What program?" he said.

"The most recently updated version of the software you use to show your clients what they'll look like when you've completed the courses of surgery you've outlined for them. The one whose code has finally been modified to take in all but one of the novel procedures to which the adversary introduced you. The one that would reproduce the face of Adam, if you could only insert that last missing element into the code—the tantalizing element that the Devil has carefully reserved to his own custody."

Victory tried hard to control his own expression, lest it give too much away. He had known, of course, that he had come close to a final resolution of the comprachicos' last secret, but he had not been able to determine that he was only one step short. But on what authority, he wondered, had the Monsignor decided that he was almost home? Did the Vatican have plastic surgeons and computer hackers at its disposal? If it did, would they be set to work on tasks of this bizarre sort? If so, had the men in question genius enough not only to steal his work but to read it more accurately than he had read it himself?

It was too absurd.

"Why would I give my work to anyone while it's incomplete?" Victory asked. "And why shouldn't I show it to everyone, when I've perfected it? Surely that's what you ought to want—if what Gwynplaine told me is true, it ought to put humankind back on the path to salvation."

"He's not called the father of lies without reason," the priest observed. "He was an angel himself, before his own fall. He doesn't remember what he and Adam looked like, but he knows full well that the comprachicos weren't searching for a way to set mankind on the path to salvation. Quite the reverse, in fact. Why do you think they were condemned as heretics and annihilated?"

"I understand the politics of persecution well enough to know that so-called heretics didn't need to be guilty of anything to be hounded to extinction by the Church," Victory retorted.

"I doubt that you do," Torricelli said, with a slight regretful sigh. "But that's by the by. We'll pay you for the program as it presently exists, if you wish—provided that we can obtain all rights in the intellectual property, and that you agree to desist from all further work on the project."

Victory was slightly curious to know what price the Vatican might be willing to pay, but he didn't want to waste time. "I already have more money than I can spend," he said, proudly. "The only thing I want that I don't have is the book I saw nine years ago—and I'm not entirely sure that I need it any longer. I don't have any particular interest in the faces of angels but I'm extremely curious to know what the results of the operation I performed might have been, if the boy had lived."

"You're making a mistake, Dr. Victory," said Monsignor Torricelli.

"You needn't worry about my selling out to the opposition," Victory said. "I've dealt with Gwynplaine before. This time, I'll need copies made in advance—and then we'll be even. Afterwards, I might let him look at what the program produces—but I'm certainly not going to let him walk off with it while I have the strength to stop him."

"I wish you'd reconsider," the priest persisted. "No harm will be done if you stop now, even though you're so close. The Adversary might be able to complete the program himself if he steals the present version, but he wants more than a computer-generated image. He'd still need an artist in flesh, and that he isn't. He isn't even as clever with computers as he'd like to be."

"I find that difficult to believe," Victory observed, sarcastically.

"The reason he makes so much work for other idle hands," Monsignor Torricelli said sadly, "is that his own are afflicted with too many obsolete habits. It was his part in the scheme that went wrong, remember, not yours. It's as dangerous to overestimate him as it is to underestimate him. Don't do his work for him, Dr. Victory. Don't give him what he wants. You know that he doesn't play fair. You know who and what he is, if you'll only admit it to yourself. You still have a choice in this matter. Use it wisely, I beg of you."

"That's what I'm trying to do," Victory assured him. "It's just that my wisdom and your faith don't see eye to eye."

"We're prepared to give you more than money," Torricelli said, with the air of one who obliged to play his last card, even though the game had been lost for some considerable time. "You're an art collector, I believe."

"I'm not prepared to be bribed, even with works of art," Victory said. "I'm an artist myself, and my own creativity comes first."

"Human creativity is always secondary to God's," Monsignor Torricelli riposted. "I hope you'll remember that, when the time comes."

* * * * * * *

In the wake of Torricelli's visit Victory returned to his computer model with renewed zest. There was so much obvious nonsense in what the priest had told him that there was no real reason to believe the assurance that he was only one step short of being able to reproduce—at least on paper—the face of Adam, but Victory had no need of faith to season his curiosity. He felt that he was, indeed, close to that particular goal, and the feeling was enough to lend urgency to his endeavors.

Part of his problem lay in the fact that the transformative software had to begin with the image of a child only a few weeks old. When Victory used computer imaging to inform a forty-year-old woman what she would look like when he had worked his magic, the new image was constructed on the same finished bone-structure, modifying muscles that were already in their final form, removing superfluous fat and remodeling skin whose flexibility was limited. A baby's face, by contrast, was as yet unmade. The bones were still soft, the muscles were vulnerable to all manner of influence by use and habit, the minutely-layered fat still had vital metabolic functions to perform, and the overlying skin had a great deal of growing and stretching yet to do.

Even the best conventional software could only offer the vaguest impression of the adult face that would eventually emerge from infantile innocence, because that emergence was no mere matter of predestined revelation. Integrating the effects of early surgery into conventional software usually made the results even more uncertain—and no matter how ingeniously Victory had labored to overcome these difficulties, he had not been able to set them entirely aside. He had to suppose that, if and when he could produce a perfect duplicate of the comprachicos' instructions, the surgical modifications specified therein would somehow obliterate the potential variability that infant faces usually had—but every hypothetical alteration he made by way of experiment had the opposite effect, increasing the margin of causation left to chance and circumstance.

Whatever the missing piece of the puzzle was, if there was indeed only one, it was obviously a piece of magical—perhaps miraculous—subtlety and power.

There were, in the meantime, other aspects of the comprachicos' field of expertise that continued to reveal interesting results and applications, but Victory had lost his ability to content himself with petty triumphs. No matter how much nonsense Torricelli had spouted, he had been right to call the project "tantalizing".

The five weeks that elapsed between Torricelli's attempt to bribe him and Gwynplaine's reappearance were the most tortuous of Victory's life, and the fact that the torture in question was entirely self-inflicted did not make it any easier to bear.

This time, Gwynplaine did not bother to telephone for an appointment. He simply turned up one evening, long after Meg had gone home, when Victory was still working at his computer. He was not carrying his briefcase.

"You're a very difficult man to find, Mr. Gwynplaine," Victory observed, as his visitor settled himself into the chair on the far side of his desk.

"Not according to my detractors," Gwynplaine observed, as unsmilingly as ever. "According to them, I'm impossible to avoid—urgently present in every malicious impulse and every self-indulgent whim."

"Are you telling me that you really are the Devil?"

"Don't be ridiculous, Dr. Victory. There is no Devil. He's an invention of the Church—an instrument of moral terrorism. Priests have always embraced the defeatist belief that the only way to persuade people to be good is to threaten them with eternal torment. You and I know better than that. We understand that the only worthwhile way to persuade people to be good is to show them the rewards that will flow from virtuous endeavor. There has to be more to hope for than vague promises of bliss beyond death. If anyone's living proof of that, it's you."

"So who are you, really?" Victory tried, as he said it, to meet Gwynplaine's disconcerting stare with the kind of detachment that befitted a man who could repair every horror and enhance every beauty, but it wasn't easy.

"I was sold as a child," Gwynplaine said, his eerie voice becoming peculiarly musical again. "Adam's isn't the only face the comprachicos tried to reproduce. The society is not yet extinct, no matter what the pope may think—but its members are mere butchers nowadays, while men like you follow other paths."

"That was done to you deliberately?"

"It wasn't quite the effect they intended to produce."

"And before? Were you...like the boy you brought me nine years ago."

"No. I was healthy, and fair of face. Angelic, even. I might have become....well, that's water under the bridge. Even you couldn't help me now, Dr. Victory. I hope to see the face of Adam before I die, but not in a mirror."

In spite of his impatience, Victory could not help asking one more question. "Was Torricelli lying," he asked, "or did he really believe what he told me?"

"He believed it," Gwynplaine told him, his gaze never wavering within his frightful mask. "He still believes it—but he won't interfere again, because he also believes that the Devil operates on Earth with the permission of God."

Victory decided that it was time to get down to business. "Where's the book?" he demanded.

"Safe in the custody of its rightful owners," Gwynplaine told him. "You don't need it. Nine years of nurturing the seeds I lent you has prepared you for what needs to be done. All you need now is the master key—and a child."

Victory shook his head. "No," he said. "That's not the way it's going to be done. Not this time. This time, I get all the information first. This time, I get to see the face on my computer before I make a single cut. No arguments—it's my way, or not at all. You cheated me once; I won't trust you again."

"If I broke my promise," Gwynplaine said, "it was for your own good. If I'd succeeded in my part of the project....but that's more water under the bridge. You're not the only one who's being doing things the hard way these last nine years. We're almost there—but I'd be doing you a grave disservice if I didn't warn you that you're in danger. If you'll condescend to take my advice you'll leave the program incomplete until you have to use it to guide the robot arm. Don't attempt to preview the result. No harm can come to you if you work in the flesh of a child and allow me to take him away when you've finished—but I can't protect you if you refuse to take my advice."

"And what, exactly, will become of me if I look at the face of Adam on my computer before I attempt to reproduce it in the flesh?"

"I don't know. Nobody knows—certainly not Monsignor Torricelli. In contrast to the fanciful claims of legend, the Church has never had the slightest contact with the world of the angels."

"So your warning is just so much bluster?" Victory said.

"No. I'm trying to protect my own interests. I don't want anything unfortunate to happen to you before you repeat the experiment—or afterwards, for that matter."

"But you said before that the face of Adam would bring about a religious renaissance—that it would inspire everyone who saw it to forsake sin and seek salvation."

"I said nothing of the kind," Gwynplaine said, equably. "I only said that the comprachicos believed that. You already know that the Church believes otherwise. So do I. I may be privy to the comprachicos' secrets, but I'm not one of them. I'm their victim and their emissary, but I'm also my own person. For myself, I haven't the slightest interest in the salvation or damnation of humankind."

"So what do you want out of this?"

"That's my business. The question is, doctor—what do *you* want out of it, and what are you prepared to risk in order to get it? I've given you the warning that I was duty bound to offer. If you're prepared to take the risk, having had fair warning, so am I. I can't give you the book, but I can give you the last piece that's missing from your painstaking reconstruction of its final secret. If you insist on seeing an image before you attempt to produce the real thing I won't try again to prevent it. If, after seeing the image, you're unable to conduct the operation, I'll simply take the results of all your hard work to California. My advice to you is that you should find a suitable child, and conduct the operation as before, without a preview of the likely result. Take it or leave it—in either case, I intend to proceed."

"I'll leave the advice," Victory said. "But I'll take the missing piece of the puzzle."

Gwynplaine reached into the inside pocket of his ridiculously unfashionable jacket and produced a folded piece of paper. If he really had been in hell, the inferno was obviously equipped with photocopiers. Victory unfolded the piece of paper and looked at the diagram thus revealed.

He stared at it for a minute and a half, and then he let out his breath.

"Of course," he said. "So simple, so neat—and yet I'd never have found it without the cue. Diabolically ingenious."

Gwynplaine didn't take the trouble to contradict him.

* * * * * * *

Gwynplaine sat languidly in the chair, a perfect exhibition of patience, while Victory's busy fingers flew over the keyboard and clicked the mouse again and again, weaving the final ingredient into the model that would reproduce the face of Adam when the program was run.

It wasn't a simple matter of addition, because the code had to be modified in a dozen different places to accommodate the formulas describing the final incision-and-connection.

Victory had half-expected the code itself to be mysteriously beautified, but it remained mere code, symbolizing a string of ones and zeroes as impenetrable to the naked eye and innocent mind as any other. Until the machine converted it into pictures it was inherently lifeless and vague—but when the job was done....

In the end, Victory looked up. He didn't bother to look at his wristwatch, but it was pitch dark outside and Harley Street was in the grip of the kind of silence that only fell for a brief interval in the small hours. "It's ready," he said. "You'd better join me if you want to watch."

"If you don't mind," Gwynplaine said, "I'll stay on this side of the desk and watch you. I have patience enough to wait for the real thing."

"If Torricelli were here," Victory said, "he'd probably remind me of the second commandment." He was looking at the screen as he said it, where he had set up the face of a three-week-old child. He had chosen the child at random; any one, he supposed, would do as well as another.

"If Torricelli were here," Gwynplaine said, "neither of us would give a fig for anything he said."

Victory drew the mouse across the pad, and launched the program.

He had watched its predecessors run a thousand times before, without seeing anything unusual in the adult face that formed in consequence. He had run them so many times, in fact, that he had ceased to believe that there was any conceivable human face that could have any unusual effect on his inquiring eye and mind. When he tried to imagine what the face of Adam might look like, all he could summon to mind was the image painted by Michelangelo on the ceiling of the Sistine Chapel.

But Adam didn't look like that at all.

Adam's face was unimaginable by any ordinary mortal—even an artist of genius.

While learning the basics of medicine forty-two years before, Hugo Victory had been informed that each of his eyes had a blind spot where the neurons of the optic nerve spread out to connect to the rods and cones in the retina. Because he had always been slightly myopic, his blind spots had been slightly larger than those of people with perfect vision, but they still did not show up in the image of the world formulated by his brain. Even if he placed a hand over one eye, to eliminate the exchange of visual information between the hemispheres of his cerebral cortex, he still saw the world entire and unblemished, free of any void. That, he had been told, was an illusion. It was not that the brain "filled in" the missing data to complete the image, but rather that the brain ignored the part of the image that was not present, so efficiently that its absence was imperceptible. And yet, the blind spot *was* there. Anything eclipsed by it was not merely invisible, but left no clue as to its absence.

It was a blind spot of sorts—albeit a trivial one—that had prevented Victory from being able to see or deduce the missing element in his model of the comprachicos' final secret. It was likewise a blind spot of sorts—but by no means a trivial one—that had prevented him and every other man in the world from extrapolating the face of Adam and the angels from his knowledge of the vast spectrum of ordinary human faces.

Now, the blind spot was removed. His mind was no longer able to ignore that which had previously been hidden even from the power of imagination. Hugo Victory saw an image of the proto-human face that had been made in God's image.

Quietly, he began to weep—but his tears dried up much sooner than he could have wished.

His right hand—acting, apparently, without the benefit of any conscious command—moved the mouse, very carefully, across its mat, and clicked it again in order to exit from the program.

He watched without the slightest reservation or complaint as Gwynplaine, who had waited until then to move around the desk, carefully burned the program on to a CD that he had appropriated from the storage cabinet.

"I told you so," the man with the hideous face murmured, not unkindly, as he carefully set the computer to reformat the hard disk. "I played as fair as I dared. That wasn't the real thing, of course. It was just a photograph, lacking even the resolution it might have had. You should have done as I asked and worked directly on a child, Dr. Victory. It might require a dozen more attempts, or a hundred more, but in time, one of them will survive to adulthood. That will be the real thing. At least, I hope so. The comprachicos might not have got it absolutely right, of course. Even now, I still have to bear that possibility in mind. But I remain hopeful—and now I have something that's worth taking to California, I'm one step nearer to my goal."

"It's strange," Victory said, wondering why he had utterly ceased to care. "When you first came into my office, nine years ago, I thought you were the most awfully disfigured man I'd ever seen. I couldn't imagine why the doctors who'd treated you after your accident hadn't done more to ameliorate the effect of the burns. But now I've grown used to you, you seem perfectly ordinary. Hideous, but perfectly ordinary. I thought nine years ago—and still thought, ninety minutes ago—that I could do something for you, if you'd only permit me to try, but now I see that I couldn't....that there's simply nothing to be done."

"It's not strange to me," Gwynplaine assured him. "I've lived among the comprachicos. I understand these things better than any man alive...with one possible exception, now. I hope you can find it in your heart to forgive me for that enlightenment."

"I don't feel capable of forgiveness any more," Victory said. "Or hatred either. Or...."

"Much as I'd like to hear the rest of the list," Gwynplaine said, apologetically, "I really must be going. If you see Monsignor Torricelli again, please give him my fondest regards. Unlike him, you see, I really have learned to love my enemies."

* * * * * * *

It wasn't until Meg arrived at half past eight that Victory had the opportunity to assess the full extent of the change that had come over him, but once the evidence was before him he understood its consequences easily enough.

Meg, like Janice before her, was an unusually beautiful young woman. A plastic surgeon had to surround himself with beautiful people, in order to advertise and emphasize his powers as a healer. But Meg now seemed, to Victory's unprejudiced and fully awakened sight, not one iota more or less beautiful than Gwynplaine. She looked, in fact, absolutely ordinary: aesthetically indistinguishable from every other member of the human race. Nor could Victory imagine any practicable transformation that would bring about the slightest improvement.

It was, he realized, going to be rather difficult to function efficiently as a plastic surgeon from now on. So extreme was the devastation of his aesthetic capacity, in fact, that Victory could not think of any field of human endeavor in which he might be able to function creatively or productively—but the inability didn't cause him any distress.

Even the idea that he was now in a kind of hell, beyond any possibility of escape or redemption, could not trouble him in the least. Nor could the faintly absurd suspicion that he might have provided the means for the Devil to free himself, at long last, from the voracious burden of his envy of humankind.

VERSTEHEN

The first sign that anything was wrong was the radio going dead. At first, it was possible to hope that it was a simple failure of that particular piece of equipment, but within minutes the tell-tales on the instrument panel began winking out, and Connolly knew that the whole system had a bad case of the rot. *The rot* was a slow-growing hemophilic bacterium, which thrived on the first-generation technology that was still standard throughout the archipelago. In time, it wouldn't be a problem, but for now it was a curse—especially for flyers.

The plane would have been sprayed regularly in order to keep its guts healthy; the real problem was that extensive spraying was selecting out immune strains, which could flourish regardless. For nearly a year, things had been getting worse instead of better, and Connolly knew that his name was about to be added to the statistics testifying to that deterioration. He was two thousand kilometers from Martinstown base, without so much as an atoll in between. The archipelago's nearest airbase was no closer, and if he turned the plane he'd be flying into the prevailing wind. There was little he could do except pray that the engines would hold out.

Within twenty minutes he knew that his prayers hadn't been answered. He was beginning to lose fuel; the feed-line was punctured. That meant that there was a danger of fire on top of everything else. Connolly began to regret that he'd ever left Earth for the sake of a colony world whose surface was ninety per cent ocean, the ecosphere of which was cursed with bugs that loved to live on the surface of steel wires and steel plates, turning those surfaces brittle while they did so.

He wondered whether there was a reasonable chance that his life-raft might be spotted in time by another plane. Experience suggested that the probability was low: there was simply too much ocean. There was, however, one other chance. In latitudes not too far south of his present position, great tangled masses of floating weed and gigantic lily-pads gathered at this time of year: temporary is-lands that supported a rich epiflora throughout the calm summer un-til the coming of the storms. The ocean-dwelling indigenes, called "aquamen" by the colonists, used these gargantuan rafts as breeding grounds, and it was said that if a human could figure out which fruit it was safe to eat, and could catch fish with a line, he might live on such a raft for months. The scientists at First Landing sent out boats occasionally to visit the aquamen's communities, taking their annual opportunity to study the aliens. There was also the chance of seeing a plane from the raft, whose attention he might be able attract by means of the flare-gun in the lifeboat.

While he still had some degree of control left, Connolly turned south. There was no guarantee that he'd sight a raft before he went down, but that was the way to maximize his chances—or so he fig-ured.

The feed-line problem got worse, and it wasn't too long before the engine went dead. The plane was now in a long, shallow glide. Connolly thought that he was lost for sure, when his sharp eyes picked out the floating island dead ahead. His spirits seized the op-portunity to soar, and he was still bathing in the thrill of exultation when the fuel that had leaked from the feed-line caught fire, and it began to seem that he might be roasted in the very moment of his triumph.

He baled out, as rapidly as he possibly could, and let the burn-ing plane glide on to its doom. The parachute slowed the descent of the ejector-seat, but he'd been very low and there was an almighty splash as the blue water rushed up to meet him. He was shaken, but not concussed, and he stayed calm until the seat bobbed up and let him draw air into his lungs. He had no trouble getting the lifeboat free, and, as he watched it inflate, he reflected that all was as well as could possibly be expected.

The floating island was still visible, but it seemed a long way off. There was no current, and he had to paddle to bring himself closer, but the sea was calm and it seemed easy enough to make progress. He was glad when the loose strands of floating weed be-gan to foul the paddle, and gladder still when he began to bump the edges of the vast leaves with their walled edges and huge yellow flowers. He pushed on, heading for the heart of the raft, where tow-ering tangled dendrites carried multicolored flower-heads and seed-pods high into the air, reaching for the sun. He was even glad when the aquamen suddenly broke surface around the dinghy, until one of them hauled himself into the boat, grabbed the paddle from Con-nolly's hands, and smashed him over the head with the blade.

He just had time to stop being glad before unconsciousness claimed him.

* * * * * *

Connolly came round to find himself lying on his back, on a "mattress" which seemed to be made out of woven strips of dried seaweed. When he altered the angle of his head the pain dazed him. He blinked furiously, and when his sight cleared he was looking into the face of an aquaman, blue-black and large-eyed, with long whiskers trailing from the blunt, rounded snout. The face seemed to wear an expression of anxious concern and deep sadness, but Connolly knew enough about the aliens to realize that this was mere appearance, and signified nothing in human terms.

For a few moments, the aquaman met his stare, but then the luminous eyes withdrew as the long, supple neck lifted the head away. The alien shifted his posture; he had been leaning forward supported by the knuckles of his webbed hands, but now he squatted back on his froglike haunches.

Another face came into view beyond the alien's shoulder, and Connolly saw to his astonishment that it was the face of a human woman. The aquaman turned to speak to her in his own tongue—a series of liquid syllables that sounded oddly reminiscent of gurgling water-pipes. She answered in kind, pronouncing the alien sounds easily and confidently. The aquaman then moved away, reaching out to help himself into a semi-upright position by grasping trailing straps dangling from the wooden frame of the tent-like shelter in which Connolly had been placed. Aquamen could not stand properly erect, being designed for swimming and scrambling rather than for walking.

"Am I glad to see you," said Connolly, wondering why it was that moving his lips made his head hurt so. "For a moment there, I thought I was in trouble."

"You are in trouble, Mr. Connolly," she replied, quietly. For some reason, the only implication of the comment that registered was the mysterious fact that she knew his name. Then he remembered that his name-badge was stitched on to his shirt on the rim of the breast-pocket.

"You appear," he said, with very faint humor, "to have the advantage of me."

She knelt down beside the head of the pallet. She was about fifty. Her hair was quite white and her taut skin was tanned brown. She was tall and long-limbed, but very thin. She held her body in a peculiar way, as if she were trying to assume the slanting stance of an aquaman.

"My name is Maria Asprey," she told him. "I'm an anthropologist."

Connolly narrowed his eyes, wishing that the curtain of pain would not confuse his thoughts so. He saw that she was wearing a T-shirt that was creamy white in front but had blue-black stains reaching over the shoulders and under the arms. If the back was all blue-black, as this pattern suggested, the shirt had obviously been designed in imitation of the coloring of the alien's hides. Her shorts, though, were faded blue denim. The clothes looked as if she had been wearing them for a long time.

"Look," he said, "I'm not up to much since that crack on the head. Could you get on the radio and report for me. The rot took out the radio before I could send a mayday and Martinstown won't know I'm down."

She put her fingers to the crown of his head, making him wince. "I don't think your skull's cracked," she said. Then she added: "I'm sorry, Mr. Connolly, I don't have a radio."

"What...?" His thoughts were still clouded, and he couldn't quite register sufficient astonishment. "Your boat...."

"I'm sorry," she said, taking her fingers away just as her touch had begun to soothe instead of hurt, "I'm making it worse. I don't have a boat, either. I'm afraid there's no way I can contact Martinstown, or any other part of the colony."

There was silence for some moments while he collected his reserves of strength. Finally, he managed to say: "You got shipwrecked too?"

She shook her head. "I'm a voluntary castaway," she told him. "As I said, I'm an anthropologist. I came here to learn about the *ulaquel dur'ya.* I suppose you call them aquamen. I came to learn their way of life and their way of thought. The kind of apparatus you're talking about would only get in the way. As I said, I'm an anthropologist."

For the moment, it didn't make sense.

"No radio?" he said, to make certain that he had heard correctly.

"No radio," she repeated.

"You're crazy," he said.

She didn't smile. Her face seemed set, devoid of expression.

"It's the only way to learn a new culture," she said. "Immersion in its way of life. To understand how others live—whether the others in question are human or merely humanoid—you have to be able to live as they do, to adopt their way of being in the world. You have to achieve a kind of empathy that allows you to place yourself, imaginatively, in the shoes of another person, so that you can genuinely interact with him, communicate with him...put yourself inside the context of *his* meanings so that your intuitions coincide with his—or hers, of course. It's not easy. It was difficult enough in the old days, on Earth; it's doubly difficult here, trying to operate in a *wholly* alien culture. One can't afford the risk of...distractions. I've tried to leave the objects of my own culture out of the reckoning, as far as possible."

Connolly was beginning to feel slightly better, though he had to keep perfectly still.

"No radio and no boat," he said, his voice hardly above a whisper, "seems to be taking things to absurd extremes."

"At the end of the season," she said, "a boat will come out from First Landing to pick me up. The *ulaquel dur'ya* return to the sea, then."

"Well," said Connelly, after a moment's hesitation. "I guess if you can take it, so can I. I'll try not to get in your way. I wouldn't want to be a distraction."

She didn't respond immediately, and he gradually realized that something was wrong. Belatedly, he remembered the very first words she had spoken. He tried to lift his hand in order to take her by the arm, and his head began to throb again. He had a sudden vision of the paddle coming down, wielded by the furious alien.

"He tried to kill me," said Connolly, faintly. "But they're supposed to be friendly...docile."

"They're normally non-violent," she confirmed. "You don't know what happened, do you?"

Obviously, she read in his eyes that he didn't know what she was talking about. "Your plane," she said, levelly, "crashed into the raft. It smashed up the heart pretty badly. It killed seventeen people, mostly women and children."

Maria Asprey's face was still almost devoid of expression, but he knew that she was concealing strong emotion. She was suffering inside, as the aquamen must be suffering.

"Oh my God," he said, weakly. "I didn't realize. I didn't see her go down....I guess I was fighting with the ejector-seat or trying to get the dinghy inflated. I didn't think...."

He stopped, studying her face carefully, trying to understand what he saw there. "It was an accident," he said, feeling that it was necessary to make that clear. "It wasn't my fault. They must understand that."

"That's the problem," she said. "They can't."

* * * * * * *

When Maria Asprey returned, Connolly had recovered sufficiently to sit up. She had brought him a bowl made from some kind
of vegetable gourd, which contained a lukewarm soup smelling
strongly of fish. He stirred it with a spoon made from slightly rub-
bery wood, and eventually plucked up the courage to taste it. The
salinity was so strong that it made him wince.

"Do you eat this stuff often?" he asked.

"Not so very often," she replied. "But it *is* warm."

"Almost," he said, unenthusiastically. "They have fire, then?"

"They use clear shells from swimming mollusks as burning
glasses. Their use of fire is very limited, though."

He spooned soup into his mouth for a minute or two, quickly
getting used to the taste. She offered him a shallow cup containing
fresh, if slightly murky, water and he gulped it down gratefully. She
waited, squatting on her haunches in evident imitation of the way
the aquamen sat.

"Have you explained to them—about the accident?"

She shook her head.

"Why the hell not?"

"It's not that easy, Mr. Connolly. There's no concept in their
way of thinking, no word in their vocabulary, which corresponds to
'accident'. In their way of thinking, *nothing* is accidental. There's no
such thing as chance. Everything that happens has a cause, not only
in a physical sense but in a moral sense too. Misfortunes are brought
by men upon themselves, if they offend the ancestral spirits—either
that, or they're the result of evil magic. In the case of the plane, they
don't even need to resort to magical explanation. You brought it,
and they hold you responsible."

He struggled to sit up straighter, but found it more difficult than
he had anticipated. In the end, he collapsed back until he was again
supported on one elbow.

"Do they think I *wanted* to crash?"

"No," replied the anthropologist. "But they hold desires and in-
tentions in far less respect than we do. Among the *ulaquel dur'ya*,
individuals are held responsible even for the unintended consequences of their actions—even unforeseeable consequences—except
in cases where a person's actions are held to have been guided, either by sorcery or by the ancestral spirits. There's no distinction here
between murder and manslaughter, and no such thing as accidental
death."

"Don't they ever get ill?" inquired Connolly, in surly tones.

"They hold that all illness is caused supernaturally; it's either punishment or bewitchment."

"You haven't tried to explain to them, I suppose, that they're crazy?"

She regarded him calmly, refusing to acknowledge his hostility or his irony. "They're not crazy," she told him. "They simply have a different view of the world. I'm here to learn about it, not to change it. I'm trying to understand the way they see things, to enter into their way of life. I can't impose my own ways of thinking upon the life of the tribe. I have to set aside my own judgments and my own ideas. It's the only way to achieve empathetic understanding—what social scientists call *verstehen*."

He gave her back the empty bowl.

"So you haven't explained to them that the crash was an accident—something I couldn't help."

"No," replied Maria Asprey. "No, I haven't. As I said, I couldn't begin to make them understand."

"So what happens to me?"

"I've put in a plea on your behalf to the *culumesqua*."

"What the hell's a *cul*...." He tried to get his tongue around the alien syllables, but failed.

"He's responsible for the medical and moral welfare of the clan. He deals with illness, with the detection of magic, with the everyday business of prophesy. He has nothing to do with crimes and civil wrongs, which are the elders' business, but in all issues which touch on what you'd call the supernatural, his word is law."

"What *I'd* call the supernatural?" he echoed.

"They don't think in the same terms," she reminded him.

"In other words," said Connolly, "he's the witch-doctor."

"That's rather a misleading term," she told him, "even in its original usage and implications. It carries all the wrong connotations. The *culumesqua* carries the primary responsibility for the moral wellbeing of the community. He is the one to whom they turn in times of crisis. His role is to soothe their fears, to offer them responses at times when they feel helpless, to give them confidence not only in the continued survival of the tribe, but in the rightness of their conduct."

"Great," said Connolly. "What's he going to do for me?"

"He has agreed to journey to *uru*, to obtain judgment on your guilt or innocence."

"Where?"

"*Uru*. It's...I suppose you'd call it a mythical place, beyond dreams. His spirit can journey there through the medium of a drug-induced trance. There the *culumesqua* can attain direct communication with the ancestral spirits, in symbolic dreams which only he and his kind can interpret."

Connolly could hardly believe what he was hearing. "Jesus *Christ*!" he croaked. "You've asked this goddam witch-doctor to dive into some kind of hallucination to find out whether or not I'm guilty. What the hell happens if he says I am? What's to stop him making up his mind any old how?"

Maria Asprey shifted her position slightly, to rest fatigued muscles.

"Look, Connolly," she said, "there's no other way to approach this problem except through *their* frame of reference. They're the ones who have to make a decision; they're the ones who have to come to terms with the loss of seventeen people, including nearly a third of the season's brood. There's nothing I can do except explore the avenues that their culture makes available."

"You could make them see the bloody *truth*!"

"They have their own ways of defining truth and falsehood."

"But they're crazy!"

She shook her head. "It's a way of being in the world," she told him. "It works, for them. It's coherent, in its own terms. Whenever evil manifests itself, they feel compelled to debit the moral responsibility. They have to be reassured that someone *is* responsible, because the idea that they might be the helpless victims of an uncontrollable fate would be intolerable to them—they live too close to the margins of survival for that. Belief in chance is a luxury, Mr. Connolly; we can afford it only because we're so well-equipped to preserve ourselves against its vicissitudes. Even we have trouble coming to terms with misfortune, don't we?"

"You've got to help me," he said, dully.

"I am helping you," she told him. "I'm doing everything that can be done. I can't do the impossible."

"You're letting my life hang on the whim of some hophead's dream."

"No, Mr. Connolly...I'm appealing to the Supreme Court. I'm doing everything that can be done to preserve your life. If I fail...there was nothing else I could do. Nothing."

"You half-believe that I'm guilty yourself," he accused. "You're that far ahead on the road to insanity yourself."

"I'm trying to understand the aquamen," she said, allowing herself to use the human word without inflection. "I'm trying to cultivate the ability to enter into their way of life, to be able to see situations as they see them. I'm not becoming one of them. I can still see things from your point of view, as well. The crash was an accident, caused by the rot. But Martinstown lies due west of the archipelago, and you approached the raft from the north. You did change the airplane's course, Mr. Connolly, didn't you? You did head for the raft."

"That doesn't make me a murderer," he said, spitting the words out sourly.

"I know that," she said, softly. "But we're on a floating island on an alien world. That changes…everything."

"Miss Asprey," he said, as though he was fated to repeat it over and over in an eternally hopeless attempt to win her comprehension, "*it wasn't my fault*. If anything happens to me…how are you going to square *your* conscience?"

Her voice was thin and distant, and she turned her face away to look out through the opening of the shelter even while she made her response. "Conscience," she said, "doesn't come into it. It doesn't come into it at all."

* * * * * * *

Evening fell, and the twilight slowly ebbed away. There had been plenty of light inside the shelter, whose walls were crudely-woven, but now it rapidly grew dark. The moon was nearly full, but it was a small moon, and its light was meager by comparison with the white glare of Earth's companion. The stars were bright, but they seemed impotent to interfere with the gathering gloom inside the alien nest.

Maria Asprey returned again, this time carrying a strange nightlight: a bowl made out of translucent shells cemented together, filled with a suspension of bioluminescent algae. The light it gave out was cold and very weak, but it was enough to fill the shelter with radiance and shadows.

"Get me to the boat," said Connolly, trying once again to sit up straight, hoping against hope that he could stand.

"Where could you go?" she asked. Her voice was still unnaturally calm. "The ocean is their world. You couldn't get away."

"There's a flare-gun in the emergency-kit. I could defend myself. It's a chance, but I might get clear, under cover of the darkness."

"You wouldn't," she said, squatting down as before. "They'd slit the fabric of the dinghy from below. Your flare-gun would be useless. Darkness is no cover; they see well by moonlight, and they remain active by night. It's not possible."

"Then bring the gun to me here."

"Why?" she asked, tiredly.

"Because I'm damned if I'll give in without a fight. If they're going to kill me, they're going to have to work to do it." His voice was high and urgent, but far from hysterical. His anger was under control.

"You've already been the cause of seventeen deaths," she told him, flatly.

He felt helpless even to protest against the injustices.

"How the hell are you going to explain this," he asked, "when the season ends and you have to return to your own kind? How?"

"I'll just have to do my best," she said. "If the people at First Landing think that I've done wrong, and that I should have acted differently...well, that's for them to judge."

"Maybe you can suggest that they shoot up with dope and consult the ancestors in order to figure out whether you're on the right side of fate—except that all the ancestral spirits got left behind on Earth, sixty-six light years away."

"For the *ulaquel dur'ya*," she said, "the world of *uru* is as real as this one. Even the dreams of ordinary men and women are sacred and meaningful. They're the medium in which they see *through* reality, into the greater realm where this world is simply a fragment, where the futures of men and of worlds are determined, and where the moral order of the universe is preserved. The *culumesqua* might discover in *uru* that there was a reason for those people to be killed today. He might find that it was part of some misapprehended pattern—that you were just the instrument through which other forces were working. Perhaps the responsibility for the deaths rested with the dead themselves, in consequence of some evil they harbored. Perhaps powerful sorcerers were at work, attempting to destroy the tribe, requiring the tribe to make powerful magic in reprisal. Don't mock, Mr. Connolly—your very life depends on the *culumesqua*'s journey."

"At best, on a whim of chance," he countered, "and, at worst, on a decision he's already taken. It's too easy for him to tell them what they want to hear—that I'm guilty and that they can take out their frustrations by killing me. Too bloody easy by half."

His head was on fire and he couldn't find the words to go on. Helplessly, he let his eyes close, and wondered if what was happening really mattered at all. At Martinstown, in the hospital, he'd be a sure bet to recover—but out here, in the middle of nowhere, without proper care and proper food, he might be finished anyway….already prepared by circumstance as a human sacrifice.

He didn't rouse himself from his torpor again until he heard the movements which signified that Maria Asprey was no longer alone in her vigil. She was moving round to sit still closer to his head, while three of the aliens squeezed themselves up against the walls, leaving a clear space between the pallet and the doorway. Into this space moved a fourth aquaman, whose body was decorated with an elaborate costume, decorated with shells and flowers. He was carrying some kind of staff made out of bone, intricately carved.

Connolly opened his mouth to speak—to issue some kind of formal protest—but Maria Asprey immediately laid her fingers across his lips. The pressure of her fingertips was very gentle, but the implied command stilled his protest. He looked up at her face, palely lit by the wan light. She tried to smile, and for the first time he thought that she really was on his side. She seemed to be sympathetic, hoping that things would come right for him. She didn't seem crazy any more.

There was a rustle and a sequence of clicks as the *culumesqua* squatted down before him, making passes with the staff as though he were a stage magician declaring to an imaginary audience that without the benefit of wires or mirrors he was about to make Connolly disappear. Eventually, he laid the staff down and produced a small capsule made from a leathery weed-bladder from the folds of his costume. His body was rigid, and his nimble fingers daubed some kind of ointment from the bladder upon his head and breast. Then, raising his eyes aloft, he began to rock gently from side to side, crooning softly in the liquid tones of his language.

Although the words of the song—if they *were* words—were unlike those of any human tongue, Connolly found the slow rhythm and the cadence strangely familiar. He felt as though *he* ought to be yielding to hypnosis, but in fact his mind seemed to be growing clearer. Whenever he made some involuntary movement, Maria Asprey misconstrued it, and tried to restrain him. She lowered her crouch somewhat, and both of her hands began to flow over his face, soothing him with caresses. There was sweat on his brow despite the coolness of the night, and she brushed it away with her fingertips.

At first, he thought it would be over quite quickly; the silent watchers were clearly expectant. However, they were also patient, and knew the skill of waiting. Time dragged by, and the song dragged on and on, although the *culumesqua* was clearly no longer conscious. The minutes turned to hours, and Connolly found himself slipping periodically into a trance of his own, lulled more by Maria

Asprey's touch than by the alien crooning. Always, though, he came back from the brink of sleep, letting memories flow through his mind in an unsteady train, intermingling with his hopes and his fears.

It seems, he told himself silently, *that my case is unduly confused. Perhaps the ancestral spirits have never before been faced with a problem of this nature.*

When the silence finally did come, it took him quite by surprise, although he made no convulsive movement to betray himself. The silence lasted for two or three minutes before the aquaman began to speak, the syllables spilling from his tongue in an unnaturally regular stream. The voice sounded deeper now than it had when it was singing, and more remote.

He didn't have to ask about the verdict; it was plain in the way Maria Asprey's hands suddenly gripped his shoulders. She had been praying for him, he was sure, although he had no idea as to which deity her prayers might have been directed.

He acted swiftly and reflexively, surging forward, with his own hands reaching for the *culumesqua's* unusual throat. She pulled him back, and the others went to help her, though he knew as he collapsed that he wouldn't have been able to carry through the attack. He was too weak, and they were all too strong.

* * * * * * *

When Connolly was quite dead, spread-eagled across a gigantic lily-pad, with his blood spreading out in the shape of a spiny brittle-star along the leaf-veins, Maria Asprey looked down at the fish-spear in her hands, as if surprised to find the barb stained. Then stain didn't look like blood; in the half-light of the alien night, there was no color.

Connolly hadn't screamed for mercy, but instead had shouted his wrath until the breath was gone from him. Strangely, all the anger had seemed to be directed at her, but perhaps she was just being over-sensitive. She was, after all, the one who had tried to help him. He was wrong to have taken the view that she had betrayed him in some way. Perhaps it was only to be expected, but it was still wrong. She had done everything that she could, and she had done what she had to do. She had nothing for which to reproach herself.

It was a pity...such a terrible pity.

Given more time, she felt sure that she could have enabled him to see things as she saw them, and to understand.

THE BAD SEED

Meg came round, after a fashion, while they were lifting her into the ambulance, but she couldn't quite get a grip on reality. It was as if her mind had gone limp, relaxing into a kind of exhausted passivity and refusing to take up any but the most elementary responsibilities of consciousness. She was aware of pain but it didn't seem to be particularly terrible, and she didn't give it any further thought. She couldn't seem to further her thoughts at all.

"Hello," said the ambulance-man who had sat down beside her. "Can you tell me your name?"

"Meg," she said, without hesitation.

"Good," he said. "That's good. You're going to be all right, Meg." She felt a sudden surge of pain as he pronounced the words *all right*, and it made her gasp, but she still felt strangely detached, as though the pain wasn't really hers. He placed something over her right eye, very gently. It wasn't the pain of the contact which surprised her but the fact that the point of contact seemed to be so far away, as if her face were no longer where—or perhaps what—it had been before.

"What's your full name, Meg?" the paramedic asked, when he'd fastened the dressing. His face seemed to be floating in mid-air at an odd angle. It was red and round. His hair had receded a very long way—almost as far as the tide went out in Swansea Bay, it seemed—and what was left was dappled grey.

"Hughes," she said. "Margaret Leonie Hughes." It was hard to formulate the syllables, and she realized that her lips were swollen and bleeding. Her front teeth weren't all there.

"Good. That's great. Address?"

"One-one-five Belmoredean Road." The ambulance was pulling away now. juddering over the rough ground.

"Good. Very good. Age?"

"Twenty-one," she said, wondering what was so good about anything and everything she said. The ambulance jolted one last time as it went over the pavement and on to the road.

"Great. Rest now. Just rest. We'll have you in hospital in no time. You'll be fine. I'll just put this over your mouth to help you breathe. Just a precaution. You'll be fine."

The oxygen-jet was cold. She didn't think she needed it. She let herself relax completely, listening to the throaty roar of the engine and the plaintive wail of the siren. The combination of sounds was strangely absorbing and strangely comforting.

It wasn't until the ambulance was drawing up at the hospital that she suddenly realized that she wasn't twenty-one at all. She was twenty-two, and had been for at least a month. She had forgotten how old she was!

Hell's bells, she thought, *I've got amnesia!* That was when it finally came home to her that she'd been hurt, perhaps badly, and that they were taking her to hospital in an ambulance because she was injured, and that the reason everything she said was good was that it was an achievement on her part to be able to say anything at all. She suddenly began to pay attention to the pain, to recognize it as her own, and to tick off its sources one by one.

Head. Eyebrow. Cheek. Mouth. Ribs. Oh shit. Oh shit....

She blacked out while they were hurrying the stretcher from the back of the vehicle, while she was still trying to remember what day it was and why she had been lying in the bushes: lying on the moist black soil whose earthy odor still clung to her hair and her naked, bloody legs.

* * * * * * *

Meg didn't have amnesia. *It would have been better if I had,* she thought, savagely when she finally had the opportunity to organize her thoughts and get the narrative of her life under way again. *The more the better. Not just this but all of it. Far, far better if I could start over with a clean sheet...and maybe get it right this time.*

She knew, of course, that she'd handled the rape all wrong, and was still handling it all wrong, but she didn't seem able to do anything about it. She'd always been conscious of the danger—how could one not be conscious of such dangers in this day and age?—and she'd always told herself that if ever it happened to her, she'd get it right. She'd scream and she'd scream as loudly as she could, and she'd go for his eyes with her fingernails if she couldn't reach his balls, and if the worst came to the worst, because he was too big and too well-armed and there was no help near, she'd just grit her teeth and bear it, and come out the other side, and tell herself that it was no big deal and just get on with her life....

But she hadn't managed to do any of that. Not one damn thing. There was no excuse, not even the fact that he'd hit her far too hard far too quickly, more than once and more than he really needed to, for purely practical purposes. She hadn't done anything, because she wasn't the person she'd always tried to be, the person she'd always wanted to be, the person she'd determined to be in spite of everything....in spite of her failures, in spite of her incompetence, in spite of all the faults which her over-solicitous mother had always been so over-ambitious to correct by means of judicious over-criticism.

Even before it happened, she'd had the sense of only just hanging on to her self-respect by her fingernails, never quite being able to pull herself up and away from the brink of the abyss. Now....

Now, in spite of all she'd resolved to do and be, she was in free fall into the darkness and into the cold. Her brittle fingernails had shattered, and left her nothing to hang on with, and now her mind had collapsed, and life itself had become too much for her. She wanted to die. She wanted to be dead already. She wanted to be left alone, so that she could fall forever in peace, and vanish unmourned into the void.

Naturally enough, that wasn't allowed. In this day and age, you couldn't just be raped, you had to be a victim, and you had to follow the script that had been written in blood by doctors and feminists, policemen and psychiatrists, mothers and ladies from Victim Support. You couldn't even play dead, because every time you so much as twitched an eyebrow somebody would be saying "Good, that's good", as if the very concept of badness had been banished beyond some invisible *cordon sanitaire* drawn around your bed.

It was only to be expected. They weren't going to let her get away with lying down and dying, any more than they'd let her get away with all her other sins and all her other failures. You couldn't ask to start over just because you'd fouled things up, could you? Life wasn't like that. You had to take it as it came and live with all your mistakes. Nobody got second chances.

Mother had always told her all of that. Mother had always been very free with that sort of advice. Mother had always been a great one for picking at old saws and using them to make things bleed. Not that she ever meant to be unkind—not even when she turned up at the hospital while Meg was still spaced out, and lectured her at some length on the subject of pulling herself together, telling her that for once in her life she had to be tough, for everybody's sake.

"Everybody" presumably meant Emily, but Mother wouldn't bring Emily in to see her.

Actually, Meg thought she'd always been tough, until now. Tough-minded, anyway—you couldn't really be tough in other ways when you were so small and thin. She had always been one of those people who told herself that it was better to know the truth, however horrible, than not to know. She had always been proud of being that sort of person, proud of her conviction that ignorance was anything but bliss. Until now....

Now, she found it quite impossible to be tough—especially when Mother explained, in the nicest possible way, that she hadn't brought Emily to see Meg because it would upset Emily too much to see Meg lying there all messed up. That was particularly bad because Meg thought that Emily was the one person who might be able to bring her back from the void, the one person who might be able to ameliorate her misery. After all, Emily was the one real reason she had for not wanting to start over, for not wanting to have forgotten everything, for not wanting to be dead. It was okay to forget your parents, especially when their love was so cloying, so wounding, so prolific in the misery it caused, but you couldn't want to forget your own kid. It simply wasn't on, even for a complete failure like Meg. But they wouldn't let Emily see her. Instead, she was confronted with an endless series of monstrous comforters, every one of them just as motherly as the next: the lady doctor, the lady from Victim Support, Mother herself....

Even the police, doubtless leaning over backwards to be sympathetic and diplomatic, sent a female officer to interrogate her, as soon as she could make a statement. The policewoman, whose name was WPC Lowther, told her she'd done very well indeed before recapitulating the description, checking off every single detail with the careful relish of a predator who already had the sense that this one wasn't going to get away.

"Five foot six or seven. Stocky build. Fair hair; a two-month-old razor cut growing out. Nose crooked, probably broken at some time in the past. Pale skin; lots of acne scars; right cheek scratched. Pale blue eyes. About eighteen, no more than twenty. Black T-shirt with a silver motif half-flaked away, possibly a five-pointed star inside a circle with lettering underneath, too broken up to be legible. Blue jeans, black trainers. Is that everything?"

"That's everything," said Meg, more faintly and far less distinctly than she would have liked. She hadn't yet been down to the orthodontist, and now that the stitched-up wounds around her eye had become infected that appointment was likely to be postponed for several more days.

"It's good," said the policewoman. "Very good."

"Did you get any blood from under my fingernails?" Meg asked, lifting her hand so she could look at her newly-clipped and neatly-filed nails. Manicurists were not inconvenienced by infected facial wounds.

"I think the doctors got more than enough tissue samples to get a DNA-fingerprint," WPC Lowther confirmed. "We also have a witness who saw him running away. We have a very good chance of tracking him down. These types that go berserk are the ones we almost invariably do catch—they don't plan things, you see, and they don't cover their tracks very well. Nothing's certain, but he'll need a miracle to slip through the net, and I don't think he's a likely candidate for one of those."

The last remark didn't make Meg feel as good as WPC Lowther had intended. Meg didn't feel like a likely candidate for a miracle either. Mother, who still clung to the vestiges of her religion, had often pointed out to her that she couldn't expect any favors from God, all things considered.

"In court...." Meg began, doubtfully. She stopped abruptly. The possibility of going to court was so remote as to be almost meaningless, and yet....

The WPC must have been used to dealing with this kind of case. "It's okay, Meg," she said, swiftly. "That's a long way off yet. Don't think about it. Let's catch him first." Her voice had a hint of unease about it, and she was quick to add: "You mustn't worry about the court. He isn't going to be able to say that you let him do it, is he? Thirteen stitches around your eye, three broken teeth and two broken ribs can hardly be the result of a misunderstanding, can it? We've got photographs of everything. If we catch him, he'll go away. No doubt about that. Anyway, you'll be a great witness. There aren't many people who could have given me all this." She raised her notebook triumphantly.

"But they'll ask....they'll ask about....other things." Meg's voice had shrunk to an awkward whisper, which sounded despicably feeble.

"About your sexual history?" The WPC shook her head vigorously. "Not relevant. Don't believe what the tabloids say about the worst part of any rape case being the trial. The judge won't let defending counsel take a line like that, given the violence that was used. The fact that you're a single mother won't make a shred of difference. Quite frankly, it wouldn't matter if you were on the game...." Meg watched the WPC hesitate as doubt momentarily shadowed her thoughts, but she picked up the thread effortlessly enough. "It won't be pleasant, of course, but, compared to the rape itself, it'll be no sort of ordeal at all. You can stand in the witness-box and tell the absolute truth, knowing that every word you say will paint the bastard blacker. If the defense has any sense at all they'll want you off the stage as soon as possible. They probably won't cross-examine you at all. You mustn't be afraid. You have to concentrate all your energy on getting better. That's all that matters. You have to get your life back. You have to think positively. I think you're tough enough to do it. I know you are."

"I've always been tough," Meg said, weakly, wishing the WPC wasn't such an exact clone of her mother. "Five foot nothing and thin as a rake, but tough. Always." She couldn't convince herself. *If I were tough*, she told herself, sternly, *I'd have handled it better. I'd be handling it better now. If I were tough, I wouldn't feel that I'd be better off dead.*

"That's right," said the WPC, dutifully responding to the spoken word rather than the treasonous thought that it surely couldn't have concealed. "You might have lost a battle, but you can win the war. Don't worry about your little girl—your mother's looking after her and everything's fine. You've got to get past this for her sake as well as your own, and you can. You can put it behind you and start going forwards again."

If only it were that easy, Meg thought. *If only I'd been going forwards before.*

* * * * * * *

Meg knew the news was bad because her mother and the lady from Victim Support were moved carefully into place before the doctor arrived. She didn't like to be so crowded. She felt embarrassed because the massive doses of antibiotic they were drip-feeding her to clear up the infection in the wounds around her eye had given her terrible diarrhea. It was nightmarish enough to have diarrhea while she was hooked up to a drip feed without being surrounded by people who weren't nurses and weren't immunized by experience against the effects of close proximity to the horrid and the degrading. Just as the infection was an obvious symbol of her failure to do things right and her failure to cope with having done things wrong, the diarrhea was a symbol of her inability to avoid giving offence to others, especially those who loved her most. Except, of course, that the infection would clear up, in time, and the diarrhea wouldn't last forever....

"Emily's perfectly fine," her mother assured her, while they were waiting. "She's longing to come to see you, but I knew you'd want to wait until you looked a little bit less like the Phantom of the Opera. She's such a sensitive child, isn't she?" *Not like you*, she implied, effortlessly, in spite of her sugar-sweet smile.

The doctor seemed uncomfortable, as if she too would have preferred to speak in private, without the crowd. Who, Meg wondered, had actually decided that her mother and the lady from Victim Support should be present? Who had the power to organize and orchestrate such things? Or did they just happen by coincidence, as a result of the unfortunate accumulation of a pathological superabundance of good will?

At least the doctor didn't beat around the bush. She wanted to get it over with. "The test results have all come in now," she said. "The ones we did here, that is—the police surgeon had the tissue-samples sent away. Everything's satisfactory....except that you're pregnant. I'm sorry."

The doctor went on, but Meg didn't hear what she said. She didn't hear what anybody said for two full minutes. She just chewed her new teeth furiously, wishing they didn't taste like something alien, something that didn't belong inside her mouth. All of a sudden she seemed to be full of things that didn't belong. She'd been invaded. This whole affair was an alien invasion; she was surrounded by body-snatchers, inside and out.

When Meg finally got around to paying attention again, the lady from Victim Support was talking to her mother about the abortion. "Of course it's not a trivial matter," she was saying. "No abortion ever is. But in cases like this, where it's obviously for the best, there's very little danger of long-term trauma."

Her mother was nodding, in that worldly-wise and sensitive manner she had refined by long practice.

Meg didn't want to talk shop with the lady from Victim Support. She didn't want counseling, and she didn't want reassurances about lack of long-term trauma. She just wanted to know when the alien invasion would be over, so she could have her own body back—so she could go back to being an ordinary common-or-garden human alien moving through the uncaring hostility of everyday society, instead of a victim and a host who had somehow begun to attract rapists and cuckoos and all manner of hateful monsters.

Some people, she knew, would have taken all of it in their stride. Some people would even have found things to like about it.

Some people would have been glad of the attention, glad about all the worry being expended on their behalf, flattered by all the kindness and all the planning. If only she'd been someone else, she realized, this might have been a turning-point in her life. All her life she'd felt like an outsider, an also-ran in the human race, a bad girl, an incompetent in the everyday business of living, a person incapable of maintaining any normal or rewarding social relationship—but now, if only she'd had the right attitude, and the wit and determination to seize the opportunity, she could have put all that right. Being a victim could have been a way back in, a way of building bridges. But she wasn't someone else. She was Meg, and for her the worst thing about being a victim was Victim Support—not the charity *per se* but everything the charity stood for.

If he'd only hit me a little bit harder, she thought, *if my skull had been just a little thinner, I'd never have recovered consciousness, and I'd never have known anything about it. Perhaps that's what really did happen, and all this is just a dream, a fantasy exploding in my head at the moment of death. Or maybe this is Hell. Maybe this is what I get for being a bad girl, for never being what Mum wanted me to be, for getting pregnant at school and having to leave, for going out dancing and drinking and taking drugs, for not being a good mother, for getting raped....*

"You mustn't worry," the doctor told her, with a careful kindness that seemed almost macabre. "Everything will be all right. In ten days or so you'll be able to have the abortion. After that, if there are no further complications, you can go home—to your mother, and your little girl. Just concentrate on getting back to normal. You're doing very well. It'll all be okay."

"That's right," her mother said. "Once we get you home again we'll soon have you back on your feet. You'll feel better once you're back where you belong. Everything will be fine."

These are the fictions people live by, Meg thought. *This is the way the world works. This is what I can't do, and will never be able to. It must be me that's odd, me that's mad, me that's bad, because they aren't, are they?*

"Thanks," she said, out loud. "I'll be okay. I really will."

"By the way," her mother said. "They've caught him. That nice WPC told me to pass the message on. They haven't charged him yet because they're waiting for the DNA-fingerprinting tests to be completed, but it's definitely him."

"Oh," said Meg, helplessly. "Good. That's good." And she wondered why she was such an unnatural creature that the only thing she felt was sick.

* * * * * * *

At first, when Miss Tomlinson introduced herself and sat down beside the bed, Meg didn't think there could be anything to worry about—nothing serious, at any rate. After all, her mother wasn't there, and the lady from Victim Support wasn't there, and even the doctor wasn't there. It only took her a few minutes, though, to realize that these might be indications that matters had reached a whole new level of seriousness, and that this might well be the point in time at which she realized the error of her assumption that things couldn't get any worse.

"I'm afraid this is going to be difficult," Miss Tomlinson said, ominously. "Very difficult indeed."

At least she was making no attempt to be kind. She had the grace to look stern and stiff-lipped. She was about Mother's age, but slightly better-preserved. Her hair was black and her eyes were very dark. She looked as if she could be quite fearsome if she got angry, but she wasn't angry now. She explained, quickly and efficiently, what she wanted Meg to do.

"You want to transfer me to a private clinic?" Meg repeated, tackling the easy one first. "Two hundred miles away, in Sussex?"

"That's right," Miss Tomlinson said. "I know it's asking a lot, but I have to ask. I have to ask you to trust us, completely—and I don't have any way to demonstrate to you that we're trustworthy. All I can tell you for the moment is that it's very, very important."

"I can't," Meg said, flatly. "Do you have any idea what my mother would say if I told her I was going to a private clinic in Sussex? I've got to go home as soon as possible, for Emily's sake."

"We can work out a way of bringing your daughter along," Miss Tomlinson said. "Emily's not a problem. But everyone else—not just your mother but the doctors here, and the police—have to be kept out of it. The police are easy to deal with because they know how to follow orders without asking questions or making a fuss, but the others might have to be handled more delicately if we're to avoid awkward publicity. We'll figure out a convincing pack of lies—but you'll have to be a party to it. You have to be inside the curtain of secrecy. We'll need your full co-operation."

"Who exactly are you?" Meg asked, wondering whether someone whose face was as badly puffed up as hers still was could contrive to incorporate astonishment and suspicion into her expression.

"I work for the Home Office," Miss Tomlinson told her, blandly. *A civil serpent*, Meg thought. Her father always called civil servants "civil serpents". It was his idea of a joke.

"This is crazy," Meg said. "It's like something out of Kafka." Meg had never read *The Trial* but she'd seen the Orson Welles film on TV, with Anthony Perkins pretending not to be *Psycho*. She'd watched a lot of films on TV since Emily had tied her to the house, forcing her to abandon her older and wilder ways.

Miss Tomlinson nodded. It was just a straightforward nod, without frills. "I'm sorry," she said. "But we really don't mean you any harm. If it would help at all, we're perfectly happy to offer you money. I can guarantee that all your needs will be more than adequately met for the foreseeable future. You can have anything you want, within reason, if you'll co-operate with us."

"How long is the foreseeable future?" Meg wanted to know.

"A long time," Miss Tomlinson told her, frankly. "This is going to be a long-term thing, I'm afraid. Months, at the very least. Perhaps years, if the situation warrants it and you decide you want to stay with it. It won't be easy."

Meg looked the older woman in the face, marveling at her laconic manner. Miss Tomlinson was so straightforward she seemed positively surreal. It was all surreal—as if the reality she'd only just got a grip on again was dissolving into a nightmare. She just begun to get the hang of being a victim, and now the Home Office wanted her to become....what, exactly? Oddly enough, though, the unknown didn't seem quite as terrifying as it was cracked up to be.

"They're not going to charge him, are they?" Meg said, knowing that she was guessing but knowing that there wasn't much else that could necessitate forcing the police to follow orders whether they liked it or not. "You want to get me out of the way to make sure that the whole thing will die down and be forgotten. Why?"

Miss Tomlinson didn't even raise an eyebrow. "That's only part of the reason," she said. "I'm sorry, but it's necessary."

"Who is he? Somebody's son? Somebody's spy?" Meg knew as she said it that there must be more to it. If it were just something like that, they wouldn't have cancelled the abortion which had been scheduled for the following week. If it were something as banal as that, they'd surely have rushed the abortion through.

The civil serpent shook her head soberly. Meg was glad that the black-haired woman didn't laugh at her, or try in any way to suggest that what she'd said was ridiculous.

"It's more complicated than that," Miss Tomlinson said. "Much more important. I'll explain just as soon as I can, but in the meantime I can only give you my word that it's important."

"You're not going to charge the rapist," Meg said, still trying to make sense of it, "and you want me to have the baby. You really want me to have it, in spite of everything." *It's not enough to have been invaded,* she thought. *It's not even enough to have been invaded twice. It's not enough to have your life laid waste, to have your last illusions shattered. Oh no...that's not enough for Meg—not for little Nutmeg, the runt of the litter, who never got anything right. You don't get off that easy, once you're damned to Hell.*

"That's right," said Miss Tomlinson. "I really am sorry."

"Suppose I say no," Meg said, wishing that she could inject some venom into the words as she shaped them with her alien teeth and her still-rubbery lips. "Suppose I say go to hell, that I want the abortion and if the bastard isn't charged I'll squeal to the papers—and if the papers won't listen, to the BBC or S4C or Amnesty International or MI5 or anyone at all who'll take notice?"

"We'd very much rather you didn't," said Miss Tomlinson, mildly. "And I'm afraid that we'd have to stop you if you tried. I really am sorry, but that's the way it is." If repetition meant anything, she really was sorry.

"They sent you because they thought I'd take it better from a woman, didn't they?" Meg said, trying her level best to sound vituperative. "In fact, they didn't dare to send a man, did they? Because what you're saying is that you're going to rape me all over again, and the only fucking thing I can do is lie back and let it happen."

Miss Tomlinson condescended to look faintly surprised, although it wasn't altogether clear whether she was startled by Meg's calculated rudeness or by her perspicacity. "No it isn't," she countered, smoothly. "You do have a choice—as much choice as we can give you. We don't expect you to like it, and we're prepared to compensate you as best we can. This really is an unprecedented matter, you know. If you wanted to, you could look at it as a ticket to adventure." She pronounced the word adventure without any hint of embarrassment—which, Meg thought, was quite a feat in this day and age.

"Adventure!" Meg echoed, wondering why the syllables didn't sound quite as contemptuous as she'd imagined or intended. "You must think...."

She stopped, realizing that she really didn't know what they must think, and that the fact that she didn't know, and couldn't guess, was evidence that something was going on that really was very odd, and that maybe—just maybe—the situation might not be quite as horrid as it seemed.

After a long pause, Meg said: "What am I supposed to tell my mother?" It wasn't until she had said it that she realized what a revealing question it was, and how much it said about her.

"Medical complications," Miss Tomlinson said, as quick as a flash. "I think we can swing that with the doctor, without having to be too specific. We can tell her that the tests carried out at the police forensic labs turned up something puzzling and worrying—which, in fact, they did, or I wouldn't be here. Without telling any outright lies we'd probably want to drop a hint or two about AIDS—which, I can assure you, is definitely not a problem. The same hints will excuse our taking the man who raped you out of police custody. These days, people are only too anxious to see the back of someone who might be carrying that kind of taint. You might want to be a little vaguer or a little more reassuring when you tell your mother, so as to save her any undue alarm."

Might I? Meg thought. *When was the last time she spared me any undue alarm?* But that wasn't fair, and she immediately felt guilty about it, as she'd been carefully trained to do. *This is crazy*, she thought, instead. *Completely crazy. I'm the victim here. People are supposed to be helping me, not compounding the crime.*

"This is crazy," she said, aloud. "Completely crazy. Like something out of a horror film."

"Yes it is," Miss Tomlinson admitted. "But it's intriguing, isn't it? Mysteries are so fascinating—all the more so if they have just a little suspicion of the horrific about them."

When the lady from the Home Office said that, Meg realized how cleverly she'd been weighed up, how competently she'd been judged, how safely she'd been hooked. Miss Tomlinson had known that she'd play along obediently, that she was as weak as that, as gullible as that, as habitually compliant as that—but Miss Tomlinson hadn't once tried to tell her that everything would be all right, when it patently wasn't and wouldn't be, and Miss Tomlinson hadn't once said "Good" or "That's great." On the other hand, she had said sorry.

I'm not going to get angry, Meg thought. *I'm not going to be indignant. I'm not going to be terrified. For once in my life, I'm not going to behave like some TV cliché. I don't have to do that, and the civil serpent not only doesn't expect me to, she actually expects me not to. It's not an insult. It's not another rape. It really is something important.*

"What do I have to do?" she said.

THE BEST OF BOTH WORLDS, BY BRIAN STABLEFORD * 103

* * * * * * *

As things turned out, it wasn't so hard to tell her mother, partly because her mother made the mistake of bringing Emily along with her—thus forsaking any chance of a narrow and intense confrontation—and partly because Meg was able to capitalize on her reputation for being stubborn, disputatious and downright perverse. This was one situation in which Mother couldn't win.

"Well, if you absolutely insist on going," her mother was eventually reduced to saying, "then I'm coming with you."

"You can't," Meg told her, defiantly, while keeping her eyes focused on Emily—who was sitting on the bed, as good as gold. "It'll be difficult enough finding accommodation for Emily. It's not the kind of place where mothers can come too. Anyway, I'm twenty-two years old. I'm an adult."

"Then I'll stay in a hotel in Lewes—in Brighton, if I have to."

"There's no need," Meg said. With calculated brutality she added: "You'd just be in the way."

"I can look after Emily. You can't—not properly, not, while you're ill. Anyway, she's supposed to be starting primary school in less than three weeks."

"I might be back by then," Meg said, although she had a very strong suspicion that she wouldn't be. "And I can look after her perfectly well. I'm much better now that I'm finally off the antibiotics."

Mrs. Hughes changed tack. "I don't understand this at all," she said, in the kind of aggrieved tone of one who felt that the right to understand was just as sacred as the right to life, liberty and the pursuit of middle-class respectability. "I can't get any sense out of the doctors. That monster still hasn't been charged, you know. That WPC who was so helpful to begin with has gone all tight-lipped. She says that there are problems with the medical reports. I suppose he's going to get off by claiming to be schizophrenic or something—as if that were some kind of excuse."

"That doesn't matter," Meg said, playing with Emily's fingers and smiling.

"Of course it matters! It matters that people don't believe in evil any more—that everything is some kind of illness, so nobody has to take responsibility, as if everything were just chemistry and whatever people do they couldn't help it. Time was when people knew that if they broke the law they'd be punished. Nowadays every evil-minded swine knows that the nastier he is, the easier it will be to plead insanity. It makes me sick."

Once upon a time such tirades had fallen upon Meg's head like showers of sharp stones, making her flinch and duck, but over the years she'd built up a shell. Now, the ideas didn't even rattle as they bounced off.

"I thought you believed in the *bad seed*," Meg said, maliciously. "I thought you believed that some people just went wrong, in spite of everything their long-suffering parents could do, that there was just something inside them that made them wicked and perverse."

"I never said that," her mother said, lying in her teeth. "Yes, of course some people have a perverse streak that always makes them want to do the opposite of what they're told, of course some people are just naturally contrary, but that doesn't mean they're not responsible. It doesn't mean they can't help it."

"Are we talking about the rapist or me?" Meg inquired, knowing perfectly well that she would get a dishonest answer.

"Don't try to be clever, Meg," Mrs. Hughes retorted. "I don't know how you can sit there, looking like that, with some...."—she hesitated, mindful of Emily's inhibiting presence, but plugged on gamely—"...some you-know-what inside you, just trying to make more trouble. You want to go to this place in Sussex, don't you? You don't even care enough about yourself to ask what these people are doing and why. You're so selfish."

Meg knew better than to charge her mother with inconsistency. "Sussex isn't the other side of the world, Mum," she said. "I'll phone you. I'll tell you what's happening when I can. I'll be fine. Everything will be all right."

Well, why not? she thought to herself. *Everybody does it. Why the hell not?*

"I don't like it," her mother said, bitterly, speaking the plain and simple truth for once. "I don't like any of it. I don't know what the world's coming to." But she finally calmed down, and hugged her daughter and her grand-daughter to remind them that she loved them very dearly, and only had their best interests at heart—which was true enough, in a way. In her perverse and contrary fashion, she really wanted nothing but the best for both of them.

* * * * * * *

Meg studied herself in the hand-mirror. The last vestiges of the swelling had almost disappeared from the flesh around her eye. The stitches were long-gone and it was almost impossible to see where they had been. Her chest didn't hurt much any more, although the damaged ribs were still bandaged and still let her know it if she breathed too deeply. She was almost back to normal—outwardly. As to what was happening inside, that was something Miss Tomlinson had yet to explain.

In preparation for their scheduled meeting, Meg had run through all the possible options. Perhaps she really was carrying some new venereal disease, even more exotic than AIDS. Perhaps, in spite of Miss Tomlinson's continued denials, the rapist really did have influential relatives—important enough to require the whole thing to be hushed up and important in some strange way that required her to have the baby instead of getting rid of it. She often thought, even now—but had never begun to believe—that it was all just a continuation of some morbid fantasy which was unwinding in her brain as she lay comatose in the bushes where her attacker had dragged her, while her life slowly leaked away.

Meg dismissed all of these theories, on the grounds that they were either too simple or too fanciful. It had to be something more peculiar than any of them. She had begun to want it to be something so peculiar as to be hardly imaginable. What else could possibly justify and redeem everything that she'd been through, not just since the rape but since the moment she'd been born.

"We've done a few more tests," Miss Tomlinson said, demonstrating that even she was not beyond the reach of tedious cliché, "and we've chased several other lines of enquiry to their conclusions. We have a better idea now what it's all about."

"It's *Rosemary's Baby*, isn't it?" Meg said.

One of the older woman's jet-black eyebrows twitched. "What do you mean?" she asked.

"Not in the sense that it's the Devil's only-begotten son, of course," Meg said, as casually as she could. "Just in the sense that you're going to ask me to carry it, and give birth to it, and maybe even love it, in spite of the fact that there's something seriously odd about it."

Miss Tomlinson nodded, conceding the obvious.

"Okay," Meg said, proud of her self-possession and her self-control. "So tell me—what's so special about it? What's it got that your average common-or-garden rapist's brat hasn't?"

"The rapist's name is Gary Cordling," Miss Tomlinson said, in a level tone. Meg didn't mind that her question wasn't being answered directly. She figured that the civil serpent would get there in the end, as all civil serpents invariably did. "He's sixteen years old," Miss Tomlinson continued, "although he looks older. He's been in trouble before—quite often, as a matter of fact. He's been in care since he was five. His mother just couldn't handle him, even at that age. She said at the time that she'd tried her best, but that nothing seemed to be good enough."

Meg felt slightly uncomfortable. Her own mother had told her a thousand times that she'd done her best. She didn't want to have any aspects of her own situation linked to that of the man—the boy—who'd raped her. She didn't want to be invited to sympathize, or to understand. She had a five-year-old child of her own, after all, and she would never have put her into care, however perverse and wicked she seemed.

"His mother was unmarried, of course," Miss Tomlinson went on. "Her social worker at the time wasn't surprised that she couldn't cope—according to the reports on file, the only surprise was that she lasted so long before giving up on him. The social worker she had when the child was born had already registered a prediction that it wasn't going to work out, on the basis of the mother's unrelenting insistence that Gary didn't have a father—that the conception had been some kind of freak, some kind of unnatural event. Gary's mother never suggested that the Devil might have sired him, but she always called him unnatural. The social worker interpreted this as a neurotic attempt to disclaim responsibility—but even he recorded a comment that the mother was so very insistent on this point that some people might actually have believed her, if only the baby hadn't turned out to be a boy. Do you understand why that ruled out the possibility of a virgin birth?"

Meg had sat GCSE Biology while she was pregnant. She had intended to do A level, maybe even a degree, but it hadn't happened. "Boys have Y chromosomes," she said. "Y chromosomes have to come from fathers. If virgin births ever happen, which they probably don't, the babies would have to be girls."

"Right. Except that Gary Cordling hasn't got a Y chromosome," Mr. Tomlinson said. "The mother was right. He really was unnatural—not conventionally natural, anyhow. But nobody knew that until the police forensic lab had to produce a DNA-analysis of his blood and semen, in order to compare it with the samples they obtained from you after the rape."

"I don't understand," Meg said, more by way of punctuation than anything else.

"Nor do we. There are people, apparently, who are born with an unpaired X chromosome; it's called Turner's syndrome. Almost all the reported cases are outwardly female but there are one or two on record who had male sexual organs—non-functional, of course. In any case, Gary doesn't have Turner's syndrome. His case is spectacularly different."

"How?"

"Every single one of Gary's chromosome-pairs is aberrant, and he has four additional unpaired chromosomes, which don't correspond to any of the familiar ones. There's no way he ought to be alive, let alone reproductively-functional. Ordinarily, it only requires a single breakage in a chromosome, or a pairing error, to foul up the entire process of embryonic development. Gary Cordling was no ordinary freak—if you'll pardon the expression. The baby you're carrying is proof of that, if any more were needed. There's nothing supernatural about it, but it's something that will take some explaining. In terms of the calculus of probabilities, what's happened here is some kind of miracle."

"WPC Lowther didn't think he was a likely candidate for one of those," Meg observed, although she knew that Miss Tomlinson hadn't meant the word to carry any religious connotations.

"It might not be as rare as we suppose, of course," Miss Tomlinson said, "given that we've only just started doing these kinds of tests, but even if it's not unique it's the first time anything like this has ever been identified. So you see, Gary Cordling is a very interesting specimen—and so is his child."

"He's still a rapist," Meg pointed out, "and the child is the product of a violent crime—something that was forced on me against my will."

"I'm not offering any excuses for him," Miss Tomlinson told her. "I haven't the slightest idea whether his behavioral problems have anything to do with his abnormal genetic make-up, or whether he'd have been as nice as pie if his mother hadn't been so convinced of his unnaturalness. Nor am I saying that the fact that he might be genetically unique puts him above the law. But this is something important—a problem that requires a unique solution. If we're to investigate this properly, we need you, not just as a specimen but as a collaborator. It's a hell of a way to get recruited, I know, but it happened. If you absolutely insist that you don't want anything to do with it, we'll understand—in which case we'll transplant the fetus— but we really don't want to take that risk unless we have to. We'd rather you carried it to term, and to be perfectly honest we'd like you to stick with us beyond that point....maybe for life."

Meg looked at the woman from the Home Office very carefully. "I don't suppose Gary will get much choice about helping you out," she said.

"No, he won't. But for that very reason, he might not be as helpful as you. His mother might be difficult too. But you're brighter than they are, and tougher too. You can understand what's at stake."

Flattery, Meg thought, *will get you almost anywhere, or so it's said.* "What about Emily?" she asked.

"We're not planning to separate you," Miss Tomlinson said. "You'll raise her just as you would whatever job you were doing."

"But she'll be part of it, won't she?" Meg pointed out. "Whatever I'm mother to, she'll be sister to. She'll be involved, almost as intimately as me."

I can see why they don't want me to tell my mother, she thought. *By the way, Mum, I've taken this job in Dr. Frankenstein's laboratory, and your next grandchild is going to be a lovely little monster. Won't that be fun?* Even at her calmest, even at her most supremely reasonable, her mother would surely say: "They can't do this to you. It isn't fair." And she'd be right. It wouldn't be fair. The main difference between Meg and her mother was that Meg knew far better than to expect fairness, in people or in the wayward works of time and chance.

I've always been a bad girl, Meg reminded herself, *always a misfit, always a failure as a respectable human being. Who could be better qualified to raise an alien child, and to love it cleverly and conscientiously, no matter where it came from?*

"You mentioned compensation before," Meg said, pleased with the evenness of her tone. "Anything within reason."

"Yes I did," Miss Tomlinson said, just as evenly. "You can name your price—anything within reason."

Meg laughed briefly. "The policewoman said that this case was so straightforward it wouldn't fall apart even if I were on the game," she told the civil servant. "Looks like she was wrong about that too, doesn't it?"

"It's not like that," the black-haired woman said, just a trifle primly.

"No," said Meg, "it never is. It's more like *Invasion of the Body-Snatchers,* isn't it? The rape of all mankind, of the earth itself, of the holy empire of Gaia. Was Gary Cordling's mother abducted by a flying saucer, do you think? They say it happens all the time."

"No, she wasn't," said Miss Tomlinson. "As far as we can ascertain, she just liked swimming a lot. At present, we think that whatever got into her was probably in the sea....that's our best guess, anyhow. Maybe it fell into the sea from above, maybe it came up from below—but we fear that, whatever it was and wherever it came from, it had been carefully designed by natural selection to do exactly what it did: latch on to the egg-cell of a totally unrelated species, and reproduce itself by causing the egg-cell to develop. One of our scientific advisers described it as a kind of super-virus, another as the ultimate venereal disease."

So all my guesses were right, Meg thought, *except the one about it all being a dream. And it really might be something incredibly odd, something from outside, from another planet, something authentically alien. I couldn't just get raped, could I? Oh no. I had to go the whole hog...one small step for a girl, one giant leap for life on earth. Sod Kafka, this is....*

But she couldn't think of anything to compare it to.

Miss Tomlinson was still talking, sounding more ordinary and more conventional with every well-worn phrase she uttered. "We may never be sure about its origins," she said, beginning to carve out her clichés on a wholesale basis, "but it's the future that concerns us now. It's what happens next that's important. This is just the beginning."

"You'd better ban swimming in Swansea Bay," Meg advised, "in case it happens again. Maybe you could arrange for an oil spillage or something, to poison the entire coastline. Obviously the raw sewage isn't an adequate deterrent." *That's the whole trouble*, she added, silently. *We live in an age of inadequate deterrents.* She was glad that she wasn't mindlessly scared by the thought that there was something unnatural inside her, something perverse and maybe wicked: a bad seed. She was proud of herself for having that kind of courage.

Miss Tomlinson shook her head. "I know it all sounds like some bad B-movie," she said, "but it isn't really. It's not *Rosemary's Baby* and it's not *Invasion of the Body-Snatchers* or *I Married a Monster from Outer Space*. As I said before, it's better regarded as a kind of miracle: something rare and strange and infinitely precious. It might have taken a rape to reveal it, but that was just bad luck. We shouldn't think of this as a violation of our precious species by some monstrous thing. We have to see it as an opportunity: a chance to learn, and a chance to discover something new."

"That's not how a lot of people would see it," Meg pointed out. "Even if it didn't actually drop out of the sky—even if it's a product of some incredible mutational freak here at the surface—Cordling's mother was right to call it unnatural, and calling it a super-virus or the ultimate venereal disease isn't going to help its PR any. And it *is* an insidious predator of sorts. It's something that can take over the genetic complement of a human egg-cell—maybe any kind of egg-cell—and produce a viable organism, which looks like others of its kind but isn't really. Whatever the calculus of probability says, paranoia will say that it really did come from outside—that it's some kind of spore adapted to the task of world-colonization. And paranoia will tell us that we don't know how far it's already spread. We know about Cordling, but we don't know how many more like him there are, and we don't know about the fish that aren't really fish and the crabs that aren't really crabs....in fact, the only thing we know for sure is that even poisoning the Bristol Channel might be locking the stable door long after most of the horses have bolted. You can practice your uplifting speeches all you want, but you aren't ever going to convince people like my mother to be glad that this thing's popped up out of nowhere."

"You might be right," Miss Tomlinson agreed, uneasily—and not without a trace of admiration in the expression of her dark eyes, which Meg gladly drank in—"but you and I know that the paranoid way of looking at things isn't the only way. You and I know that there are other analogies to be drawn, apart from invasions and takeovers and rapes. For the moment, at least, we have the choice of treating this as a miracle—or, if it really is a visitor from elsewhere, as an honored guest, extending the hand of friendship across the void; or as the basis of a whole new branch of biotechnology: a whole new set of biological systems to explore and domesticate and turn to our advantage."

"So we do," Meg said, lukewarmly. All of that, she realized, had been put together with the immediate aim of persuading her to play her part, willingly—but in time, the world at large would have to be persuaded too. She knew that if she did play her part, if she did throw in with Miss Tomlinson, she would have to stay with it for a long time. She would have to be more than tough. But she could see that even if Miss Tomlinson's optimistic reassurances were just so much hot air and this really were phase one of the body-snatcher invasion—especially if this were phase one of the body-snatcher invasion—it had to be studied as carefully and as cleverly as possible.

Through the window of her nicely-decorated sick-room, Meg could see Emily poking around in the flower-beds with a stick she had picked up, concentrating fiercely on whatever she was stirring up. Emily, at least, was taking everything in her stride—as she always did. Emily was not yet old enough to be afraid of rape, to be afraid of life collapsing around her, to be afraid of life itself.

Serene, Meg thought. *That's what she is. Did I do that, or was it just the lottery of fate? Can I take the credit for her, or was she just thrown up haphazardly by life's unfolding pattern? How will she turn out, when she's got an alien for a brother—and would she turn out any different if we went back Swansea, so that Mum could*

breathe down our necks all the time, hanging over us like some aw-
ful black shadow, trying to stifle us with tender loving care and her
mistaken sense of certainty?

All of a sudden, despite the cloying warmth of the September afternoon, she shivered. She regretted having agreed to come here, having half-agreed to take all this on board and become a part of it. She should have known that there would be no comforting revelation to be obtained here, no healing abreaction. There were no final explanations here, no promises that everything was going to be all right, or even that she was doing really well. There was nothing here but brutally honest uncertainty, and something strange, something alien.

She raised a hand to touch the eyebrow that hid a faint but all-too-tangible scar. "I bet she didn't feel a thing," she said, meaning Gary Cordling's mother. "She wasn't that unlucky."

"But she couldn't cope," said Miss Tomlinson, who was very quick on the uptake. "You can. At the end of the day, it's better to know the truth than to be ignorant, and better to be tough than to be lucky."

"The trouble is," Meg said, "nobody actually has the choice." But her mind was already made up. She was in, entirely and whole-heartedly—not necessarily for life, but for anything within reason.

THE MAN WHO CAME BACK

There was a pool of light above him and he was staring straight into it. His eyes refused to focus and the pool seemed to eddy and swirl gently. The light seemed to emanate from a brighter, but still indistinct patch, which he thought was a light bulb. There was something wrong with his eyes, as though he couldn't use them properly.

A round object appeared at the side of the pool. He couldn't make it out, but he knew that it was a human face, looking down on him. A second dark blob eclipsed another section of his pool of light.

Oh God! They're here again.

"Can you hear me?"

Don't answer. Perhaps they'll go away.

"Hello? Jason, can you hear me?"

"Yes. Away." The words were slurred, as if pronounced through a mouth full of saliva.

"Now, Jason, listen carefully. You know me. I'm Doctor Yorke. This is Doctor Angeli. You remember us, don't you?"

"Yes." *You were here yesterday with your bloody questions. And I'm not answering them today either.*

"You must try to remember, Jason." Yorke was pronouncing the words slowly and deliberately. They echoed hollowly in the pool of light. "Try to remember exactly what happened. We'll try to help you, as much as we can. You were on a ship—the *Stella*. Remember?"

"Yes." *Of course I remember. I remember everything. But I'm not telling. You go on thinking I can't remember.* Pleased, he nodded his head.

"What is he doing?" asked a new voice—Doctor Angeli.

"I think he probably imagines that he's nodding his head," replied Yorke, in a low voice, which Jason found hard to make out.

You think. Can't you see? You know what a head looks like, don't you? Well, I'm nodding mine.

"At least," Yorke amended, "I think that's what he's trying to do."

"Remember, Jason." The voice was slow and clear again. "The *Stella*. All right? You were traveling to Vesta. Vesta is an asteroid."

I know what Vesta is. I haven't lost my mind. Stop talking to me as though I were a bloody child.

"While you were going to Vesta, the alarms rang, didn't they?"

He nodded his head again. There was no question or commentary this time.

"Those alarms meant that a slug ship was on the screens. Did you know that?"

Another nod. *Of course I know that. I'm an officer in the navy. I told you that. Do you think I'm mad?*

"Now, when the ship was attacked, you escaped in a liferaft. The liferaft was picked up by the slugs after they blasted the *Stella* apart. They took you prisoner. Is that all right so far?"

Nothing. *No, it isn't right. Imbecile. And that's where I stop answering, and your logic goes off the rails.*

Yorke started talking in his low voice again, addressing himself to Angeli. "He always stops there. I don't know what happened then or afterwards. He closes up entirely, and I can't worm even another nod out of him. The only thing he says is 'Away'."

"Try again," requested Angeli.

"Jason, I'm talking again. Understand?"

"Yes." Nod.

"You were captured by slugs. What does a slug look like, Jason?"

Nothing. *A slug looks like a colossal coenocytic mass, with thousands of nuclear blobs, including one major protuberance with modifications to serve for eyes and ears, and a mouth with no lips. It can repeat most of the things we say, but it can't make all the sounds we can. Its vocal apparatus is too different. God what an understatement! All of its apparatus is too different. Alien. But I'm not going tell you any of that, in case there's something you don't know, something you might use. You can't be allowed to hurt the slugs.*

"Could it be just that he can't speak?"

"Oh, he can speak all right—after a fashion, anyway. He can't say everything we can, but with a little improvisation and indistinct mutter, he can manage enough syllables to get along. He did quite a lot of talking in the beginning. About his family and his naval career, mostly. He had to, in order to convince us that he was—or, rather, *is*—William Jason."

"Then why won't he tell us what happened after the ship was attacked, when he was taken prisoner?"

"I don't know. We can only keep trying." Louder again. "Jason, what did the slugs do to you after they picked up your liferaft?"

Nothing. *There was no liferaft.*

"Jason, you must tell us. We're at war with the slugs, now that they've begun attacking our ships. You're the only man, so far as we know, who might have seen one in the flesh. We need every last little bit of information you can give us. Now, what did they do to you to make you look like this?"

Look like what? I'm Bill Jason. I've always been Bill Jason. I look like Bill Jason.

"Jason, this body you have. Is it a slug's body?"

A slug's body? What the hell? Of course it's not a slug's body. I'm Bill Jason, human being. I always have been. I'm tired. Go away. He tried to shake his head, but he wasn't sure that he'd achieved it.

Angeli chipped in again. "How can we be sure that it *is* Jason, anyhow, wearing a body like that. Couldn't the slugs have picked Jason's mind clean, and sent a spy with his knowledge, maybe even his memories?"

"What would be the point?" said Yorke tiredly. "What good would a spy be to them, locked up in this place. He isn't ever going to get out, whether he's Jason or not."

"Then why won't he talk about the slugs?"

"I don't know. If he can talk, and he can, I can only think of one possible reason, and that's that he doesn't *want* to talk about the slugs. But that doesn't fit either. Why should he withhold valuable information after they did *this* to him?"

Did what to me? I'm Bill Jason, and I'm not talking about the slugs. Do what you like, but you'll get nothing out of me except the things that I want to say.

"Jason!" began Yorke again. "Can you remember when you were picked up? You were in a slug spacecraft. Now, can you remember getting into the liferaft when the *Stella* was hit? What happened afterwards? How did you get away from the alien vessel? Were you released, or did you escape?"

Nothing. *I'm not telling you any of that. You'll get nothing from me, except for my life-story. It's my life-story that matters.*

"Jason! Where did the slugs take you? What did they do to you? How did you get away?"

Nothing.

"Look, please Jason, you have to tell us—for the sake of your family, if not for your own sake. Now, you escaped from the *Stella* in a liferaft. That's right isn't it?"

"No." This time, he condescended to pronounce the word instead of trying to shake his head.

"But you must have. The *Stella* was wrecked. You could only have survived in a liferaft."

There was a pause; then Angeli said: "He's not going to talk about any of that. I suspect that he honestly believes that *we*'re the enemy. After all, he *is* in a slug body—or what we suspect to be a slug body. He may even *be* a slug, pretending to be Jason."

One of the round black blobs moved from side to side, as if it were being shaken. It was an oddly bizarre and meaningless gesture

"You must tell us, Jason," said Yorke desperately. "What did the slugs do to you? Why on Earth won't you tell us?"

Oh hell! If I tell them that, maybe they'll stop plaguing me about all the rest.

Slowly, and with difficulty, his lipless mouth formed the requisite syllables. He managed to slobber out the barely intelligible words.

"They killed me."

APPEARANCES

1.

Because Angie and her mother were making the car journey on their own Angie was allowed to sit in the front seat. It made little difference to the experience, because Angie spent the entire time solving the mazes in the new puzzle book her mother had bought her for the journey.

"You might save a few for later, precious," her mother said. "We'll be at the cottage on our own for nearly a week—Cathy and your father won't be coming down until Friday."

"I'm just doing the mazes now," Angie said. "I'll save the others for later. Anyway, I'll be helping you, so I won't get bored. If I do, I can go exploring."

"I'm not sure about that," her mother said. "We'll have to find out how safe it is before you go wandering off on your own. You can play in the garden, though—the front garden, that is. We won't be able to sort out the back one for quite a while."

The cottage in the South Downs that Mr. and Mrs. Martindale had bought the previous year was called Orchard Cottage, because there had once been an orchard behind the property. Unfortunately, all the apple trees had died a long time ago, and the former orchard was now a jungle of hawthorn trees and brambles, topped off by a layer of bindweed.

"I'll be okay," Angie assured her mother, as she began to trace a path through yet another maze with the point of her pencil. "I've got my library books and my drawing pad, and now the electricity's on the TV will be working."

"You'll be able to get out and about more when Cathy comes down," her mother said, although she wasn't able to make it sound convincing. Cathy wasn't keen on "getting out and about". Cathy disapproved of what she called "the whole cottage thing"—that was why she'd insisted on staying in Kingston with her father, who could only get time off work to come down for the Easter weekend itself.

Angie didn't bother to point out that Cathy wouldn't be much use in assisting her to explore the neighborhood of the cottage. It would only have drawn the conversation out, and she needed to concentrate on the track she was following with her pencil.

Her mother took the hint and concentrated on the road ahead of her. The A29 was a straight road, built on the course of one of the ancient Roman roads, but Mrs. Martindale was very scrupulous about not letting her attention wander. She was always reminding her daughters that driving required the utmost concentration, even though Cathy wouldn't be legally able to drive for another three years, and Angie for nearly three years longer than that.

When they arrived at Orchard Cottage Angie had to get out and open the gate so that her mother could back the car into the narrow drive, all the way up to the front door. Then they had to unload the bags from the boot, and transfer them into the house two at a time. They'd brought a lot of luggage, because the kitchen had to be properly equipped, now that it was properly fitted, and the new beds had to be made up.

Once the bags were safely inside Angie went back into the garden to admire the new roof. The slates were exactly the same shade of grey as the broken ones they had replaced, but they seemed much brighter, almost as if they'd been polished.

The front garden was still in a mess. The builders had piled up all their materials here while they were fixing the roof and doing the other repairs inside the house. They'd cleared up after them, but it would be some time before the crushed grass and trampled flowers would recover. As a play area, it wasn't very inviting—although it still had a clear advantage over the thicket at the back of the house, which offered no scope at all.

Angie went back inside, where her mother was busy putting things away.

"There you are, treasure," Mrs. Martindale said, "Could you take some of this stuff up to the bedrooms, please?"

"Sure," Angie said. "Which is which?"

"Those are for your room, those are for Cathy's. Cathy's bedding could have waited until Friday, but I couldn't trust your father to remember it in addition to his own stuff. That's the trouble with engineers—too intent on the task in hand to remember anything else."

"Cathy could have reminded him," Angie pointed out. Angie was still a little jealous because Cathy had got her own way, and would have the house all to herself while her father was at work. Angie couldn't see why a fourteen-year-old had any greater need to be able to see her friends than an eleven-year-old. The argument that Cathy was better able to look after herself than Angie was silly, given that Cathy was so proud of her inability to boil an egg.

"Cathy would have reminded him of all the wrong things," her mother replied, proving Angie's point. Her parents were always commenting on the fact that while Angie obviously "took after" her father, Cathy didn't seem to resemble either of her parents, being far less tidy-minded.

Angie distributed the two sets of bedding between Cathy's room and her own. Cathy's room was at the front of the house, next to what her father called the "master bedroom", while Angie's was at the back, next to the bathroom. Cathy's room was larger, but Angie preferred her own because it had a lattice window.

The window was one of the few "original features" the cottage had left, apart from the grey stone walls and the big fireplace downstairs. The window had a frame of seasoned wood that seemed as hard as stone, and instead of a single pane it had a lead lattice supporting more than forty smaller pieces of glass. The pieces were diamond-shaped, except for the triangular ones at the edges.

The glass in all the downstairs windows had had to be replaced, but most of the glass in Angie's window had survived the centuries of neglect that had left almost everything else in the building irreparably damaged. One central cluster of five diamonds had had to be replaced, but the others had only needed the thick layers of grime to be wiped away. The five new diamonds didn't distort the light as much as the older ones, but that only added to the window's individuality.

Angie's father had tried to explain to her why the older glass was slightly distorted. Because he was an engineer, he was very fond of explanations.

"What you have to understand, treasure," he'd said, the first time he'd shown her the as-yet-repaired window, the previous October, "is that making liquid glass set in flat sheets wasn't always as easy as it is nowadays. When your window was first put together some glass-makers were still using a method that involved swirling the hot liquid glass around to make it spread out. The parts near the centre of the swirl were thicker, and they retained the traces of circular waves. Those were the bits they used to make the cheapest windows. People didn't worry much about views in those days—they just wanted to let in enough light for a room to serve its purpose. Luckily, you've got enough new sections to let you appreciate the view—which will be well worth looking at, once we've sorted out the back garden."

Angie remembered that she had looked out through the gap left by the missing diamonds at the overgrown orchard and said: "That won't be easy." She'd only said it because she knew exactly what her father's reply would be.

"Of course it won't," he'd said, "but you have to remember the engineer's motto." Then they had joined their voices together to say: "The difficult we do at once; the impossible sometimes takes a little longer."

When Angie had made up her bed and put her puzzle book down on the bedside table she went to the window in order to look out through the new diamonds.

The plot of land behind the cottage extended for about forty meters to the rear wall of the property. The field beyond belonged to a farmer, who sometimes grazed cattle there, although it had been left to lie fallow this year. The estate agent had explained, when the family had first come to view the property, that the orchard wasn't an "original feature". The house's name had been changed by a former owner, some time in the 1930s, when the doomed apple trees had first been planted.

"Before the orchard there was probably some kind of vegetable garden," the estate agent had said, during that first visit, "but you'll be able to clear the hawthorns and the brambles and put in a *proper* garden. The cottage deserves that, don't you think?"

The estate agent had spent almost as much time talking about what the cottage *deserved* as he had about its *potential*. According to him, it deserved new and careful owners, who would make it into the kind of cottage it really ought to have been, but had never succeeded in becoming.

Looking at the overgrown orchard now, from her high vantage-point, Angie wasn't at all sure what it deserved to be, or what it was trying to be. The dense sheet of bindweed overlaying the various dead and stunted trees and the coiled-up brambles certainly seemed to be a commanding presence, which would resist any attempt to destroy it.

In the 1930s, Angie supposed—a historical era so distant that her grandparents had been children younger than her—someone must have thought that the cottage *deserved* an orchard, but the land behind it obviously hadn't wanted to be one. She could hardly see the lumps in the thicket where the dead crowns of the old apple trees must be.

After looking through the new glass for half a minute, Angie moved her head sideways to look through the older glass. The greens became slightly darker, and the leaves of the bindweed seemed to become even greedier as they flooded over the underlying branches. The gentle movements stirred by the breeze gave the former orchard the appearance of a green sea billowing up in response to some mysterious force emanating from below.

"Perhaps the cottage didn't deserve an orchard because it had been naughty," Angie murmured. "Or maybe it thought that getting an orchard wasn't really a reward." She knew that coming here with her mother to spend the entire fortnight of the school holiday didn't really qualify as a reward, although her parents had been careful to talk about it as if it were, but she hadn't been naughty. Cathy was the one who had started a big row in order to avoid coming here, and had got her own way in the end—which she clearly didn't deserve.

"I don't want to go to your stupid cottage!" Cathy had yelled. "I didn't want you to buy a stupid cottage in the first place. Don't you realize that it's people like us, buying second homes, who are ruining the countryside for the people who were born there and the people who work there, pricing them out of the market?"

Her father had, of course, taken the trouble to explain to Angie, once Cathy had stormed out, why that argument was untrue, or at least irrelevant.

"We're not taking a home away from anyone else, Angie," he told her. "No one's lived in Orchard Cottage for almost fifty years. It's not that the local people couldn't afford to buy it—they just couldn't afford to fix it up. What we're doing is *rescuing* a property that would otherwise have to lie derelict until it was too badly ruined ever to be saved. We're doing a *good* thing. You'll like it, when it's finished. It'll be *so* beautiful. The perfect place to *get away*."

The problem with that perfection, Angie knew, was that Cathy didn't want to *get away* at all. Everything in life she needed and wanted, at present, was in Kingston, or a short train ride away in London. It was different for her parents, who both had jobs and were always competing with one another to establish who had had the most stressful day. For them, the office and the sites where her father worked, and the primary school where her mother taught, were things that really did need to be escaped occasionally. For them, the opportunity to construct a refuge in the South Downs was a dream come true.

But what about me? Angie wondered, as she stared down at the thorny jungle that would surely require the use of some kind of heavy machinery before it stood any chance of becoming a "proper garden". *Do I need to get away or not?*

She had felt a need to get away a year before, when she had still been at the primary school at which her mother was a teacher. She had made that escape, though, when she'd moved up to the secondary school. Being in a school where she had a sister in year nine wasn't at all the same thing as being in a school where she had a mother who taught year three. It might even be reckoned an advantage to have an older sister around if Cathy wasn't quite so determine to ignore her during school hours.

Angie wondered whether she still needed to *get away*, or whether she too would now be better off in Kingston, hanging out with friends—or, at least, making some friends...or trying to.

Angie turned away from the window, still uncertain. She honestly didn't know whether she wanted to be at the cottage or not. Time would tell, she supposed. She didn't know, as yet, whether she could be comfortable in the cottage—whether it was the kind of place where she wouldn't feel the pressure of *needing* something to do, in order not to feel awkward and out of place.

She tried to put on a smile before she went back downstairs, though. She knew that she ought to pretend to be glad to be here, for her mother's sake. Her mother wanted her to be glad to be here, to count the time they spent here as a reward and not a punishment, and she had to keep up that appearance. She didn't want her mother to be disappointed—not, at least, in her.

2.

Angie's mother was still in the kitchen, looking round proudly at all the utensils for which she had found proper and permanent places. She was nursing a freshly-made cup of tea. "Do you want a drink, darling?" she asked. "It'll have to be tea, I'm afraid, until I can get some juice from the village shop."

"I'll just get a drink of water," Angie said, hunting for a glass. "When are we going to start stripping?" The first job on their list was to scrape the remains of the ancient wallpaper off the walls in all the rooms, so that when her father drove down on Friday with a cargo of plaster and paint-cans he could start straight away on doing the repair work that had to be done before they could start "brightening the place up with a lick of paint".

Angie knew that the painting would make a big difference to the way the interior of the cottage looked. The wallpaper patterned with apple-blossom must have seemed cheerful enough when it was put up in the 1930s, to reflect the cottage's new name, but the building work that had been done in recent months had added massively to the ravages of ordinary dirt. The walls were now so filthy that the apple-blossom inside had been obliterated almost as successfully as the apple-blossom outside.

"We've got to finish stocking the fridge today," her mother said. "It's Sunday tomorrow, and shops still shut on Sundays in these parts. You'll have to come to the village with me and help me carry things back. There won't be time to do much today. The best plan is to settle in and make an early start on the walls tomorrow morning."

"Fine," Angie said.

"We'll walk to the village instead of taking the car," her mother went on. "It'll give us a chance to look around, and it'll do us good to use our legs for once. We can get a taste of what life used to be like in the olden days, when your granny was your age."

"And all the glass was swirled around, so the world was always slightly blurred when you looked out through your windows," Angie added—although she knew perfectly well, thanks to her father's careful explanation, that glass of that sort dated from a much earlier era.

Her mother removed her spectacles and squinted at them. "I really should have booked an optician's appointment over Easter," she said. "It'll probably have to wait till summer now."

"So much to do," Angie observed, trying in vain to imitate her father's voice. "So little time."

The village of Little Wychwood was about half a mile away on the map, but the map didn't take account of the ups and downs. In spite of their name, and in spite of the fact that the appearance was plainly paradoxical, the South Downs seemed to Angie to have far more ups than downs. The ones between Orchard Cottage and Little Wychwood seemed much steeper on foot than they had in a car.

On the return journey, of course, the ups became downs and the downs became ups, but the ups *still* seemed more numerous and more awkward, even though it didn't make sense. The fact that Angie had to carry a bag full of shopping didn't help.

They had looked around the village for more than an hour, but there was so little to see that they hadn't really needed that long. The heart of the village was a pub called The Elms, whose most notable feature seemed to Angie to be the incongruous reach of its car park. The shop was much tinier than their local supermarket in Kingston. There was a church too, and a graveyard, but the church was no longer in use and the graveyard was overgrown by long grass.

"Is it called Little Wychwood because people used to hunt witches around here?" Angie asked, once they were safely out of earshot of any villagers who might take offence.

"I don't think so," her mother replied. "I think it's something to do with a kind of tree called a wych-elm. If the name of the pub signifies anything at all, there must have been a grove of them hereabouts, in the days before we were invaded by Dutch elm disease."

"Just like the cottage, then," Angie remarked. "One's called after apple trees that died, the other after elm trees that died."

"Don't be so morbid," her mother advised. "Look—here's Mrs. Lamb on her way to the village."

Mrs. Lamb was their only close neighbor; they had met her for the fist time back in October. She lived in a house set back from the road between the cottage and Little Wychwood, hidden behind a tall hedge. Its gate bore the name Well House, although Angie suspected that any well that might once have been in its grounds had run dry long before the 1930s.

Mrs. Lamb was older than either of Angie's grandmothers and she kept a black cat, but she didn't look like the kind of witch after which Little Wychwood hadn't been named. In fact, her blue-rimmed spectacles and her tied-back hair made her look like a retired primary school teacher, which was what she was. According to Angie's mother, however, she and Mrs. Lamb had nothing in common, because Mrs. Lamb had done her teaching in a very different era, in a very different school.

"Good afternoon, Mrs. Lamb," Angie's mother said, cheerfully.

"Good afternoon, Mrs. Martindale," Mrs. Lamb replied. "Hello, Angela."

"Hello, Mrs. Lamb," Angie replied, dutifully.

"We're down for the whole school holiday," Angie's mother explained. "There's just the decorating to do now—and the back garden, of course."

"Clearing that dead orchard will be back-breaking work," Mrs. Lamb observed. "You'll need more people in to do that, I suppose."

"Rob's going to hire a chainsaw and a heavy strimmer, to see how difficult it is," Angie's mother said. "Not this time, though—it'll have to wait until summer. With luck, we'll get most of the painting done over Easter, and the rest on the odd weekend in May and June. It'll be so nice to get it all finished—it was a big job. I don't think Rob realized how much we were taking on."

"You'll want to be careful with that old orchard," Mrs. Lamb said, looking at Angie rather than her mother.

"We will," Angie's mother assured her. "If Rob has to use heavy duty weed-killer he'll wear a mask. We'll be sure to warn you when we burn the rubbish—but it won't be this trip."

"Lots of nasty things under that bindweed," Mrs. Lamb continued, still looking down at Angie from behind her blue-rimmed spectacles. "Two weeks is a long time for little folk with nothing much to do, but you don't want to go rooting around in there. Townsfolk are always allergic—not used to country plants, see."

"There can't be much pollen about yet," Angie's mother said. "The bindweed's beginning to flower, but the jungle seems to be mostly hawthorn, brambles and dead apple trees. Angie doesn't suffer from allergies, though—Cathy's the one who gets hay fever."

"I'll be helping with the stripping," Angie put in, because she didn't want Mrs. Lamb to think that she'd be idling around for two whole weeks.

"Must get on," Mrs. Lamb said, continuing on her way towards the village.

"Have a nice day," Angie's mother said, to the older woman's retreating back.

"Aren't country people supposed to be friendly?" Angie asked, when Mrs. Lamb was safely out of range.

"She *is* friendly," her mother insisted. "Just not very talkative. Comes of living alone, I suppose. I couldn't. Not without a car, at any rate."

"What *nasty things* might there be under the bindweed? Why was she looking at me when she said it?"

"Thorns, I suppose," her mother told her. "She's right, though—you don't want to go burrowing around in there."

"Poisonous thorns?" Angie asked.

"No, of course not—but scratches can start allergic reactions, even in people who don't get hay fever. When your father's cleared it we can make a nice big lawn, with flower beds. Until then, best let it alone."

The natural result of this advice was that Angie immediately began to take a greater interest in the dead orchard than she had before. While her mother put the shopping away, Angie ran around to the back of the cottage, along the paved path that ran beside it to the left.

From ground level the tangle of vegetation didn't look like a carpet or a sea, although it wasn't tall enough to be a forest. It was more like a huge square hedge, like a country house maze without any internal pathways. Because of her fondness for puzzle-book mazes, her father had sought out some real ones for her to get lost in—and she *had* got lost at first, because being inside a maze was quite different from looking down at a drawing. Her father had explained the trick of finding one's way out, though. "Like any other problem, it's just a matter of method," he'd told her. "Remember the motto."

It looked as if Mrs. Lamb's advice to stay out of the thicket would be very easy to follow, because there seemed to be no way in. There was no gap at all between the vegetation and the garden wall, whose uppermost stones were so irregular that trying to walk along the top of it would be highly dangerous. A path of sorts had been cleared between the brambles and the wall of the house, so that the builders could fix their scaffolding and go in and out of the back door, but all they'd done was to stamp everything down with heavy boots, and now they'd gone the brambles had begun to rear up again much more forcefully than the feebler plants in the front garden. The greenery facing Angie, extending between the garden wall and the house, was like a solid wall itself.

Angie went around the other side of the house. The wall of the house was much closer to the wall of the property on that side and the unpaved path was much narrower; the mass of green blocking its far end seemed even denser, in spite of the builders' attempts to clear a way for themselves. It was so difficult to see anything within the thicket that Angie settled for leaning over and putting her ear close to the green surface, hoping that she might hear something interesting within. She didn't know what sort of animals might be using it as a refuge, but she felt sure that there must be some—mice, at least. If there were, they were being just as quiet as she was trying to be.

"Daddy had better hire a bulldozer instead of a strimmer," she said, with a sigh. She straightened up, intending to turn away—but as she did, a movement caught her eye. It was in the higher branches, where the nearest apple tree must have been planted, but it wasn't a bird moving inside the thicket. The movement seemed to be on the surface created by the bindweed, as if something invisible were moving *over* it, leaving brief footprints behind.

"Trick of the wind," she said.

"What's that, treasure?" her mother asked, from the corner at the front of the house. "What are you doing down there?"

"Nothing," Angie replied, to both questions.

"I wondered where you'd got to," her mother said, as Angie joined her and they went inside. "Your case is still on your bed—you haven't unpacked yet. We're here for a fortnight, remember. This isn't just an overnight stay, like the other times. It'll be the first taste we've had of *living* here. I do hope you like it." Angie guessed that her mother must be thinking anxiously about Cathy's reaction to the possibility of spending an entire fortnight in the cottage.

They went into the kitchen, where her mother immediately set about making preparations for dinner. "Cathy will like it too, when it's all done," Angie said, supportively. "When we've got a lawn and flower-beds. She'll be able to bring her friends down to visit."

"Not if we're not here, she won't," her mother was quick to say. "Special friends, maybe—one at a time. This place is for your father, really—so he can get away at weekends and have a rest. I do wish Cathy wouldn't be so *difficult*."

"She's a teenager," Angie said, echoing her father's all-purpose explanation for Cathy's difficulties. Angie would be a teenager herself in not much more than a year's time, and she couldn't help wondering whether she, too, might turn out to be *difficult*.

Angie's mother was busy chopping carrots and made no response to the ritual remark. Mrs. Martindale didn't cook much during the week but she always made an extra effort at weekends. She believed in making sure that her children ate lots of healthy food, even if she had to cram it into them in two days rather than spreading it out over seven.

"I'll go unpack, then," Angie said.

She went back up to her room, but instead of making a start on moving her clothes from the small suitcase to the chest of drawers she went to the window and looked out over the bindweed-tiled roof of the dead orchard. The green surface was still moving, and it was easy to imagine that the movements were slow waves and ripples on the surface of a heavy sea—or that invisible creatures really were moving over it, pushing it down where their big feet landed for a moment before moving on.

Angie tried to make a mental map of the positions of the wave-crests, expecting to find that they would be arranged in a series of neat rows, because that seemed the obvious pattern in which to plant apple trees in an orchard. She couldn't make out any neat rows, though, whether running from the house to the back wall of the garden or across the garden from side wall to side wall. Indeed, when she tried to find some sense in the arrangement of the dead tree-tops, it was more reminiscent of a spiral than a grid.

"Perhaps that's how they planted orchards back in the 1930s," Angie murmured. "Perhaps they always have. Or maybe the hawthorn trees have grown so big by now that they're taller than the dead apple-trees. The spiral's just an illusion—like the idea that something invisible might be moving over the bindweed."

She moved sideways to look through pieces of the old glass instead of the clearer ones. The impression of a spiral seemed to become even stronger, as did the suggestion that something was moving over—or perhaps under—the surface of the wind-stirred bindweed.

After she had put her clothes away Angie went back downstairs. "Has anyone in the village said anything about the cottage being haunted?" She asked her mother.

"No, precious," her mother replied. "Why? Were you talking to a ghost just now? You talk to yourself so often at home that I didn't think anything of it."

"No," Angie said. "I was just watching the invisible monsters scuttling and slithering about on the bushes in the back garden."

"You'll need to be careful, watching invisible monsters," her mother said, without a trace of anxiety in her voice. "Sometimes, if you look hard enough, you begin to see them. That's when you need to start worrying."

Angie was glad that her mother trusted her enough to know that any talk of ghosts and invisible monsters was just a joke. Like her father, her mother often told her that she was an engineer's daughter through and through.

"It's okay," Angie assured her mother. "If they put on enough weight to be seen, they'll fall right through into the heart of the maze—and then the poisonous thorns will tear them to pieces, or make them sneeze themselves to death."

"That's why there are so few invisible monsters about nowadays, treasure," her mother said. "It's the allergies that get them, every time."

3.

Although the next day was Sunday, Angie and her mother were up early, eager to make a start on stripping the walls. They were each armed with a scraper and a bucket of soapy water.

By the time they'd been working for an hour in the lounge-dining room—where there were already big gaps in the paper left by the builders when they'd knocked down the partition wall—Angie had begun to wonder how she'd ever got the idea that stripping wallpaper might be fun. It was much harder work than she had expected, because the wallpaper was much more resistant to being stripped than she'd imagined. Whenever she seemed to have a nice fat strip that got broader as she pulled it would suddenly decide to narrow itself down. Whenever a piece seemed to be coming away cleanly it would suddenly stick hard and leave a stubborn patch behind.

Angie was interested to discover that there were three layers of paper, which had been laid one atop another. The apple-blossom paper had been put on top of an elaborately-textured paper whose colors ranged from beige to chestnut brown. Beneath that was something thicker and more fibrous, whose colors included royal blue and silver.

There was a certain pleasure in taking an edge turned up by the scraper between her fingernails and pulling steadily, hoping that a huge strip might come away. More often than not she'd be left with a piece in her fingertips that was only a little larger than the edge she'd turned up, but on the rare occasions when things worked out the strip would curl up in her hand, as if it were finally able to revert to the shape it wanted to be after a hundred years of being forced to lie flat.

Wherever the plaster underneath the paper was uneven, little islands of paper were left behind, clinging hard—and when the plaster wasn't uneven to start with, it often became uneven as it cracked and crumbled under the pressure of the scrapers.

"Don't worry about the plaster coming away, precious," her mother told her, as a whole section melted into dust and miniature rubble. "Daddy will skim the whole surface before he paints it."

"Do we have to do one room at a time?" Angie asked. "I think I'd rather make a start in my bedroom."

"It's all got to come off eventually, I suppose. You can make a start upstairs if you like. It won't be any easier, though, even if there aren't so many layers."

As predicted, the wallpaper in Angie's bedroom proved just as hard to remove from the wall as the paper downstairs—although there were, indeed, fewer layers and the outer layer of paper wasn't as dirty. Here, a relatively plain paper patterned in pink and blue had been laid over something very similar to the bottom layer in the downstairs room. On the other hand, because the bedroom was so much smaller than the lounge-dining room, the job seemed far less daunting. The ceiling was lower too, although Angie still had to stand on a chair to reach the higher parts of the wall.

Once she'd figured out that the paper became much easier to strip away after it had been soaked for some time, Angie doused the entire wall around the window while she was still working on the narrow strip between that wall and the doorway. By the time she'd cleared the strip, the paper around the window was ready to come off a little more easily.

The plaster underneath the wallpaper was more grey than white, and sometimes stained with yellow and brown. It had occasional pencil marks on it, which the first of the two paper-hangers—presumably working long before the 1930s—must have used in calculating how much paper he would use and how it would need to be cut.

In mid-afternoon, when she returned to work after spending a leisurely break reading on her bed, Angie peeled back an unusually satisfying strip to find more markings on the plaster, in black ink rather than pencil. They seemed to have been made by a fine brush rather than a pen.

At first, Angie thought that the first drawing she uncovered must be a doodle of some kind—the kind of thing her father drew absent-mindedly on the message-pad beside the phone, consisting of a series of interlocking shapes or an expanding spiral. It looked like something that the wallpaper-hanger might have done in an idle moment, while taking a short break and staring out of the window.

Because bits of plaster tended to come away with the wallpaper, or crumble under the scraper, some of the lines had been lost or blurred. Even so, it soon became obvious that the drawing was more extensive and more elaborate than Angie had initially imagined. It *was* a spiral of sorts, but instead of approximating closely to a series of circles, the line wandered eccentrically, so that each successive cyclic sweep of the brush became more peculiar in shape.

Then she discovered the second drawing, which seemed to be a slight variation on the same theme. Again, instead of trying as hard as possible to make each loop of the spiral follow a near-circular path, the line began to wander as soon as it moved away from the central dot, and its wandering became more adventurous with each loop. Seen in isolation, this drawing too might have been mistaken for a mere doodle, but seeing the two of them together gave the impression that they were two attempts to produce a particular design: sketches aiming for a particular result.

Because the divergences from circularity became more exaggerated the further each line extended from the centre, each whole pattern ended up looking more like an amoeba than a coiled watch-spring. Both patterns reminded Angie quite forcefully of the puzzle-book mazes she liked so much—except, of course, that a spiral had no side-turnings. If the space enclosed by the looping line were regarded as a path, it was impossible to get lost, because all the pencil tracing the way out had to do was keep going, around and around and around, untroubled by all the kinks in the route.

Scraping away with increasing urgency, Angie soon uncovered parts of a third design, and then the edges of a fourth and a fifth. She immediately moved over to the other side of the window and began scraping there. It didn't take long to determine that there were two more spirals there, making seven in all, but the artist seemed to have been less comfortable working on that side.

Angie knew that it would take time to uncover all seven sketches completely—especially if she did it carefully enough to minimize the damage to the plaster—but she was in no doubt that each of the seven was subtly different in shape from all the others.

Angie looked back at the first spiral she had found—the only one she had so far uncovered in its entirety. The line had been broken in numerous places where plaster had flaked away, but it was easy enough to complete the spiral in her mind if she looked at it intently enough. She found, however, that when she did stare hard enough to reconstruct the pattern in her mind it seemed to acquire a kind of flowing movement, as if it were continually attempting to change its own shape. It was an interesting optical illusion—and it helped her to guess what it was that she was looking at.

She ran downstairs then, shouting; "Mum! Come and see what I've found."

Her mother put down her own scraper, without bothering to pretend that she was annoyed by the interruption, and followed Angie up to the bedroom.

"It's just graffiti, treasure," she said, having glanced at the near-complete sketch and the other six fragments. "People have always scrawled on walls. You see it all over the place in Rome, from the finest palaces to the ancient sewers and catacombs—you get it in all the cathedrals of Europe. The temptation to scrawl must be even stronger when people are about to hang wallpaper and cover the plaster over."

"No, you don't understand," Angie told her. "Look out of the window."

Her mother looked out of the window. "What am I looking for, treasure?" she asked, after a few seconds.

"The old orchard," Angie said impatiently. "The apple trees weren't planted in rows. They were planted in some kind of wonky spiral pattern—a spiral that gets less and less circular as it expands."

"I can't see anything," her mother told her, after a few more seconds. "I can't tell whether the bumps in the bindweed are apple trees or hawthorn, or something else entirely—there's no pattern at all, so far as I can see. Anyway, there are seven drawings and there's only one garden."

"That's just it," Angie said. "Somebody was trying to draw the pattern, but they needed seven goes—maybe more, if there are others I haven't uncovered yet."

"I don't think so, precious," her mother said, sympathetically. "The bottom layer of paper here is the same type as the bottom layer downstairs. It's Victorian, I think—the downstairs rooms were decorated again before the apple-blossom was pasted over it by the man who planted the orchard. The trees weren't there when that wall was last bare."

Angie hadn't thought of that. She frowned.

"Keep up the good work," her mother said, as she made her way back to the door. "I'll do a little bit more, then we'll leave it for today. We can go for a walk before dinner, if you like."

It wasn't until her mother was downstairs again, scraping away, that Angie wondered whether there might have been some kind of spiral formation in the garden *before* it was replanted as a orchard, and whether the layout of the trees, like the sketches, might have been an attempt to reproduce it.

They did go for a walk, heading away from the village along the road that ran past the front gate, but they didn't go far. They were both too tired. Somewhat to Angie's disappointment—although it was only to be expected, given that they were moving away from Well House—they didn't meet Mrs. Lamb.

Later, as they ate dinner, Angie said: "How long has Mrs. Lamb lived in the cottage down the road?"

"I don't know, treasure," her mother replied. "Since she retired, I suppose—maybe since the 1980s. Why?"

"I just wondered whether she knew what the back garden was like before it was turned into an orchard."

"Whether it had trees planted in a spiral pattern, you mean? It's not likely—but I think she retired here because she knew the area. If she didn't spend her childhood hereabouts, you might find someone in the village who did, but I doubt that you'll find anyone alive now who can remember anything earlier than the 1930s."

"What about the local library?" Angie asked.

"What passes for a local library in these parts is a van that comes around once a fortnight," her mother observed. "There must be parish records somewhere, I suppose, but wherever they are, they'll only be lists of births, marriages, and deaths—nothing about gardens. Does it matter?"

"I suppose not," Angie said. "If there aren't any more sketches on the other side of the window, whoever drew them was probably left-handed."

"That's a clever deduction," her mother said. "Your father will be proud of you. You'll be able to show him the designs when he comes up on Friday—by then you'll have the whole room scraped clean."

"I'll finish tomorrow," Angie predicted, confidently.

"Maybe you can. The big room downstairs will take a little longer, though. Do you think you can bear to help me out with it when you've finished your room, or would you rather do Cathy's room?"

"I'll do Cathy's," Angie said.

"So you can be on your own?"

Angie hadn't realized soon enough that the question was a kind of trap. "I'll help you with the living room if you want me to," she was quick to say—although she realized immediately afterwards was that what her mother really wanted was for her to *want* to. "That might be better," she added—too late.

"No, you're right," her mother said. "We'll probably drive one another crazy if we're under one another's feet the whole time. Best to work on two fronts anyway—we'll see quite enough of one another when we're not actually scraping, I dare say."

On the following day they continued to work in separate rooms, but on the Tuesday Angie made a point of helping her mother in the lounge-dining room before starting work on Cathy's bedroom. When they had finished downstairs, her mother made a start on the master bedroom, for the sake of "a change of scenery".

Because Angie was able to finish Cathy's room on Wednesday, she and her mother were able to spend Thursday morning working together to finish off the larger bedroom. By that time, however, Angie was only working in sporadic spells, most of which lasted little more than half an hour. She spent the rest of the time on other pursuits. She finished off the puzzle-book, although the other puzzles weren't nearly as fascinating as the mazes. "That's an engineer's mind," her father had told her, proudly. "The words and the numbers are just things you need—all the beauty is in the spatial constructs."

"Did you ever get a chance to ask Mrs. Lamb about the back garden?" her mother asked, as they walked past the gate of Well House on Thursday afternoon. They were on the way to the village for the third time to stock up on groceries. They had to lay in supplies for the new arrivals expected on the following day, because it would be Good Friday.

"Yes, I bumped into her yesterday," Angie said, innocently. Although she still wasn't supposed to leave the garden, she had spent more than an hour hanging about in the lane outside Well House before Mrs. Lamb had put in an appearance outdoors, creating the opportunity for her to shout a greeting and strike up a conversation.

"What did she say?"

"She did grow up not far from here, but she never saw Orchard Cottage in the days before it was Orchard Cottage. She's heard talk, though."

"And what does the talk say?"

"Not very much. Before there was an orchard the people in the cottage used to grow vegetables there, and herbs."

"Nothing planted in spirals, then? No fancy rockeries, or anything of that sort?"

"No," Angie admitted. "Nothing of that sort."

"No ghosts, either? No resident witches?"

"No witches," Angie confirmed. "As for ghosts, she said that everywhere's haunted, *The dead can't do us any harm if we pay them no attention*, she said—her exact words. She didn't laugh at me, though, the way some people might. When she warned me off last Saturday, she meant it. She does seem to have the idea that there's *something nasty* under the bindweed, even though she can't say what it is."

"Just thorns and dirt, precious," her mother assured her. "Even if it doesn't make you sneeze or bring you out in a rash, it'll make you absolutely filthy. Better stay out of it, even if it's not haunted. You've been copying those sketches, I see. Daddy will be pleased. He's very fond of diagrams."

Angie had left her drawing-pad shut, so her mother couldn't have seen her sketches by accident, but she didn't protest that her mother had been snooping because she knew that Mrs. Martindale would retaliate by asking her exactly where she'd "bumped into" Mrs. Lamb.

"They'll be painted over soon," Angie explained. "I wanted to keep a record. The copies aren't very good, though. The spirals loop around anti-clockwise, and it's easier to draw anti-clockwise spirals left-handed than right-handed, especially if you're naturally left-handed. I'm right-handed. Maybe I was wrong about him being left-handed, and that's why he never got the design exactly right."

"How do you know he didn't?" Her mother asked. "Come to that, how do you know he wasn't a she?"

"I suppose I don't," Angie conceded, although she was certain in her own mind on the first point, at least.

"Maybe the sketches on the walls really are preliminary sketches," her mother suggested. "Maybe he went on to do a painting, once he'd had enough practice. Maybe he got it right when he used charcoal on the canvas. That kind of painting would have seemed a bit weird back in the nineteenth century, though, when they hadn't any idea what modern art would be like."

"I don't think he ever did a painting," Angie said, "or even a drawing on paper." She was quick to add, before the question was put to her: "Not that I can know that for sure, of course."

"It seems a bit disappointing to me," her mother said. "It would have been so much more interesting to uncover a long-lost mural of the battle of Trafalgar, or an inscription saying *Queen Victoria slept here*."

"That would have been in Cathy's room," Angie said. "From there you can see the road. Queen Victoria wouldn't have wanted a room overlooking a vegetable garden, would she?"

"Queens are funny like that," her mother agreed. "Are you looking forward to seeing Daddy and Cathy, after being cooped up in the cottage for a whole week with your mum?"

"It'll be nice to see them," Angie admitted, carefully. "But it's been an interesting week—and I expect you'll be looking forward to seeing Daddy too, even if he does have a teenager in tow."

"It won't be as quiet, that's for sure," her mother said, glancing disapprovingly into the almost-empty car park of The Elms as they passed by. "Cathy ought to be grateful that you've done her room, but she won't let on—and I dare say she'll find plenty of things to complain about. If she becomes unbearable, I suppose I can always give her a pair of scissors and tell her to make a start on the orchard."

"She'll claim that she can't do it because of her hay fever," Angie pointed out. "You might be able to change her mind by offering her the use of the chainsaw—except that the only thing worse than a bad-tempered teenager is a bad-tempered teenager with a chainsaw."

"Tell that one to your father," her mother said. "But wait until Cathy's well out of earshot before you do."

4.

Angie's father and sister didn't arrive at Orchard Cottage until mid-afternoon on Good Friday, but the fact that they were due to arrive combined with the fact that it was an official holiday to provide a good excuse for not working too hard in the morning. Although the wallpaper was almost all stripped, there was still a lot of cleaning to do, but Angie's mother decided that it could wait a little longer.

After five days, Angie felt that she had done enough soaking and scraping to last her a lifetime, although she was looking forward to helping out with the painting, which would be more creative.

She wasn't entirely happy about the prospect of her unexpected discovery being plastered and painted over, but she knew that it had to be done. There was no way that the walls of her bedroom could be left bare and crumbling. It was partly for that reason that she had what effort she could to preserve the mysterious finding by trying to copy the designs on to sheets of paper in her drawing pad. She decided to use the Friday morning to make one last attempt to get the drawings exactly right.

Because her mother was idling too, she came up to Angie's room to see what her precious daughter was doing. Knowing that her mother had already seen the drawings, Angie didn't try to hide them.

"We used to have tracing paper when I was a girl," her mother said, when she saw Angie had done. "I don't suppose there's much demand for it, now that we've got photocopiers and scanners."

Angie had already tried to trace the drawings using ordinary printer paper, but had proved too difficult. She didn't bother to mention it.

Her mother joined her at the window and imitated her, first looking out through the diamond-shaped miniature panes, then looking carefully at all seven of the fully-exposed sketches on the wall.

"I still can't see anything out there that looks remotely like these drawings, treasure," she said. "The lumps under the bindweed seem quite random to me."

"Perhaps it's just my imagination," Angie said, anticipating the suggestion.

"Perhaps it is, treasure. But that's good. Imagination is a precious gift, especially when you're eleven. When you're younger, you haven't really got enough ideas and images in store to make the most of it, and when you're older...."

"You turn into a teenager," Angie said.

"That as well," her mother agreed. "What I was going to say is that when you're older—and it lasts much longer than being a teenager—your horizons get narrower. You concentrate on the ordinary things. You start not being able to see the forest for the trees—or the pattern of the orchard for the bindweed that's overgrown it. It's too easy to see *appearances*, and to hard to see things as they really are."

Angie reached the end of a spiral and stopped drawing. "Are you all right, mum?" she asked.

"Fine," her mother assured her. "Engineers don't have a monopoly on little flights of philosophical fancy, you know—schoolteachers can do it too." She turned round then and left the room.

Angie carried on drawing, moving her pencil as carefully as she would have done if she'd been solving a maze. She eventually managed to produce copies of all seven diagrams that seemed *almost* correct—except, of course, that none of the seven was *really* correct, as a representation of whatever lay beneath the thicket that now occupied the area behind the house. Given that the original artist seemed to have had so much trouble getting the effect that he—or she—wanted, Angie thought that her efforts were just as good as his.

It was easier to compare the view from her window to her own drawings than it was the compare it to the sketches on the wall because she could place the sheets of paper flat on the older diamonds, one by one, while peering through the newer ones directly alongside. It was very difficult to figure out exactly where the discrepancy was between the drawings and the actual spiral, though. The weather was still breezy, and the bindweed overlaying the bushes and brambles was moving about restlessly. The illusory movement in the spiral drawings might have helped, if it had only matched the stirrings of the wind, but it didn't; indeed, it seemed perversely contrary, always working in opposition.

It was even easier now to imagine that there were invisible creatures wandering over the surface of the overgrown orchard, or moving about beneath the bindweed, but they no longer seemed as monstrous as they had when Angie had first imagined them. It was easy enough to picture them as ordinary animals of an ordinary size—sheep, perhaps, or dogs—or even as people, more likely children than adults. It was easy enough, too, to imagine small people wandering in the gaps between the lines of her spirals, as if they were lost in a maze. Even though they couldn't *really* be lost, Angie realized, they might still *feel* lost. If they didn't know that the path would eventually lead them out, if only they stuck to it stubbornly, they could easily become convinced that they were wandering hopelessly around in wonky circles.

When her father and Cathy finally arrived Angie tried to put the puzzle out of her mind for a while, but she couldn't help dragging her father upstairs at the first possible opportunity to show him what she'd uncovered.

"That's interesting," he said obligingly. "I wonder when that first layer of wallpaper was stuck on. Before nineteen hundred, probably—more than a century ago."

"The person who drew them must have been looking out of the window," Angie said. "What do you suppose he could have been looking *at*?"

"Staring into infinity, constructing mandalas," her father replied. "He must have been left-handed, you know."

"I figured that out," Angie was quick to say. "The left-handed bit I mean. What's a mandala?"

"Just a design—anything like a maze or spiral, however simple. There's a famous psychoanalyst called Jung, who thought that they were reflections of something fundamental in the unconscious mind—maybe ways of symbolizing space, or time; I'm not sure."

"I thought it might be something in the garden," Angie said.

Her father obligingly looked down. "I can't imagine what it could have been," he said. "Certainly can't tell now, with all that convolvulus getting in the way."

Angie knew that *convolvulus* was just a fancy term for bindweed. She gave up on her father at that point, but she made another bid for support when she finally persuaded Cathy to come in and take a look.

"I've seen better tags on railway bridges and tube trains," was Cathy's judgment of the drawings on the wall.

"Look out of the window," Angie said. "Try to match the lines to the pattern of the treetops."

"There aren't any treetops," Cathy objected. "There's just that green stuff with the white flowers, drowning everything."

"You can still see vague shapes underneath it," Angie persisted.

"I guess," Cathy said. "You could imagine it as a miniature model of the downs, if you tried hard—except that the real hills don't sway like that."

"That's just the invisible monsters walking about on it," Angie said, with a sigh of disappointment.

"Right," Cathy said. "So *that*'s what the wind is: invisible monsters wandering back and forth. Good job I found out before I sit my GCSEs."

"Actually, they're not *that* monstrous," Angie said, resentfully. "They're just ghosts, really. Animals, mostly, except for *the boy*. You can hear him at night, you know, crying—and sometimes you can hear his footsteps running over the roof. He's looking for something, but I don't know what. Maybe you'll remind him of his mother and he'll come to sit on your bed."

"*You* think you can scare *me* with silly ghost stories?" Cathy said, incredulously. "Listen, kid—I know all about ghosts. Dad says they can't exist, because if they did there'd be at least six ghosts hanging around for every living person, most of them left over from prehistoric times—but what he doesn't take into account is that only a few unlucky spirits get trapped here on Earth, while the rest make it through to the afterlife. If there's a little boy ghost hanging around here, he's far more likely to be interested in you than me. Misery loves company, they say."

"Maybe he's not that little," Angie countered. "Maybe he's more of a teenager, still yearning for his first kiss after a hundred years of loneliness. He'll be in your room tonight, there's no doubt about it—*watching* you."

Cathy decided to laugh instead of getting angry; she was right about Angie's inability to scare her by making things up. "In that case," she said, "it's up to me to help him out, isn't it? You're a weird kid, Ange—but I have to admit that you're pretty good with a scraper. I'm glad I don't have to do my room. Do you think Mum will be crazy enough to trust you with a paintbrush next week?"

"Only in your room," Angie replied. "Don't worry—I'll be sure to cover up all the magic mandalas on the walls."

"There aren't any whatsits on *my* walls," Cathy said, walking straight into the trap that Angie had set.

"There could be, now that I've practiced drawing them," Angie said. "But you'll never know, once the walls are painted over, what anyone might have drawn or written there—or what they might be *for*."

"Sticks and stones might break my bones," Cathy retorted, serenely, as she went back to her own room, "but the ghosts of little boys and invisible magical graffiti will never hurt me."

The topic came up again at dinner, this time raised by Angie's mother—who was trying to help rather than to add to the rain of mockery.

"Angie asked Mrs. Lamb what was out back before the orchard was planted," Mrs. Martindale told her husband. "Apparently it was a vegetable garden and a herb garden. Is there any possibility, do you think, that there are still herb seeds lying dormant beneath all that rubbish? I quite like the idea of having a herb garden."

"I don't think so," Angie's father replied. "It wouldn't matter if there were. I'll have to use weed-killer to kill off the roots of the hawthorns and the brambles once the actual growth's cleared away. We'll never get a lawn otherwise. What sort of herb garden was it, Angie?"

"Is there more than one sort?" Angie asked.

"There used to be. Your mother is thinking about herbs used in cooking—thyme, fennel, rosemary and the like. There was a time, though, when people grew herbs for medicinal purposes."

"Witches, you mean?" Cathy put in. "Must have been a lot of *them* around here, since the village is named after them."

"It's not," Angie said, quick to score a point. "It's named after wych-elms."

"Oh yeah?" said Cathy. "So what are wych-elms named after, then?"

"It's possible that people who had herb gardens might have been more likely to be accused of witchcraft than people who didn't," their father said, cutting off the argument, "but that would have been back in the seventeenth century. If there was a medicinal herb garden behind the cottage in the 1920s, before the house became Orchard Cottage, its owner would have been perfectly respectable. Anyway, the Romans used to think that hawthorn was a charm against sorcery, so any witchcraft in our garden must have been obliterated long ago, along with the apple-trees."

"That's a pity," Cathy said. "It might have explained Angie's ghost."

"What ghost?" Mrs. Martindale asked, while her husband frowned.

"Nothing," Angie was quick to say. "I just made it up to tease Cathy. She started it."

"I did not!" Cathy retorted, evidently feeling unjustly accused. "*She* started it, with her silly graffiti. She says there's a little boy haunting the place. I just thought that if there's a witch's garden buried underneath all those brambles, it might be the ghost of some child sacrifice whose innocent blood had been used to fertilize the ground where the plants used to make love potions once grew."

"Where do you get such nasty ideas?" her mother complained.

"She's a teenager," her father said, dismissively.

"I never said any of that," Angie added. "The witches and the human sacrifice were all Cathy's idea."

"Unlike the invisible monsters and the magic graffiti," Cathy pointed out.

"That was just a joke," Mrs. Martindale said.

"Well, it's probably best to get these things into the open and out of the way as soon as possible," Mr. Martindale said, deliberately making light of it all. "We've bought an old ruined house built in the seventeenth century, which has been left to lie derelict for more than fifty years—exactly the sort of place that generates talk of hauntings. If you can cook up a good enough story between the two of you, my darlings, maybe we can get the place on TV, in one of those shows where people walk around in the dark, lit by infra-red, with glowing eyes, squawking in terror every time the director drops a paper-clip. I suppose I'd better take some photographs of those drawings on Angie's wall. That's the sort of thing the TV people like—the camera can zoom in on them over and over again, while they spin around suggestively. The entire audience will be hypnotized into seeing ghosts."

"I never thought of that," Angie said, suddenly feeling stupid.

"Getting the house on TV?" her father said.

"No—taking photographs. I wasted all that time trying to copy them by hand."

"That's because you don't have a mobile phone yet," Cathy put in, to emphasize the fact that she did have one. "If you'd borrowed Mum's, you could have sent us pictures when you first found them."

"The time wasn't wasted, love," her father said. "Drawing's good for hand and eye co-ordination, and very useful to an engineer. You should draw more."

"Have you got your digital camera with you?" Angie asked. "Can you take the photos anyway?"

"I brought it down to take family photographs," her father said. "And the house too, of course. I'll certainly make a record of your discovery—and anything else we might unearth."

"You don't really want the girls to go on one of those TV shows, do you, Rob?" Mrs. Martindale asked.

"Of course not. Our girls are far too sensible to believe in ghosts, and far too honest to pretend. I was joking."

"Pity," Cathy said. "The story was getting better every time we told it."

"That's how these silly things develop," her father said. "Every teller adds an extra twist. The sooner we get the walls painted and the back garden sorted, the sooner we'll be able to see the cottage for what it really is, and what it *deserves* to be: our home-away-from-home, a place to rest and recuperate from the stress of city life."

"A place to get bored to death instead of scared to death," Cathy added. "Personally, I'd rather be on TV, faking ghosts."

5.

On Saturday Angie's father drove the family to a large supermarket just outside Chichester. They stocked up enough food to see them all through the holiday weekend and make sure that Angie and her mother didn't starve in the remainder of the week, when they'd be abandoned again. Mr. and Mrs. Martindale also bought lots of other oddments for the house, and items that would help with the cleaning and decorating.

After lunch, there was supposed to be an all-out assault on the last of the wallpaper stripping, but among all the things they had bought no one had remembered to include a fourth scraper. Angie argued that she'd already done her share and more during the week, and that Cathy had a lot of catching up to do, so she was let off. Her delight in the unusual experience of watching Cathy work soon faded away, and she began to feel slightly uncomfortable being the only idle person is a busy house, so she went out into the front garden.

Mrs. Lamb, who must have been taking a walk, had just paused in the road to inspect the house. "Hello Angela," she said. "How's the decorating coming along?"

"Daddy's going to start the plastering tomorrow," Angie told her. "He'll try to get it done before he goes back to Kingston, so that Mummy and I can start painting on Tuesday."

"It's strange to see the place looking lived-in," Mrs. Lamb observed. "I've got used to seeing it as a ruin."

"I found some drawings behind the wallpaper in my bedroom," Angie told her. "Spirals, but bent out of shape. They're beside the window—as if someone were trying to draw something that was in the garden before it was an orchard."

"Is that why you asked me if I knew what was there before the orchard?" Mrs. Lamb asked.

"Yes," Angie admitted. "You'd already said there was something nasty in there—I thought you might know something."

"No," Mrs. Lamb said, thoughtfully. "Nothing specific, at any rate. I mentioned it in the village, though. Some of the regulars in The Elms said they remembered talk of a ghost—a little boy—but they're the type who'd make up that sort of thing just to get a rise out of you."

"Cathy and I made up a ghost of our own," Angie told her. "He's a boy, too. I think he might be trapped in the old orchard because he can't find his way out of the spiral, even though it's not a real maze. All he has to do is keep on going, but he doesn't know that, because he just seems to be going round and round and getting nowhere."

Mrs. Lamb looked at her sharply, then. The story had awakened her interest, as it had been intended to do, but this didn't seem to be the right kind of interest.

"You shouldn't joke about things like that," Mrs. Lamb said. "You shouldn't make up stories, any more than those old fools in The Elms. Sometimes, spirits *do* become trapped between this world and the next, and it's very frightening for them."

Angie could see by the pained expression on Mrs. Lamb's face that she had accidentally touched a nerve. "I'm sorry," she said. "Our story doesn't make sense, anyway—if the boy who made the drawings had been the one who got trapped in the maze, he'd *know* that it was just a spiral, not a real maze."

"Never you mind about ghosts," the old lady said. "It's not them you need to look out for." Angie could tell that as soon as the final sentence was out of her mouth, the old lady wished she hadn't said it.

"What *do* we need to look out for?" Angie asked, immediately.

"Townsfolk on motorbikes," Mrs. Lamb replied, sharply—although Angie was quite certain that it wasn't what she'd previously had in mind.

"No, really," Angie said.

"Seeing things that aren't there," the old lady retorted, just as sharply—except that this time she did seem to mean it.

Some day, Angie thought—perhaps a long time ago now—Mrs. Lamb must have seen something that *wasn't there*. "What kind of herb garden was behind the house before the orchard?" she was quick to ask, to keep the conversation going. "Was it for cooking, or medicines—or magic?"

"What an imagination you've got," Mrs. Lamb observed, grimly. "For cooking, I expect." The old lady's manner suggested that there was still something that she was deliberately not saying.

"It wouldn't matter anyway," Angie said, stubbornly plugging on. "Dad says that hawthorn wards off sorcery, so any magic there ever was in the orchard is dead now, just like the apple trees."

Mrs. Lamb tried to smile, and almost managed it. "I expect that's right," she said. "But you'd best remember what I said. Don't go looking for things you don't want to see."

"Maybe I do want to see them," Angie said, teasingly.

"If we only had to see what we wanted to see," Mrs. Lamb retorted, "the world would be a nicer place. What I should have said was that you shouldn't look too hard in places where there might be things you definitely wouldn't want to see. Curiosity killed the cat, remember."

Having said that, Mrs. Lamb turned on her heel and marched off in the direction of Well House. She didn't give Angie the opportunity to mention that cats were also supposed to have nine lives, and could probably afford a certain amount of curiosity. There was nothing to be done then but to go round to the back of the house and stare hard at the overgrown orchard, to see what might be seen.

In order to get a better view, Angie climbed up on to the side wall of the property. She wasn't sure that she could keep her balance if she stood up on it, so she contented herself with sitting down. That left her at just the right height to look out over the waves of greenery from the same sort of viewpoint she'd have had if she'd been on a harbor at high tide, looking out over the waves of a wind-tossed sea.

This view was quite different from the one from the bedroom window. There was no point in trying to find patterns in the waves of the sort for which the boy who'd made the drawings must have been searching. Here, the bumps in the green carpet where the crowd of the trees pushed up against the bindweed stood out purely by virtue of their height, not their distance from one another. Nor were the movements of their leaves blurred by distance; from here, it was obvious that the wind was stirring the foliage, and that each individual bump was quivering. It was equally obvious that the regions in between weren't being depressed by the passage of invisible bodies. It was easy to see the hawthorn branches and brambles that protruded through the bindweed in hundreds of different places, so it was obvious that the greenery *wasn't* a single oceanic mass at all, but a confusion of different things.

Angie looked hard. The bumps on the apparent surface were squat and rounded, impossible to imagine as people or animals, but it *was* possible to imagine creatures hiding behind them or moving beneath them—except that they only seemed to move when she wasn't looking directly at them. Angie knew that it was an illusion. She knew that the movements glimpsed from the corners of her eyes were just branches of different kinds shifted in different ways by the wind. The reason she could imagine animate *creatures* making those movements was that the information transmitted to her brain by her eye was incomplete, allowing her brain to make things up. She was an engineer's daughter, after all. Her father was always enthusiastic to explain those sorts of things.

That wasn't the point, though. She wanted to know what *kind* of creatures she wasn't really seeing. She wanted to know what it was that Mrs. Lamb had avoided saying. So she tried very hard to see exactly what wasn't there. She tried to work out exactly what her brain might want to invent, if it were given a license to do so.

Then she guessed, and giggled.

"There are fairies at the bottom of the garden," she quoted. That was what Mrs. Lamb had been too embarrassed to mention. It wasn't ghosts that lurked in impenetrable thickets, in the old lady's mind, but mischievous fairy folk.

Angie was eleven years old, and she knew better than to think of fairies as tiny people with butterfly wings. It wasn't the kind of fairies that featured in children's fairy tales and their illustrations that Mrs. Lamb had been thinking about. She had been imagining tricky things that moved in the borderlands of existence as well as the borderlands of sight: things that teased belief as well as sight.

"Well, if *that*'s all they are," Angie said, "there really isn't any need to be afraid, is there?"

"What's that, treasure?" her mother's voice put in. Her mother had opened the back door of the cottage, perhaps to look for Angie and perhaps to let in some fresh air.

"Nothing," Angie said. "I'm just going upstairs to my room."

That was, indeed, what she had decided to do. She wanted to take another look at the dead orchard from her bedroom window, to see if she could make any more sense out of the designs drawn beside it, now that she had made her new guess as to what it all might mean.

She ran up the stairs, and went into her grey-walled room, which now seemed to be waiting to be rescued from its own unfinished state. It deserved to be made into a thoroughly human habitation again, by the careful repair of its crumbling plaster and the application of two layers of cheerfully-colored paint, and it expected to be given what it deserved.

"All in good time," Angie told the walls.

She took her drawings from the drawer of her bedside table and took them to the window. She looked out intently, staring as hard as she could, and then looked at one of the drawings. She repeated the procedure with another, and then another.

The artist never got it quite right, she reminded herself. *Not while he was drawing on the wall, any rate. None of these is exactly accurate—but there's a wonky spiral in there somewhere, if only I can figure out how to see it and draw. It's difficult because it's a fairy thing—a tricky thing. Maybe it is a kind of trap. Maybe there is someone in there, after all, who can't go on to wherever he's supposed to go, because he's trapped in the fairy ring. Even though he knows that, in theory, all he has to do to get out is to keep on going, he can't actually do it because the fairies keep tricking him, the way fairies do.*

It occurred to her, after she'd finished formulating the thought, that she now had it firmly fixed in her mind that the unknown artist was a boy. What Cathy had said about him being a human sacrifice whose blood had been used to fertilize a witch's garden was nonsense, because there was no witches' garden, but he had been trapped there nevertheless. The orchard hadn't failed because the apple trees had been planted in poisoned ground; it had failed because it had been planted on a fairy ring—which was actually a fairy spiral.

That was nonsense too, of course—but it was a different kind of nonsense. It couldn't make the kind of sense that an engineer's thinking could recognize, but it might make a kind of sense that the artist standing by the window, looking out through the old lattice with its ill-matched fragments of distorted glass, had recognized quite naturally. Even her father had conceded that what he called mandalas might reflect something basic in the unconscious mind—something that hovered on the brink of perception and believability, teasingly.

Angie put the completed drawings back in the drawer and took out her pad and a soft pencil. She took them back to the window, and looked out. At first she looked through the cluster of new diamonds, but then she moved her head sideways, to look out through the older glass, which blurred the image of the green waves just a little bit more.

She began to sketch, trying to find the *right* eccentric spiral, the *right* mandala. She wanted to see the trap as it really was. She wasn't in the least afraid, because she thought that if she could only succeed in making an accurate map, she would know exactly how to get out of the trap should she ever find herself in it.

Her first attempt was a dismal failure, worse than the examples scribbled in the yielding plaster. Her second was no better—but she could feel that the practice was doing her good. She was getting a feel for the work now. She was beginning to see what was *really* there, and beginning to guide her hand in such a way as to reproduce what she saw on paper.

She carried on drawing, relentlessly.

6.

When Angie's mother finally called her down to dinner, she took her best effort yet downstairs to show her parents.

"It's not quite right," she told them, "but it's very nearly right. I don't think the light's quite right at this time of day. I'll try again later, when the sun's gone down."

Her mother looked at the drawing, and then passed it on to Mr. Martindale. Angie could see that they were gathering themselves to be complimentary, although they wouldn't really mean it. They couldn't see what it was that she had almost drawn. To them, it was just a glorified doodle.

"It's a load of crap," was Cathy's verdict. "If you're going to be an artist, you might as well try to be a real artist first, before you settle for passing off scribbles as *abstracts*."

"Not these days," her father observed. "These days, you might as well skip the drawing entirely and go straight to pickled sharks, unmade beds and video loops."

"You were wrong about the ghost, by the way," Angie said to Cathy. "He wasn't killed. He just got lost. He knows that he's in a spiral rather than a maze, but he still can't get out because he doesn't have an accurate map. It's not just a matter of going on walking, you see—you have to be able to see through the tricks."

"What *are* you talking about?" Cathy demanded.

"I'm not at all sure that he's a *ghost* at all," Angie said, blithely. "At any rate, he's not the sort of ghost they hunt for in those TV shows. The TV people are looking for the wrong things, so they never get to see anything clearly."

"You're off your head," Cathy said dismissively.

"Don't be nasty," her father instructed. "What should they be looking for, precious? What *are* you talking about?"

Angie hesitated, knowing that it wouldn't be a good idea to try talking to her father about fairies.

"I don't think they've got a name," she said. "In fact, I think that's what they are: the kind of thing you can't put a name to. Mrs. Lamb wouldn't, when I talked to her this afternoon. She believes in spirits that get trapped here, and she believes in something else, but she couldn't say exactly what it was, because it doesn't have a name. Something you can't see unless you look really hard, and might wish you hadn't seen if you did."

"Stark raving bonkers," Cathy observed.

"No," said Mr. Martindale, making an obvious effort. "I think I understand what Angie's getting at. From what your mother tells me, Mrs. Lamb's a country person, born and bred. She hasn't always lived and worked in the same place, but she's always lived in the same area. She taught village children in a village school. She's never lived in a town, let alone a city. She's an intelligent and sensible woman, no doubt, but she's never entirely got away from the folklore she grew up with. She doesn't believe it, exactly, but she doesn't reject it either. People of that sort don't put names to such things, because that would compel them to think about them more clearly, and come to a firmer decision about whether to take them seriously or not. But we're not like that, are we? So what are we talking about, Angie? Fairies?"

Angie was surprised to hear her father make that guess, even though she knew how smart he was.

"You might call them that, I suppose," she said, serenely. "Not the silly kind, though. Not the kind those two little girls cut out of soap ads so that they could fake photographs."

"What little girls?" her mother asked.

"She means the girls who faked the Cottingley photographs that fooled Conan Doyle," her father supplied, helpfully. "Are we talking about *sinister* fairies, love—sly things that steal the milk and knock things over in the kitchen while everyone's asleep?"

"No," said Angie, defensively.

"No?" her father echoed. Then, like the intelligent man he was, he looked at her drawing again, and studied it more carefully. "Ah!" he said. "I'm getting it now—the right folklore, that is. Tales of traps where people are becalmed in time—tales of wanderers who stray over some invisible barrier, into a world where time stands still, then return home to find that years have passed, or centuries."

"Kids' stuff," Cathy said, scornfully.

"Not at all," Mr. Martindale replied. "It's a kind of story found all over the British isles, and very old. There was a time, you see, when fairyland and the land of the dead were the same thing. That's why time doesn't move in fairyland: because the dead are outside time, and unaffected by it. In that way of thinking, fairyland's in-habitants *are* ghosts, of a sort—and Angie might be right when she says that it isn't appropriate to name them, to see and know them for what they really are. Ignorance, you see, is what sometimes allows the living who stray into fairyland by mistake—especially chil-dren—to get back again unscathed. If they ever realize where they are, they get stuck, perhaps because they die themselves but perhaps because they just *get stuck*."

"What's the drawing got to do with it?" Angie's mother asked.

"It's a mandala," Mr. Martindale said. "A map of time and life as a kind of maze—a maze that you can't really get lost in, as you proceed from birth to death, by way of the eternal sequence of days and years, but in which you always *seem* to be lost, because you never know where you're headed, and always seem to be going around in circles."

"I don't get it," Mrs. Martindale said, flatly.

Angie was still looking at her father, and he was looking at her. "The thing you have to remember," her father said softly, "is that you *can* always get out, even if you think you're stuck. You understand that, don't you, treasure?"

Angie knew that her father wasn't talking about what was in the back garden, or about ghosts, or about fairyland. He meant that it was okay for her to let her imagination run wild occasionally, as long as she knew the way back and didn't ever accept that she was stuck.

"Sure," she said. "I know what I'm doing."

She honestly thought that she did. As soon as she'd finished dinner, without even glancing in the direction of the TV set, she went back upstairs to see if the grey twilight would allow her to see what she hadn't quite been able to grasp in the sunlight.

She drew one pattern, and then another—and then, finally, she got it right. She managed to capture the exact pattern of the fairy ring.

She didn't take it downstairs to show her parents and sister. She knew that it would just be one more meaningless doodle to her mother and Cathy, and one more arbitrary mandala to her father. None of them would be able to see it properly, and recognize it for what it was.

Among the various things her father had bought in the supermarket to help with the decorating was some masking tape, which he was going to put around the edges of the windows while he painted the frames, so he wouldn't get paint on the glass. Angie went down to the kitchen and used the kitchen scissors to cut a few inches off the roll.

She took the piece of masking tape back to her bedroom, and stuck her drawing on to the wall beside the window, on top of two of the sketches that had been made directly on the wall. Then she spent a few minutes looking back and forth from the drawing to the window, checking that it really was right.

After that, she went downstairs and watched TV with Cathy. She didn't mention ghosts or fairies between then and bedtime, and was quite happy to listen while Cathy talked about her friends, and all the things they planned to do once she was back in Kingston, having returned to civilization from the desolate of wilderness of Sussex.

Angie and Cathy stayed up late, because it was Saturday, and because the work that had to be done the following day was not work with which they could be expected or asked to help. Scraping wallpaper was something the entire family could do, but plastering wasn't. Plastering was specialist work—the difficult sort that an engineer had to do on his own.

"Mind you don't have bad dreams," Cathy said, when they finally went up to their rooms, probably hoping that that was exactly what Angie would have.

"I'll be fine," Angie assured her.

She was confident that she would be fine. Indeed, she was so confident that she would be fine that she wasn't in the least afraid when she woke up with a start to see that the starlight streaming through her window was falling at an angle upon the face of a boy who was studying her drawing raptly.

After a minute or so, he turned to face her. "You've got it right," he said. "I never could." He pointed at Angie's drawing using his left forefinger.

Although he wasn't very tall and was wearing knee-length trousers, Angie judged that the boy was at least as old as Cathy—plus an extra hundred years or so that didn't show.

The most peculiar thing about the boy was that his clothes seemed brand new, as if he'd only just put them on for the first time. His trousers and socks were clean, without a thread out of place. His white shirt looked freshly-washed, and the black waistcoat he wore over it was equally unstained. His face had been scrubbed and his hair newly-combed.

All of that seemed much stranger than the fact that there was something slightly odd about the way he spoke, or seemed to speak. It was almost as if Angie weren't hearing his actual voice, but some kind of substitute, like the voice-overs they sometimes used on the TV news to translate what foreign speakers were saying into English.

"You're not a ghost, are you?" Angie said.

"No," he replied.

"But you don't belong here."

"Oh yes I do," the boy said, with a sigh. "That's the trouble."

"I mean that you don't belong in this *time*."

"Why not?" he said, innocently. "What time is it?"

"Two thousand and six," she said. "What year was it when you got lost?"

"I don't know," he said. "But it was Whitsun—I remember that."

"Might you be able to find your way out," Angie asked, "now that you have the right map? You can borrow it if you like."

"Is that why you drew it?" the boy asked. "I thought *you* were trying to find a way *in*. I tried to warn you twice, when you were looking at the bushes, but you couldn't see me then."

"Could you see me?" Angie asked, interestedly.

"I can see everything, after a fashion," the boy told her. "Not well enough, though. I've never been able to see *well enough*." He didn't sound happy about it. Angie figured that he had been born into an era when there were no regular eye tests, and maybe no opticians at all, but she suspected that he wasn't just talking about being short-sighted.

"What's your name?" Angie asked.

"Jesse."

"Mine's Angela—Angie for short."

"I know. I can hear too. I can see time go by and I can hear time go by; I just can't seem to get *into* it any more. I'm not sure that I'm in it even now. I think you might be out of it."

Angie had put her wristwatch on the bedside table, as she always did. The hands glowed in the dark, so she was able to see what time it was, but she couldn't tell whether they were still moving or not. She assumed that they were, but she couldn't be sure. The boy could watch time going by, even though he couldn't *get into* it, so time *might* still be going by...except that the significant thing wasn't that Jesse could see her, but that she could see him.

"Am I like you now?" she asked.

"I don't know," he said. "You're not the first I've talked to. Other people have tried to see me, and looked hard enough to do it, just about—but it never lasts. Time carries them away. They didn't have *this*, though." He pointed to the drawing. "It's not seeing *me* you have to worry about, in any case—it's seeing *them*."

"Who's *them*?"

"I don't know," he said, again. "They can talk, I think, but they don't—not to me. Not any more. They don't *explain* things."

Angie reminded herself that she was an engineer's daughter, who didn't have to be afraid of anything, but she wasn't entirely convinced. "They don't tear you apart and gobble up the pieces, though," she observed. "They don't use your blood to fertilize their garden."

"No," Jesse admitted. "They don't do things like that. At least, I've never seen them do things like that—but I can't really *see* them at all. Not well enough. That's always been the problem. I can see *through*, but I can't quite see what's on the other side."

"So what's so terrible about *them*?"

"Nothing, except that once you've seen them—even if you can't see them well enough—they can take you out of time, the way they took me."

"And what's so terrible about *that*?" Angie wanted to know.

"Nothing," he said, again. "There's no hunger, no thirst, no pain, no loneliness, no boredom. It's just that I can't *go* anywhere— except *here* and *there*. I can't go home."

Again, he used his left hand as a pointer, stabbing his forefinger at the floor of the bedroom when he said "here" and at the window when he said "there". When he said "home" the palm of his hand opened up, and he made a gesture of helplessness. Angie knew that Orchard Cottage must have been his home once, long before it became Orchard Cottage—but he had been watching time go by for long enough to know that it wasn't his home any longer. For a while, it had been a ruin, but now it was going to be something else: a weekend cottage; a place to *get away*.

Angie still didn't know whether she wanted to get away from her life in Kingston, but she knew that she had to find out what was in the mandala. She didn't imagine for a moment that it would be something she wanted to see, but she felt that she had to look anyway, as hard as she could.

7.

Angie got out of bed, feeling more than a little self-conscious about her night-dress. Before going to join Jesse at the window she pulled on her jeans and put on a sweater of her own. She put her trainers on too, although she didn't bother with socks.

She went to the window and looked out. There was nothing visible through the new glass but the same old lumpy green carpet. The old glass, on the other hand, displayed something quite different. The distorted diamonds filtered out the bindweed, the hawthorn, the dead apple trees and much more, leaving the mandala beneath exposed.

Angie had imagined the spiral as a kind of hedge, but it wasn't. It wasn't made out of vegetation at all, or of anything solid. The sight of it was slightly suggestive of the kind of glass that made up the older parts of the lattice window, but Angie knew that it wasn't actually glass. Whatever was making up the mandala was only *imitating* substance. It was one of those things that was invisible unless you tried really hard to see it—and which only a very few people could see even then. There was a sense, Angie knew, in which the fairy ring wasn't really there—but she could see it now, and because she could see it, she could look past everything else.

Should I have wanted to see it, though? she asked herself, in a moment of self-doubt. *Would I have been better off following Mrs. Lamb's advice, and looking the other way?*

"You can't really be trapped in it," Angie told Jesse. "You're outside it now."

"No I'm not," he told her. "Or if I am, this spot right here is the only other place I can be. This is where I first saw it, and once I'd seen it, I was inside it. You're probably inside it too, now that you've seen it. I'm not sure, though—I'm never sure of anything. Can you turn around and go back to bed?"

Angie turned around without any difficulty—but when she tried to take a step back into the room, she couldn't. Her legs wouldn't obey the instruction. She could watch time going by around her, but she wasn't *in* it any more.

Her parents, she realized, would think that she had disappeared—vanished into thin air. Except, of course, that her father wouldn't believe that anyone *could* vanish into air, however thin it might be. Her father would take note of the fact that her jeans, sweater and trainers were missing, and would assume that she'd put them on in order to leave the room, and maybe go outside. He'd think that she'd run away, or that she'd been kidnapped.

Angie didn't want him to think either of those things.

"I can get back," she told Jesse, hoping that it was true. "It's just a matter of figuring out how. What's at the other end of the maze?"

"I don't know," Jesse said. "I can never get there. It doesn't matter how long I keep going, I never get there. I think that's because I'm not really going anywhere at all. I seem to be moving, but I'm really still *here*."

Angie looked at the diagram she had drawn with such painstaking care. If you imagined the space contained within the spiral line as a space in which someone could move, she thought, then the someone could start from where the line ended and move around and around and around, until they eventually came to....what? The little covert where the line first curled away from the initial dot: a small enclosed space from which there was no escape but to go back.

The only way *out* of the maze, if one cared to think of it as a kind of maze, was also the way *in*. From where she and Jesse were standing, it appeared that the only way they could go was in. Perhaps, she thought, that was the way they had to go if they were ever going to get out.

"Right," she said. "I need to see what it looks like from the inside. How do we get from here to there, since we can't go down the stairs?"

"That's easy," Jesse said. "You just do *this*."

What Jesse did was to go through the window. It wasn't obvious how he managed it, because it wasn't a very large window, even if you ignored the leaden latticework, and the sill was chest-high. Even so, he went out that way, without climbing or jumping.

Perhaps I won't be able to do that, Angie thought, almost hoping that she might find that she couldn't. She paused to pluck her drawing from the wall, figuring that if she could go out that way she would surely need a map to get back.

When she tried to do what Jesse had done, she found that she could—and that it was, as Jesse had said, ridiculously easy. It was the only step she could actually take, now that she was no longer able to turn back.

Once through the glass, she was inside the maze; it was as simple as that. And once she was inside the maze, she realized why the exact shape mattered so much. If the walls had been opaque, like the walls of her room, the way they curved and wound around wouldn't have been important, because they'd just have been boundaries containing the path within. Because they were transparent, though, the curvature had dramatic effects. The walls distorted the light they let through, like the walls of a bottle or the glass in her mother's spectacles, creating all manner of strange images.

The walls of the maze weren't glass, though. They weren't even solid. They weren't just something that happened to get in the way of the light that was shining through them, she realized. They were, in some strange sense, a product of the light. They were there in order to transmit it, and they were shaped in order to transmit it in the way that it had to be transmitted—the way it wanted and needed to be transmitted.

Angie guessed immediately where that light came from. It came from—or, rather, *through*—the point from which the spiral started. Perhaps, within or behind that point, it was only the merest spark, but as it moved through the walls, reflected and refracted this way and that, it was multiplied and amplified. Invisible as it was to eyes that hadn't yet caught a glimpse of it, that light was glorious and dazzling, and *alive*.

Angie saw immediately what Jesse meant by *them*, and understood why they were so mysterious. There were no clear shapes visible through the walls of the maze—it wasn't in the least like looking into an aquarium—but it was extremely easy to catch glimpses of things that might have been trying to *become* shapes, if only they could be captured and clarified.

"It's quite safe," Jesse said, reaching out to take her left hand in his. "They won't hurt you. It's best not to try look directly at them though. It can't be done. Every time you think you've got a clear sight of one, it vanishes. Then you get a sort of feeling—nothing painful, or even very unpleasant, but odd...as if you'd lost something."

"You have lost something," Angie pointed out. "You've lost your mother, your father, your brothers and sisters and the time where you belong. Unless...."

"Unless what?" the boy asked.

"Unless there's a way back *then* as well as a way back *now*, if only you can master the trick of it. That's not in the fairy tales, but that doesn't mean it isn't possible. Maybe you have to step *through* the walls instead of letting the spiral pattern guide you."

"You can't step through the walls," Jesse told her. "It's like when you tried to go back to your bed. You just can't go *that way*. You can only go further and further in—and even then, you never arrive anywhere."

"I don't believe that," Angie said. "Just because you always seem to end up where you started, it doesn't mean that you haven't been anywhere. If there's an answer, it has to lie at the heart of the maze. It always does. Let's go."

Without letting go of his hand, she pulled him along. She didn't have to look at the map, because there was only one way she could go while she consented to be guided by the walls. It was, as Jesse had said, exactly like standing at the window; no other step was possible. Her right hand was clinging hard to the map, though, because she thought the time might come when she did need it. She still intended to get out if she could. She didn't want to become trapped the way Jesse had.

While they walked, knowing that they were going round and round and round, though not in a perfect circle, Angie looked into the walls, searching for *them*.

As Jesse had said, anything she glimpsed had a tendency to vanish as son as she tried to look directly at it, and when it did she felt a curious sense of regret. At least, there was a sense of regret *there*, although she wasn't completely convinced that she was the one who was feeling it.

"How long had you lived in the cottage when you began to see the maze?" she asked him.

"Not long," he told her. "Less than a year. It belongs to Lord Halcombe. My father is one of his stewards. We had a smaller house before, on the home estate."

"It belongs to my father now," Angie told him. "I never even heard of Lord Halcombe. You're talking about a long time ago, maybe when Queen Victoria was on the throne."

"Is she not?" Jesse asked, in surprise. Although he could see and hear time go by, he obviously couldn't keep up with the news.

The light was getting brighter all the time. It was brighter than daylight now. The walls of the maze seemed to be made out of liquid light—but it wasn't like the dazzle of a light-bulb or the even blue of a cloudless sky. All the colors of the spectrum were in there, but they weren't arranged in a neat order running from red to violet, with all the others taking strict turns. Even in the maze, the colors might not be free to wander as they wished, but they seemed quite chaotic from where Angie was.

As the light grew brighter *they* became less numerous—but they also became more complicated. In the outer parts of the spiral the glimpses had been mere patches, like fragments of shadow. In the inner regions they were composed of brighter colors, which seemed much closer to patterns or shapes. They still vanished when she looked at them directly, but Angie thought that she was getting nearer all the time to a moment of capture, when the thing she had glimpsed would remain a thing, and increase its *thinginess* dramatically, while she looked at it squarely.

That possibility seemed strangely exciting. There was, at least, an excitement of sorts in the air, although she couldn't be absolutely certain that it was she who was feeling it.

"You see," Jesse said to her. "We're getting nowhere."

"That's not true," Angie told him. "We're getting closer and closer to the heart of the maze—to the spiral's point of origin. Can't you see that?"

"No," he said.

She stopped, and let go of his hand. She showed him her drawing, and pointed to the exact spot on the map that described their location.

"Can you see it now?" she asked.

"No," he said. "I *can't* see. That's the trouble. I can only see *so much*. I'm useless." There was a note of plaintive desperation in his voice—except, Angie remembered, that it wasn't really *his* voice. They were his words—at least, they conserved the meaning of his words—but it wasn't his voice. His own voice was lost in the past.

Can he hear my voice? Angie wondered. *Or can he only hear them, repeating what I'm saying.* If that was true, she thought, then perhaps what she was seeing wasn't the real him, and what he was seeing wasn't the real her. The fact that they could see one another was just another trick of the maze. Ordinarily, that would have made no sense at all, but they were in the maze now, and seeing wasn't the same here as it was in the world of engineers and schoolteachers, brambles and dead apple trees.

"It's not far now," she said. "The heart of the maze is just around the corner. It's a long and winding corner, but we really are almost there."

She took his left hand in hers again, and led him on: around and around and around, but not in perfect circles. She didn't get dizzy, in spite of the peculiar effects of the dazzling light.

Within the walls that they couldn't touch, the light and its color danced with excitement. Angie knew exactly where she was, without having to glance at the map again. The map was only a drawing; the maze was in her mind. She wasn't just walking it but thinking it and living it. She really was *going somewhere*, even if the somewhere was inside herself as much as it was in the dead orchard.

In no time at all, they arrived.

"If you stand *just here*," Angie told her companion, "You'll be at the dead centre, the point of origin."

"I can't," Jesse said. "I've tried, but I can't. I saw the maze, but I can't see *them*. I've tried. I'm useless. I saw you, though. I could see *you*. I could do that."

Angie looked around before taking the final step. The walls were very close here, wrapped around the two of them so tightly that there was hardly room to move. There was only one of *them* that was not-quite-visible now, hovering at the spiral's point of origin. It was a riot of color that was just one small step short of acquiring an actual *appearance*. There were many others strung out in the maze, but they were only reflections of reflections. Here at the centre there was just one.

Perhaps things of a similar kind had been taken in the past for the fairy king or queen, but Angie knew that names like that, and titles too, were just a part of the attempt to give the thing a definite shape, and a real presence.

The air was alive with anticipation.

"Don't do it," Jesse said, suddenly. His voice became distorted as he spoke, as if the air were reluctant to transmit what he said.

"Why not?" Angie asked.

"Because it's bad," he croaked, having to make a visible effort to speak. "It's...." He could say no more.

"If I don't," Angie reminded him, "I'll probably be stuck here, just like you. To get back, I'll have to be able to find the way. I'll have to be able to *see*. Anyway, I want to see."

Having said that, there was no point in further delay. She let go of Jesse's hand and took the extra step—the one that Jesse had never been able to take. She stepped into the point that was the heart of the maze, and *became* the heart of the maze.

Then she tried, as hard as she could, to see what there was to see.

This time, the image didn't vanish. She was finally able to look directly at the creature made of light, and it immediately began to take on a definite shape. It began to *appear*.

Angie realized then that it was using her to discover how to appear and what to be. It wasn't reading her mind, but it was using her imagination. That was why it tried to capture people. That was why it had captured Jesse. Jesse had not been able to see well enough, but Angie could.

Angela understood, too, that Jesse had been right to say that it *was* bad. It wasn't bad because it had any innate desire to hurt her, or anyone else; it was too strange a thing to have any such motive. It wasn't *evil*, in any ordinary sense of the world. It was only bad because its existence—the existence she was granting it by trying to see it—would be the beginning of a *contest* for existence: a battle to determine what could and would be real from this moment on, in which there would be losers. If *they* became real, then *their* reality might prove more powerful than the one from which Angie had come.

There was no going back, though. Now that Angie had found that she really could see, there was no way to deny what she saw. She couldn't turn away.

She had never been so excited before in all her life, although it wasn't really *her* excitement at all.

8.

The monster—because it *was* a monster of sorts; there was no doubt at all about that—seemed to have considerable difficulty figuring out exactly what it ought to be.

Because it was so brightly colored, Angie's first inclination was to see it as some kind of bird: a peacock, maybe, or a parrot, or a bird of paradise. At second glance, though, it seemed too *shiny* to be a bird, no matter how glossy a bird's feathers could be, and Angie wondered whether it might actually be a snake with highly-polished scales. That seemed more appropriate, given that it was, after all, a monster. It might be an intricately-patterned python, although it was probably more likely to be something poisonous, like an adder or a hooded cobra.

When she looked more intently, however, Angie saw that it wasn't really a bird or a snake. Nor was it any weird combination of the two. It wasn't a dragon, or anything mythical at all. It wasn't anything that retained the least taint of *unreality*. It wasn't content to be anything out of a story, even though Angie's imagination had been formed and educated by stories to a greater extent than anything real.

The monster was striving, in spite of all its *vivid* qualities born of light, for a kind of appearance that was both ordinary and extraordinary at the same time. It was striving for an appearance that no one would ever suspect, even for a moment, to be monstrous, even though everyone would be forced to recognize that it was exceptional and magnificent.

It was, Angie realized, striving for *beauty*. It wanted to be seen as something marvelous, but also something irresistibly attractive. For a moment or two, Angie was almost on the point of seeing it as a child: a child more like herself than Jesse, but better-looking, more charming, not quite so *odd*. The moment didn't last, though. If the thing were to appear human, Angie knew, then it had to appear as an adult: a *young* adult, to be sure—not someone as old as her mother, let alone Mrs. Lamb—but an adult nevertheless.

Perhaps, if Jesse had been able to see all that *they* wanted him to be able to see, the creature at the heart of the maze would have been a strong man, a regal Hercules—but it was Angie Martindale who had turned out to possess the gift in its fullest measure, and what she saw was born of a twenty-first-century imagination, whose educative stories had been taken as much from films and TV shows as from books and oral tales. Angie's imagination was highly visual, and its visual images had been tailored to a high level of distinction.

What Angie saw, when she finally managed to make out the form within the light, was not a fairy queen but a *beauty* queen, or an actress equipped with a designer dress for a red-carpet walk at an award ceremony. There was a moment then when the whole business seemed perfectly ridiculous, and rather comical, but that didn't last. As soon as the monster fixed Angie with her piercing blue eyes, Angie knew that the manifestation was no laughing matter.

"Oh yes," the creature said. "That's neat, and stylish. Have you any idea how precious you are, my child? Have you any idea what a *treasure* you are?"

"Mum and Dad are always mentioning it," Angie replied, "but I never really believe them. It's just a habit they have."

"Believe it, my precious angel," the monster said. "There was a time, I think, when sight such as yours wasn't quite as rare—but time passes in the world of human beings, and there never was a time when sight was as *sharp*. You should be grateful that you've had the opportunity to use your gift—and will have the opportunity now to use it to the full. Gifts that people don't realize they have, whose use they don't practice, can so easily vanish...but once you take possession of a gift, and practice it...."

The monster was complete now. Angie decided to think of her as "the Diva" now that she existed, because everything that existed needed a name, and it might be undiplomatic, as well as unfair, to keep on thinking of her as "the monster".

"There is a way out, isn't there?" Angie said. "Now that I've got to the centre, I can find a way out, can't I?"

"What does that matter?" the Diva said, "That's not what you wanted. You wanted a way *in*, and you've found it. You've found your destiny. You've found the one place in the whole of your dismal and confused world in which you're absolutely perfect and absolutely precious. There's so much to see, Angela—*so much to see*."

Angie knew what the Diva meant. *They* were very numerous— or could be, with the aid of the spiral maze, which multiplied them by reflection. They wanted her to see them all. They wanted to *appear*. They wanted to *be*. And she could do it. She could make them all real. She could make a whole new reality, and she could be at the heart of it.

She knew that Jesse had been right, though. That would be bad—not because *they* were evil, intent on doing harm for the sake of doing harm, but simply because their existence would eclipse all the things that already existed. There was a sense, Angie knew, in which the universe wasn't big enough for *them* as well as *us*—and *us*, in this instance didn't mean just human beings, or even everything living, but everything material.

Angie shut her eyes, but that didn't work. She knew, even before she opened them, that the Diva would still be there, smiling.

"I've changed my mind," Angie whispered.

"Now why would you want to do that?" the Diva asked. "Even if you could. That's not what you *really* want at all, is it?"

Angie realized that the Diva wasn't just making conversation. Here in the maze, her feelings weren't entirely her own any more, any more than her sight and her voice were her own. She could feel *their* excitement, *their* pleasure, *their* anticipation. If she wasn't careful, that would soon be all she'd be able to feel—but she could resist it. She could resist the Diva's power of suggestion. She could resist the Diva and the way the walls of the maze forced her into its centre in spite of the fact that they weren't solid. She could still set things right, if only she could figure out how. She ought to be able to do that. She was the daughter of an engineer. The difficult she had done at once; now it was time to attempt the impossible.

"I'm glad I came here," Angie told the Diva. "I had to find out what this was all about. Now I know—not everything, of course, but I do understand know why curiosity kills cats, and why it's sometimes not a good idea to want to see *everything*. I'm sorry."

"What are you sorry about?" the Diva asked.

"About having to send you back again. About having to deny you what you want. It's a pity—you're very beautiful. I didn't know I had that much imagination. I'll never be able to draw anything like you."

"You can't *unsee* me, Angela," the Lady said. "You couldn't send me back even if you wanted to. And you can't get out. That drawing can't help you—it's not really a map."

For a moment or two, Angie thought that what the Diva was saying might actually be true: that the drawing couldn't help her, because it wasn't really a map; that she wouldn't be able to get out, even though there was a way to do it; that she couldn't send the Diva back into the light, because she couldn't *unsee* what she had now consented to see.

Then she realized that the Diva was trying to trick her: to deflect her attention away from the solution to the mystery. Of course she couldn't *un*see, because there was no such thing—but that wasn't what she had to do at all. The gift she had was the gift of *sight*, and what she had to do was *see*...and that was why the drawing was not only useful, in spite of the fact that it wasn't a map, but quite invaluable.

She realized, now, what the drawing really was, and why it had been so important that she get it right. She realized why Jesse had been trapped, because he'd never been able to get it right, even though he could see well enough to know why the maze was there.

She knew that she had time in hand, now. Maybe not much—because the impossible was only supposed to take a *little* longer—but enough to look around. So she looked around, not *at* the walls but through them. She looked past *them* into the vast wilderness of time.

She felt a momentary pang of disappointment because she could only see the past, not the as-yet-unmade future, and felt slightly frustrated because so much of the past was darkness, and life so very sparse, but she caught glimpses of the big bang and supernovas, dinosaurs and mammoths, Babylon and Rome, the rediscovery of America and the French Revolution. She had no chance to capture any details, but she did get a sense of the whole.

"Right," she said. "I know where I am, now, and I know where you are. I'm not trapped in the maze—the maze is trapped in me. When I finally drew it right, I captured it."

"Don't be silly, Angela," the Diva said. "The maze existed long before you were born, and it'll be here long after you're dead. It's much bigger than you are."

"The bigger things are," Angie observed, "The easier they are to see. The trick is not to focus too intently on the things that catch you up and try to take over your life. The trick is to see the bigger picture."

"You could do *so much*," the Diva said. "With us to help you, you can see anything you want to see, do anything you want to do. *You wouldn't be trapped!*"

"It's nothing personal," Angie told the Diva. "You are what you are, and you can't help it. If you were a snake, you couldn't help being poisonous. But there's only one way out of here. If I don't use it, I'll be going round in wonky circles forever."

The Diva might have leapt upon her then like some savage beast. The monster might have torn her into little pieces and flooded the maze with her blood. But that wasn't the kind of monster the Diva was—and Angie felt that she was entitled to take a little of the credit for that herself.

"You're mad," the Diva said. "You'd be throwing away *everything*. Believe me, child, we can give you more than you could ever dream of having. You're too young to know, as yet, what a meager thing human life is—but you've seen the maze, and you've seen me. You can imagine, I know, what we might make of you."

"Yes," Angie said. "But that's not what I am."

She lifted the sheet of paper on which she'd drawn the maze to eye-level and ripped it in two. Then she tore the two pieces into four and the four to eight, and crumpled the fragments in her hand. Then she dropped them, knowing *exactly* what it was that she was throwing away.

It was a symbolic gesture. The maze wasn't contained in the pieces of paper—but the drawing was the means by which she'd seen it for what it was and brought it into her mind.

She looked around at the walls full of light, and looked through them. She used her gift for seeing what was *really* there. She had enough presence of mind to shout: "Crouch down!" to Jesse before she put her hands up to protect her face and crouched down herself—but she peeped through her fingers, so that she could see what happened to the Diva.

The light stayed bright for a few seconds longer, but it couldn't compete with the darkness. Because it was Easter, the moon was a long way from full, but it wouldn't have mattered, because the bindweed would have screened out its light just as it screened out the fainter light of the stars.

The walls of the maze had no substance, and they couldn't sustain themselves against the brutal reality of the brambles and the hawthorn, or even the dead apple trees. Angie had to make an initial effort to see through the glamorous illusion of the maze, but as soon as she had caught the merest glimpse of a thorny branch there was no stopping the violent solidity of the overgrown orchard. Its force was overwhelming.

The Diva spread her arms wide, and screamed at the top of her voice, using the sound in a determined attempt to assert her reality. She *was* real, thanks to Angie; she had found the form that she wanted and needed, thanks to Angie—but the very fact of becoming real rendered her vulnerable. The thorns slashed at her solid arms, her solid throat and her solid eyes. The delicate designer dress was cut to chiffon ribbons, and rivers of red began to stain its tatters.

The Diva was standing exactly where a hawthorn tree needed and deserved to be, and the hawthorn reclaimed its space with savage efficiency. It wasn't content to flay her from without; its twisted trunk invaded her body, churning through her like a corkscrew.

Fortunately—for Angie as well as the monster itself—the Diva's agony didn't last long. No blood rained down on to the ground, either to fertilize it or poison it. The substance granted by Angie's sight was exploded by her determination to see through it, and it vanished into the thinnest air imaginable.

The decision was not without penalty, of course. The thorns had not been able to hurt Angie while she was in the maze—or, to be strictly accurate, while the maze was in her—but now that she was back in the overgrown orchard there was nothing to restrain them.

Jesse was in exactly the same predicament, although he did no more than gasp when he suddenly found himself oppressed from every side, as well as from above and below, by thrusting branches and brambles. He was solid enough to turn them aside, though, and they had been too long beneath the bindweed to have much strength left in them.

Angie felt herself poked and prodded, but she too was able to turn the branches aside.

The difficult part, she knew, would begin when she and Jesse had to move—to fight their way out from the heart of the thicket to its edge. She didn't doubt that they could do it, though.

Nor did Jesse. "Follow me," he said. "Stay close. I'll clear a path for us."

Angie was grateful, then, that the boy was bigger than she was, and a good deal more muscular. His gift of sight might be incomplete, but he was tough and he was brave. He used his arms and his legs with grim determination, smashing a way through the brittle boughs. He must have been terribly scratched by the hawthorn and the brambles alike, but he never flinched. He would have won free within a minute if Angie hadn't grabbed him around the waist and said: "Wait!"

He stopped immediately. "What is it?" he asked.

"Just a moment," she said. "I've still got the shape of the maze in my head. I've got to get it *exactly* right."

"What do you mean?" he asked.

"It's still here," she said. "The maze, I mean. We can't see it any longer, but it's still here. What was the garden like when you first saw it? Were there herbs and vegetables?"

"No," Jesse told her. "There were bushes—myrtles, I think."

"That's what we need to find, then," Angie told him. "You need to find the bushes you remember—and you can, I think, if only I can get the maze *just right*."

"I can't see...," he began—but then Angie figured out exactly where they were in the maze, and she shoved him sideways, to the left. She guessed that he hadn't finished the sentence because he'd suddenly found that he *could* see, and that the hawthorn had abruptly let him alone, consigning him to the gentler care of another kind of growth entirely—which might or might not have been myrtle.

"You *can* go through the walls," she told him. "You just have to master the trick of it."

The night was too dark to allow her to see much of the nineteenth-century house, and what she could see looked very similar in outline to the twenty-first century cottage, but Angie could sense several differences during the glimpse that she obtained. There was a momentary odor that was pleasantly sharp and strangely sweet, which she didn't recognize but which seemed strangely appealing. She wasn't tempted, even though she knew that the reverse step she would have to take when she let go of Jesse's waist would take her back to odors of a very different kind: dank and dusty odors, mingled with the stench of rotting wood.

When she did let him go, he was able to stand up and step clear. The moonlight caught him then, and she saw that his new clothes were utterly ruined. They were badly torn and hideously dirty—as if he'd just fought his way through a filthy thicket.

Jesse looked down at himself and said: "My father will *kill* me."

"That depends how long you've been gone," Angie said. "You haven't been away a hundred years and more, but I'm pretty sure it's not Whitsun here any longer. It might be as late as Midsummer. I think I can hit my own Easter dead on, though—it's a much closer target."

"You could stay here," he pointed out. He seemed to be speaking with his own voice now.

"I could go to any time at all," she said, "except the future. But there's only one that's mine. You might do better, I suppose, to come with me—to a world with supermarkets, antibiotics and opticians—but you'd be a stranger. Your father might not approve of the state of your clothes, but he'll know that you're back where you belong."

"Good luck, Miss," Jesse said, politely, "and thank you."

"You're welcome," Angie said. "Any time."

She stepped back, then, into the ruined orchard, but she didn't linger long before hauling herself out of her own exit, thrusting the thorns aside as bravely as Jesse had.

Unfortunately, the exit didn't take her back to her bedroom; it deposited her in the narrow alley between the thicket and the back of the house, which the builders had cleared in order to erect their scaffolding. She'd made the effort to see the world as it was, and she was subject to its limitations again. The back door was only a few yards away, but it was locked.

Angie made her way around the house without any difficulty, but the front door was locked too. She considered ringing the doorbell, but decided against it. Luckily, even though the builders had cleaned up after them, there was plenty of fine rubble lying around. Angie picked up a handful, and began throwing little pieces at Cathy's window.

It took more than ten minutes, but Cathy eventually came to the window and looked out.

"Come down and let me in," Angie said, in a stage-whisper. "Don't wake Mum and Dad."

Cathy was reliable in situations like that. She came downstairs and opened the door. She looked Angie up and down, and said: "You're absolutely *filthy*. Is that *blood*?"

Angie looked down at herself. The sweater had given some protection to her upper body, but not as much as her jeans had given to her legs. Her hands and forearms were badly scratched, and her bare ankles too. There wasn't very much blood, but some of the scratches had swollen up and were beginning to itch.

It's the allergies that get you, Angie thought. Aloud, she said: "I'll clean myself up. Don't tell on me."

"Tell what?" Cathy said. "What on earth are you doing outside? And why didn't you leave the door on the latch so you could get back in?"

"I went out through my window," Angie told her.

"That's impossible," Cathy retorted.

"I'm an engineer's daughter," Angie reminded her, as she pushed past her sister and made for the stairs, feeling suddenly very tired. "The impossible sometimes takes more than a little longer, but if you don't give it a try, you never make progress."

9.

Angie managed to get in and out of the bathroom without being seen or heard, and clean up her scratches as best she could. She slept late the next morning, and put on a long-sleeved blouse instead of a T-shirt when she got up. It couldn't hide the backs of her hands and her wrists, but the injuries didn't look bad enough to attract too much attention. She crept downstairs discreetly, to make sure that no one was waiting for her, expecting explanations.

In the lounge-dining room, Mr. Martindale was already mixing pink plaster, ready to begin his bold attempt to make the walls smooth and fit for painting. He was wearing his light brown overalls, and seemed to be in a very cheerful mood. The furniture had all been covered in protective sheets, including the TV.

"Morning, treasure," Mr. Martindale said, when Angie looked in.

Cathy had obviously done as she'd been asked, and had kept her mouth shut.

Her mother was in the kitchen. "How did you get those scratches, precious?" she asked Angie, when Angie reached up to the cupboard to get a cereal bowl.

"Playing in the garden," Angie said, vaguely.

"We told you to be careful," her mother reminded her, but said no more.

When she'd finished breakfast Angie went back up to her room, armed with a washing-up sponge. She carefully scoured away the four diagrams drawn beside the window. Then she tore up all her failed attempts to draw the maze and took them downstairs to put them in the kitchen bin. She didn't want to have anything around that might prompt her to see the maze again. If ever she needed to go back in the maze, she would be able to reconstruct it, but for the time being, it seemed best to let the weeds keep possession of the back garden, at least until her father got busy with his chainsaw and heavy-duty strimmer.

She went outside later, and made her way round to the back of the house to look at the overgrown orchard, but she wasn't looking for the maze.

The path that Jesse had cleared for them as they had made their reckless journey from the heart of the maze was still clearly visible, although it was by no means straight. Indeed, it wound around the trunks of the hawthorn trees in such in a tortuous manner that Angie could only marvel at the fact that Jesse had picked it out unaided. Even though his sight hadn't been quite as keen as hers, he had obviously stared at the maze long enough to get a feel for its contours. The light-starved branches beneath the bindweed canopy had become so brittle that he had broken hundreds.

She could even make out the exact point at which his path had diverged from hers. His now ended suddenly, in what seemed to be a blind alley, but hers extended all the way to the outside. Angie made no attempt to go into the thicket.

Cathy came up behind her, curiously.

"Is that where you went last night?" the teenager asked.

"Not exactly," Angie replied, vaguely.

"You couldn't have climbed out of your window," Cathy insisted. "You made that up, because you were embarrassed because you'd let the front door close and lock itself behind you, so you couldn't get back in."

"Something like that," Angie said. Vagueness seemed to be working for her.

"So what were you looking for? I can't remember exactly where we were up to when we were making things up, but it was something to do with fairies and fairyland being the land of the dead. You thought there was an entrance to fairyland in there, I suppose—but you figured that you had to get to it at the right time, the stroke of midnight, or whatever."

"Pretty much," Angie agreed.

"You're mad," Cathy said. "What did you expect to happen?"

"Oh, I thought I might meet a beauty queen and save the universe—you know the sort of thing."

"I suppose I do," Cathy said, although she really didn't. "You might need tetanus shots, you know. Who knows what might have got under your skin? Weren't you afraid of rats? I mean, take a good look in there—it's *filthy*."

Angie knew that Cathy was just trying to scare her with talk of tetanus and rats, and she wasn't in the least intimidated. "I'm okay," she said.

"No you're not. You're off your head. You're not thinking of going in there *again*, are you? You're eleven years old—you should have got it into your head by now that there are no secret entrances to fairyland."

Angie knew that there as no more point in trying to tell Cathy what had happened than there was in trying to explain it to her mother and father. The spirals she'd drawn had meant nothing to any of them, and never would. They'd never be able to catch the slightest glimpse of the maze, even when the hawthorn, the brambles and the dead apple trees had all been cleared away, to be replaced by a lawn and flower beds. She'd be able to see it, though, if she ever wanted or needed to. She'd *always* be able to see it, even if she refrained from drawing it again.

"I think we ought to have a single tree in the middle of the lawn," Angie said. "Maybe we should keep one of the hawthorns, but clear everything else away so that it has a chance to grow properly. Or maybe we should plant one of our own: an oak, say. I know *exactly* where it ought to go."

"That won't get you into fairyland either," Cathy said.

"You really should stop going on about fairyland," Angie advised her. "You're fourteen, and that's a bit old for that sort of thing. Stick to ghosts and witches."

"I would have stuck to ghosts and witches, given the chance. You and Dad were the ones who insisted on complicating it. If we'd just focused, we might have got the house on TV. It's not too late to invent a really good haunting, left over from the days when this was a witch's cottage and local farm-boys disappeared mysteriously every time there was a full moon."

"They'd check," Angie said. "TV shows have researchers. They'd find out that this wasn't a witch's cottage. It was where the landowner lodged the family of one of his stewards, who had the job of managing this bit of his estate. And nobody disappeared mysteriously—not for very long, at any rate. From Whitsun to Midsummer Day, at the very most."

"You don't know that," Cathy said. "Whatever the researchers found, there'd be all sorts of gaps in it. You can never prove that things didn't happen. People can make up what they like, and there's never any way to prove that it wasn't true. Once the past's dead and gone, *anything* might have happened. All that remains are relics, like those scratches on your arms."

Angie thought it was time to change the subject. "Are you looking forward to going back to Kingston?" she said. "Is it as much fun as you thought it would be, with Dad at work all day and Mum and me down here?"

"Absolutely," Cathy said. "Can't wait. I'm going to avoid this place as much as I can, no matter how pretty it looks when Dad's finished painting it. I'm not going to need a country retreat until I'm ninety—not if I can help it. Give it a year or two, and you won't want to come down here either. You'll have far better things to do."

"Maybe," Angie said. "Mum and Dad will like it, though."

"Will they, though? They go on and on about needing *a change of scene*, but it's probably the sort of thing that's nicer to think about than actually to do. I think Dad will get bored once it's all fixed up and there's no more *engineering* to do—no more building-plans and timetables. Once he's finished the garden and it's all *complete*, I bet he'll give it a year or so, and then put it back on the market. We'll sell it to someone who really *is* ready to retire and put down roots— and then Dad will probably want to buy another ruin somewhere. If we don't make it on to one of those haunting shows, I suppose we can probably get on TV anyway, on one of those house-rebuilding shows. At least they go out on the main channels instead of digital backwaters."

Angie hadn't thought about the possibility that her father might find that he didn't need to *get away* as much as he thought he did. She didn't know how she felt about the notion that Orchard Cottage might be sold on once it the house and grounds were fixed up. She decided after a few seconds thought, however, that her business here was probably finished. She wouldn't be going back to the heart of the maze again, whether there was a protective tree there or not. She didn't need a place to get away.

"There must be spirals everywhere," she murmured. "In Kingston, in the middle of London. It's just a matter of learning to see them."

Cathy had already lost interest. "I'm going back indoors," she declared. "The TV's covered up, but I've got my laptop and my phone. I've got better things to do than grub around in bushes."

Angie followed her sister to the back door, and went with her into the kitchen. "I'll need some curtains for my room," she said to her mother.

THE BEST OF BOTH WORLDS, BY BRIAN STABLEFORD * 169

"Of course you will, precious," her mother said. "We all will. But we need to get the plastering and the painting done first. Your father's never going to finish all the plastering this weekend, you know. There's just too much. I'll be able to start the painting on Tuesday, but we're going to have to do the job in stages. It'll be nice when it's finished, though."

Angie went into the lounge-dining room then to watch her father at work. She stood quietly to one side, not wanting to disturb him. For ten or fifteen minutes he got on with the job, almost as if he didn't know that she was there, but eventually he looked round at her. "I'm sorry you can't help, treasure," he said, "but even if you had the knack, you're not tall enough." He turned back to his work immediately, but it wasn't necessary for them to maintain eye contact to continue the conversation now that it had started.

"That's okay," Angie said. "Do you suppose, now that I'm nearly twelve, that you and Mummy could stop calling me *precious* and *treasure*?"

"If that's what you want, tr...I mean, Angel. Is Angel still all right?"

"I suppose so. I thought we might keep a tree in the middle of the back garden. Just one, somewhere near the middle. I'll be able to pick the exact spot, once most of it's been cleared."

"That might be nice," her father agreed. "It's good to plant something that might live for centuries, growing all the while. An oak, maybe? This is England, after all. You know how to pick the spot, do you? Does it have anything to do with those drawings you found? Is it the mysterious centre from which all the spirals spread out, perhaps?"

"I scrubbed out the drawings on the wall," Angie told him, evasively.

"I thought you wanted me to take photographs—I hadn't got round to it yet."

"It's okay," Angie said. "It would be a good idea to plant the tree, even if you decide to sell the cottage once you've finished fixing it up."

"You've been talking to Cathy," her father observed. "She's got her own ideas about the way things ought to go. Can't blame her—she's a teenager. I might forget, once now and again, you now, and call you *treasure* by mistake."

"The world's not as safe and simple as we think, Daddy," Angie said, thinking that she ought to make *some* attempt to tell him, and to warn him. There are more ways to get lost than you might imagine, and there are things that try to get in where they aren't wanted."

"You're nearly twelve years old, all right," her father observed. "You're right, I'm afraid—and the awareness will never go away. We just have to learn to live with it, and do the best we can. Plaster over the cracks, make things as smooth as possible—and then paint over the plaster, to produce exactly the appearance that you want, exactly the appearance that you need. Don't ever let anyone tell you that fixing things up and decorating are a waste of time. You're an engineer's daughter, remember. You know the motto."

"Sure," Angie said. "It's true. The impossible did take a little bit longer—but it was worth the trouble."

It was strange, she thought, as she went back into the kitchen, how two people could talk to one another so easily, and so comfortably, without either of them really knowing what the other was talking *about*. It was strange, too, how little that mattered, if the people could find the right things to say, even without knowing.

She told her mother what she'd said to her father about not calling her *precious* and *treasure* any more.

"Well, I'll do my best," her mother said, "but I'm making no promises. Will you be calling me *Mother* from now on, instead of *Mummy*?"

"Probably," Angie said.

"Well," Her mother said, with a sigh, "I suppose you'll be a teenager soon, and you'll have to keep up appearances, just like Cathy. You'll always be precious, though, even if we're not allowed to say so."

"I know that," Angie said. "I won't ever forget it."

www.ingramcontent.com/pod-product-compliance
Lightning Source LLC
Chambersburg PA
CBHW020643180626
46816CB00003B/1105